Coyote Ridge

a novel by

Barb Mihaljevich

Bright Eagle Publishing
Fort Collins, Colorado

First printing 2003

Printed in the United States of America

ISBN 0-9726528-0-9

LCCN 2002096659

Bright Eagle Publishing
604 Hindsdale Court
Fort Collins, CO 80526-3933
970-282-0782

acknowledgments

Many people gave freely of their time and expertise in helping me write this book. Dr. Morris Burns pointed me toward *Marat Sade* and Steve Hill, who shared what it is like to be Gothic. Eric Nielson of Larimer County Search and Rescue, Diane Jaso, Larimer County Dispatch Supervisor, and Corporal Dan Gillham, Larimer County Sheriff's Department, supplied information about rescue operations and evidentiary process. Kathleen Lewis of the *Fort Collins Coloradoan* provided research assistance while Dr. Tom Moore, Wyoming Game and Fish Laboratory, is the real expert on animal hair and author of *Identification of Dorsal Guard Hairs*. Thank you all!

In addition, I'd especially like to thank Betty Mason of Casper, Wyoming, for her information about cardiac surgery and my sister, Deb Williams, RNC, for obstetrical details. Thanks so much, you two—your patience outshines my knowledge, and if I erred in the translation please forgive me.

My editor, Sue Collier, wore more hats than I could count and switched them cheerfully at a moment's notice.

Finally, thanks to Alan, for everything.

the prairie breathes

The prairie breathes. In. Out. In. Out. And the animals that roam her feel the rhythm of her breaths, and the grasses grow according to their cadence. And though her respirations are but shallow now compared to the great in- and outpourings of air she exchanged in bygone days (when the least flutter of her mammoth breast invoked the rise and fall of thousands of square miles of grasslands), still, she breathes. In. Out. In. Out.

Can she remember those bygone days when she had *stretched*, vast and not wholly knowable, a limitless pasture for the countless creatures that dwelt upon her? Does she mourn her former glory, weeping for the loss of her wholeness?

None can say, for the small pieces into which she has been riven by the hatchet civilization no longer speak aloud. Afraid to draw attention to themselves, perhaps these fragments do whisper of past might, but none hear, for none bend so close to the ground as to listen. Thus the whispers hitchhike on the wind.

Does their fairy passage across Kaia's warm and riffling fur invade her afternoon dreams with images of yesteryear? Can she remember what life on the prairie had been like for her ancestors, the way tiny pigeon brains remember their way home across untold miles? Or are pictures of the ancient prairie etched so deeply in some neuronal crevice of her mind she can call them forth only in her dreams?

Perhaps. Who can say for sure whether the minute flicker of a tawny ear means it is catching whispers on the wind even as its owner sleeps? Only Kaia, of course, who, though she *can* speak, does so in a language not understandable to those who also fail to hear the prairie breathe.

trading goods

Like a tiny prairie blossom hit by its first hard frost, Pat's tolerance for her physical position (on her knees, bent over the snow-in-summer lining her front walk) expires suddenly. As she stiffly shifts from a kneel to a squat, her changing center of gravity continues to tug her backwards. The next instant, her feet piston out from under her and her butt smacks the cold sidewalk. This new position, though awkward, at least relieves her aching knees. She stretches her legs gratefully and reaches for the kneeling pad beside her.

The ugly thing had been old when she'd scooped it up at a garage sale years ago; now, after a couple decades in her own service, it is battered to a laughable degree. The tough vinyl exterior—originally a hideous loud yellow—is stained dull brown around the edges by years of ground-in dirt. Paint speckled across the pad's surface is a memento of home improvement projects she can identify by color: here, the grayish-white they'd painted the interior of the garage— oh, it must be six years ago now, but it still seems just recently to her; there, the eggshell of the downstairs family room.

Why was it, Pat wonders, she always started such projects on a high note of enthusiasm and always finished desperate to escape the bondage they entailed? Lopsided, like so many things in life. It wasn't so bad when her enthusiasm waned and she still had Hal to egg her on or—more likely—finish the job himself. Pat smiles at the memory. Around their house, she was always the inspired project instigator but dear Hal the guy who saw things through to completion. Now that he is gone, Pat knows she better be careful what she starts, or she'll end up with loose ends from one end of her life to the other.

So what else is new? To Pat, her lack of ability to finish things is just another in a humiliating list of limitations that grows longer by the minute. With fingers encased in garden gloves, she pulls crumpled Kleenex from her sweatshirt pocket and swipes impatiently at the tears that trickle down behind her glasses. She blows her nose loudly, then cuts another handful of snow-in-summer and flings it into her half-full bucket of clippings. Only early spring, but if she doesn't keep tabs on the darn stuff, it will overgrow the sidewalk overnight.

Whether in response to the sound of blowing her nose or her silent tears—she never underestimates animals' ability to read people—a cold, wet nose followed by a pair of limpid brown eyes insert themselves forcefully into Pat's lap. Next, the furred owner of these items opens his mouth and drops a slimy red ball into her possession, then just stands there, waiting. Pat caresses the young dog's golden head but complains as well: "You're a pest, Jethie, you know that?" The dog wags his tail. Pat gives in and from her sitting place on the sidewalk, raises her arm and awkwardly throws the ball overhand. Following its trajectory with her eyes, she is horrified to see she has thrown the thing into the middle of the street in front of her house, where a vehicle is fast approaching.

"JETHIE!" Pat's scream is full of the helpless panic of an old woman who has lost much. But the dog, usually so perceptive, is in total play mode. Eyes and body focused on the ball, he dashes down the front walk heedless of her cry. Pat shuts her eyes but can't block out the loud squeal of brakes and heartbreaking yelps that follow. Unable to witness her pet's destruction, she tucks her gray-haired head between her filthy denim-clad knees and wraps her arms around herself to hide from yet more hurt. Even after the offending car departs, she remains wrapped within herself, beaten, old, and alone.

Long seconds pass. To Pat, the tuneless chirping of the nearby birds is cold commentary on the utter disregard of the universe for her presence in it. Oh, why was she hanging around so long, anyway? Since Hal died, her life was a mess. She was just a useless old woman overdue for escape. Tears for Jethie's demise mingle with, then become more tears for her own sorry self. Salty droplets course down small ravines in softly wrinkled cheeks and splatter in tiny puddles onto the concrete below. Though it's against the rules, for once Pat gives herself permission to wallow. What difference does it make, anyway?

Just then, as if in remonstrance for her rebellious thoughts, something touches her shoulder. She jumps in guilty alarm. Has God caught her red-handed? But the voice that intrudes upon her train of thought is not godlike. "Yours?" it asks with some trepidation. Pat looks up. Some of her tears have fallen onto the lenses of her glasses so that now, looking into the sunlight, all she can see is a blurry mass. She blinks, and the shape contracts slightly. "Yours?" the voice asks again.

Pat is conscious of motion, then a shape disattaches itself from the larger one and lands heavily in her lap. Immediately she recognizes the juvenile form of Jethie, who rights himself, puts his forepaws on her shoulders and slathers her with doggie saliva. Pat's arms likewise go around the dog. Tears forgotten, she buries her face in wriggling fur. When a muttered "Guess so" causes her to look up, she sees her dog's savior retreating down the sidewalk at a rapid pace.

"Wait!" hollers Pat, and this time her voice carries all the authority her sixty-eight years command. As she struggles to get back on her feet, the stranger retraces his steps and offers her a hand. Only after she takes it and rights herself is she finally able to look fully at her dog's rescuer. When her shocked brain registers what her eyes see, she can't help but take a frightened step backwards. *This* is Jethie's savior?

The young man standing before Pat notes her discomfort and, with a smirk of disdain, again turns to leave, but Pat hastily reaches out with both hands and grabs one of his. "I'm sorry," she apologizes, leaving it at that. If he has half a brain, he must have *some* idea of his effect on people. "I do so want to thank you for saving my dog," she says, feeling her way to more confidence. "Would you please come in for a minute?"

The young man's eyes narrow, as if he now suspects her of treachery, but he says nothing.

Still grasping his hand, Pat turns, saying, "Oh, come on, I owe you," in the open, friendly manner that is her norm. Dog bumping eagerly alongside, she leads both through the garage into her back hallway, then across the house and into her kitchen. The thought that the fellow could be casing the joint while she does this crosses her mind, but she squashes it promptly. She has enough trouble without imagining what hasn't occurred. Once in the kitchen, she seats her visitor at her table, pours two glasses of iced tea, and fills a plate with fresh oatmeal cookies before seating herself opposite him. "Sugar?" she asks.

"Uh, no thanks," replies her guest. Pat looks him over carefully. Close up, she can see that, in spite of his intimidating get-up, he is just a tall, thin young man with the uncertainty of adolescence on his pale face. Dressed in black from head to toe—black T-shirt, black pants, shoes, and socks topped by an oversized black overcoat and black fedora—this is the creature she has often glimpsed walking up and down the road in front of her house. She had nicknamed him *The Grim Reaper* because of his dreary outfit, which never changes despite the season or outside temperature.

"I've seen you around, haven't I?" she asks by way of introduction.

The boy eyes her warily. "I live down the road," he admits.

"And you walk to school?" Pat hints.

The boy grimaces. "Nah. I just walk to the bottom of the hill, where a friend picks me up." He pauses as if considering something, then shrugs in a "what-the-hell" motion that makes his tomb of clothing first lift, then droop disconsolately over his bony shoulders. "My dad won't buy me a car. He says it's because of the way I dress, but really it's because he's going broke," he blurts to the old woman regarding him across the table.

Pat can tell her visitor has deliberately chosen to confide this harsh reality to her for the simple reason that she is a total stranger. She looks at him with new respect. Not bad logic for a kid who was probably sick to death of walking around wondering what his future would be like. It wasn't the kind of thing you could discuss at length with friends, she knew, nor would it now be tactful of her to ask why in God's name he traipsed around all day looking half dead.

"I'm sorry," she says, having borne a few of her own scary secrets over the years, but still wondering how his parents would react if he appeared tomorrow in a sunny yellow plaid shirt and tan Dockers.

The kid accepts her condolence with a brief nod, then reaches for a cookie with the resilience of youth. Pat smiles to herself. "And again, I do thank you for saving Jethie." Upon hearing his name, the dog pads into the kitchen expectantly. Pat fondles the animal's ears. "Yes, I made a stupid mistake today, didn't I, Jethro?

"But you know, he's really a very smart dog," she continues, looking at her visitor. "And he's not really mine after all, so I'm doubly grateful to you."

"Whose is he, then?" asks the young man.

"Well, nobody's really, yet," Pat explains. "I'm raising him to see if he can make it as a seeing-eye dog for the blind. If he proves to have what it takes, then he'll go on to intensive training as he gets older and eventually be assigned to a blind person."

"And if he flunks out?" asks the boy.

Pat smiles. "Oh, we don't call it flunking out, we call it changing careers," she corrects. "Then he'll just go to some fine family probably like your own and be a normal dog. But nonetheless, I've already got a lot of hours invested in him, so you are absolutely the unqualified hero of the moment. May I please know your name?" she asks.

"Davin," mumbles the young man with his mouth full. To her raised eyebrows he amends his moniker: "Davin Hassletree."

"Pleasure to meet you, Davin," says Pat. His last name sounds vaguely familiar but she is unable to place it. That happened so often these days—if she's lucky, it will come to her later. Pat extends her hand across the table. When Davin takes it for the second time that afternoon and shakes it briefly, she can't help but notice the thinness of the boy's wrist as it protrudes from its black covering. Funny how, after just a few minutes with Davin, his black get-up now strikes Pat more as protection for its owner than a threat to anyone else.

When Pat offers, "I'm Pat Schreveport," Davin's eyebrows rise in surprised recognition.

"Like in Schreveport Ford, Lincoln, Mercury?" he asks. The dealership was well known as one of the oldest and largest in Fort Collins and indeed, all of northern Colorado.

Pat laughs. Leave it to a teenaged male to cue in on the car businesses in town. "The very same. My late husband started that business and ran it for thirty-nine years before he died last year. It was his pride and joy," confesses Pat.

"Hmm." Seeming uncomfortable at the turn the conversation has taken, Davin pushes his chair back from the table and rises to leave, in spite of the fact that he hasn't even finished his cookie. Pat feels bad. She rises also and accompanies Davin back out to the still-open garage which, had the boy looked, is so clean it could be part of the home's interior. But the boy has other things on his mind.

Pat does some quick thinking herself. "Davin," she says. Already halfway across the garage, Davin turns back with a question in his eyes. "Have you got a dollar I could have?"

It was a strange question, Pat knew, but the kid doesn't seem put off by it, which is what she would expect from most guys his age. "Sure," he says, digging into his side pocket and coming out with a wrinkled dollar bill. He retraces his steps and hands her the crumpled buck.

"Thanks," says Pat as she pockets the bill. "Now I can tell my darling daughter I sold the darn thing." So saying, she reaches up to a nail hanging beside the door and removes a set of keys, which she then offers to the young man standing in front of her. He looks from the keys to her with a mystified expression on his face. "Take them," urges Pat.

Davin takes the keys. "What for?"

"That." Pat tips her head toward the left, where sits a buttery-yellow 1977 fully restored Lincoln Town Car. The car—a great beast of a machine with a vinyl top colored to match the exterior—hunkers in the left garage bay as if waiting for the arrival of a commander-in-chief to take it out.

Davin still doesn't get it. "You mean you want me to take it for a spin or something?"

"Nope," says Pat firmly. "I want you to take it home."

"Why? I'm not a mechanic or anything, you know."

Pat laughs. "Well, actually, Davin, I *don't* know, but it doesn't really matter, because I'm giving you the darn thing," she explains.

"*What?*" This nice old lady wasn't making herself clear to Davin at all.

"I would like for you to have this car as a token of my appreciation for your saving Jethro this afternoon." Pat spells out her intentions slowly and clearly.

Finally, understanding registers on Davin's face, but he shakes his head from side to side in disbelief and tries to give her back the keys. "Oh, Mrs. Schreveport, I couldn't take your *car* just because I was in the right place at the right time for saving Jethro. That's ridiculous."

At this, Pat throws her head back and laughs merrily. She hasn't had this much fun in a long time. "You know what, Davin? That's exactly what my daughter's going to say when she finds out I did this, and you know what else?" She doesn't wait for the young man's reply. "I'm gonna do it anyway!" she insists.

"Just look at the facts, Davin," continues Pat excitedly.

"One: I don't need this darn thing. It was my late husband's car, not mine, and all it does is sit here in the garage and remind me of him and take up space I'd rather have for my gardening equipment, and

"Two: You *most certainly* could use this darn thing, and having satisfactorily met the asking price, are now free to take it. Obviously, this afternoon was meant to be, Davin!" she burbles happily.

Davin rocks nervously back and forth on his toes. He has heard of people with Alzheimer's doing strange things, and he wonders if the lady in front of him is a sufferer. Still…she doesn't act like she's sick in any other way. Could she be for real? He wonders, but can't exactly come out and ask if she is in her right mind. What should he do?

He struggles between indecision and the biggest "what if?" he has ever had to consider. What if she *knows* what she is doing, and still wants to give him the car? Davin's pulse quickens at the very idea of such a thing. What would his father say? What *could* his father say, anyway? He is still standing there awash in his own debate when Pat briskly interrupts.

"All right, son, that's enough polite declining. Now get your ass over here and get in this car!" So saying, she again grabs hold of Davin's arm and pulls him over to the driver's-side door of the vehicle, which, he notes just before she shoves him inside, is one of the old Signature Series signed by Oleg Cassini. Davin wasn't up on vintage cars, but he at least knew enough to know this was a collector's dream.

"Mrs. Schreveport," he stammers from the soft leather interior, gripping the leather-wrapped steering wheel so hard his knuckles turn white.

"Pat. It's Pat, please," says the old lady. "Kindly remember that, Davin. Can you come by tomorrow after school and take me down to the courthouse so we can change the title and plates?" she asks. "I'm too much of a mess to go now," she admits, looking down at her filthy yard clothes.

"Well, yeah, sure," agrees Davin, still dazed from the strange turn the afternoon has taken.

"Okay, then, turn it on, for pete's sake, and I'll see you tomorrow!" promises Pat. As Davin backs out of the garage in his new chariot, the goofy old lady hollers through the open window that he might come to hate her eventually because the thing only gets nine miles to the gallon.

an heir looms

Later that same week, Bonnie Blackburn steps back from her easel, removes her big straw hat, wipes the sweat that beads her forehead in spite of the day's mild temperatures, and looks critically at her work. Her heat tolerance has dropped to absolute zero, she reflects, studying her watercolor landscape of the prairie that rolls away beneath the ridge upon which their house sits. She wants her picture to capture the sense of peace the view from her deck affords her but, as usual, it's easier said than done.

Painting is so limited, thinks Bonnie. It can't capture the feel of the gentle breeze riffling the grasses, the smell of winter-weary vegetation coming alive after harsh months of dormancy, or the sound of birds chirping in that way peculiar to spring that signals their utter preoccupation with mating and nest-building. So even the best works by the greatest masters will never be more than just poor approximations of the real thing. Nonetheless, even to hint at how certain scenes make her feel still gives Bonnie enough of a kick to keep trying.

But enough for today. Ankles swollen again from standing so long, she needs to get off her feet to ease the pressure. She dunks her brushes in the jar of muddy-colored water standing next to her palette, closes up her paint tray, then collapses on a cushioned chaise lounge. Watching the fabric of her green jumper take on a life of its own over her middle, Bonnie wonders whether, eight weeks from now when the person inside her finally escapes what it surely must regard as her too-small body, Richard will spend more time at home. She knows the two of them have not sat out on this beautiful deck more than, oh, say, a couple of times all last summer. Will that change when their child is born? Sighing, the weight of her thoughts heavier on her mind than the weight of the baby on her belly, Bonnie closes her eyes.

Almost immediately, the neighbor's backyard gate clanks open, then shut. Wheels crunch noisily over gravel. Sighing and rising to her feet again, Bonnie walks to the deck railing and peers down toward the adjoining yard. "Hey, Pat, what're you up to?" she asks.

Surprised, Pat looks up from the wheelbarrow she is manhandling down a pink crushed-gravel path that leads to an enclosure in the back corner of her yard. "Hi, Bonnie," she smiles up at her young, rotund neighbor. "I'm just carting another load back to my compost pile. Things are sprouting again, you know!" she states happily.

"I'd say *sprouting* is an understatement," replies Bonnie, placing both palms under the large load in her abdomen and lifting slightly for emphasis.

"You might be right," agrees Pat, eyeing the young woman's girth. "You feeling okay, honey?"

"I'm fine. Maybe just a little tired," admits Bonnie.

"Well, I'm not surprised," said Pat. "That's a lot of weight you're toting, sweetheart. Now, let me dump this, then I've got just what you need for a little pick-me-up if you have a few minutes."

If only you knew, thinks Bonnie, but aloud she replies, "Sure, Pat, but don't go to any trouble."

"No trouble," counters the spry old woman. "Be right there. I'll let myself in, you just stay put." So saying, she maneuvers the heavy wheelbarrow back to the compost pile and upends it to dump its contents, which she stirs with a pitchfork she keeps right inside the compost enclosure. Then she briskly pushes the empty barrow to the back door of her garage, which swallows her up inside.

Watching, Bonnie knows she'll be doing well if she has the older woman's energy at fifty, much less seventy. Still leaning over her deck railing, she smiles at the view she has of both her and Pat's backyards. If it is true that opposites attract, then the adjoining yards are destined for a torrid affair. While she and Richard have decided to xeriscape their property in keeping with Colorado's semi-arid status (a designation derived from the state's fourteen measly inches of rainfall per year), Pat fights back for all she is worth.

Thus, land on the Blackburn side of the fence sports no sod, but what Bonnie considers a visually interesting combination of stone, native grasses, and drought-resistant plants such as yucca and prickly pear. Theirs is an open, unfenced yard that blends neatly in with its natural surroundings. It requires no sprinkler system and virtually no maintenance, thank God. Richard is never home, and Bonnie's pregnancy presently precludes bending over.

Pat's yard, on the other hand, is a study in lushness. Enclosed within its tall privacy fence, her backyard is a rich emerald green Bonnie swears Pat waters at least five times a week. (Bonnie knows this because Pat's sprinkler system comes on with a loud whoosh at 3 A.M., when she is either tossing restlessly trying to find a comfortable position for sleep or up for another of her countless trips to the bathroom to relieve her compressed bladder.) Even now, though it's just spring, the yard is dotted with beds of flowers of all sizes and colors, and littered with the most amazing collection of whimsical paraphernalia Bonnie has ever seen.

Terra cotta bunnies and frogs peep out here and there from among the flowers, which seem to be randomly interspersed with round patio stones covered with multi-colored mosaics that wink in the sunshine. Birdfeeders of various sizes and shapes swing gently from poles placed around the edges of the patio, while a tiny pond containing live goldfish captures the spill from a fat stone urchin's urn. A wooden bench with wrought-iron trim faces the pond; next to it, a small windmill spins merrily.

The whimsical touches continue on the wall of the house next to the patio, where hang a large terra cotta sun face, a clock-like thermometer with dial pointing to terra cotta numerals, and wrought-iron holders filled with baskets of still more flowers. Next to the patio, under a striped canvas awning, sits a sandbox for the grandkids, and resting against the base of a small decorative tree growing in the middle of the yard, some kind of weather-beaten old brass plate. Bonnie shakes her head and smiles at the older woman's folly. What mishmash!

But then Bonnie's deck door slides open, and the creator of the mishmash herself appears, burdened with a large blue glass pitcher and a closed tin. "Can I use your glasses, Bonnie?" asks Pat.

"Sure, I'll get some," says Bonnie.

"Uh-uh," Pat orders, putting her hands on Bonnie's shoulders and pushing her firmly down onto the chaise again. "*Sit,* girl—just look at those ankles!" she chides, catching a glimpse of the swollen joints and shaking her finger accusingly. She disappears into the house again, momentarily reappearing with tall ice-filled glasses and napkins. She fills a glass with ruby-red liquid from the pitcher, opens the tin, and puts what look like two large oatmeal cookies on a napkin. She hands all to Bonnie, then serves herself and sits nearby.

Bonnie takes a sip of her drink, which indeed has a refreshing tang. "Mmmm, this is really good, Pat. What is it?" she asks curiously.

"That, my dear, is what in my family we've always called Raspberry Renew. It's good because it's not so sicky sweet, don't you think?"

Bonnie, lips to her glass again, nods agreement.

"The secret's the cider vinegar in it," says Pat knowingly.

"Well, whatever, it's delicious," Bonnie says again. "But I'll probably gain another five pounds just *looking* at these," she adds, pointing ruefully to the cookies. "I couldn't believe at my last checkup they told me to watch how much *fruit* I was eating, because it has so many calories!"

Pat waves her hand dismissively. "You know, some of those doctors get mighty carried away with that weight thing, Bonnie. Maybe this is a time in your life when you just shouldn't worry about it, as long as you eat right yada yada yada, and I'm sure you're doing all that, aren't you?"

"I'm trying, but I do eat more when Richard's not home," confesses Bonnie.

"Will he be home soon?" asks Pat politely.

"Ten days down, four to go," complains Bonnie. "Do you think he'll be home more after the baby's born?" she asks wistfully, biting into her cookie.

Pat says the only thing she can say. "Oh, honey, I don't know."

Bonnie nods. "That's just it, because I don't, either." Over her glass, she gazes sadly out over the prairie below. On the distant nature trail she can just make out the tall figure of a man she has seen before. Always dressed completely in black, the guy doesn't jog or blade or bicycle but just seems to saunter around. Though the day is warm, Bonnie shivers slightly. She doesn't know that man's business, but she does know that he gives her the creeps.

That night Bonnie, her back aching no matter what position she tries, shifts restlessly on her lonesome mattress. She has heard Pat's sprinklers go on and she has heard them go off. Now—it is 4:24 A.M.— a band of coyotes starts to howl. Bonnie smiles to herself. She doesn't wonder whether the music of the animals outside signifies anything more than an undignified reunion of compatriots. She only knows that she wants badly to *see* the creatures hosting this crazy songfest in the middle of the night.

She heaves herself from bed and, arms akimbo for protection and balance, clumsily works her way through the darkened house to her deck. Leaving the lights off, Bonnie quietly slides the deck door open, steps barefooted onto her deck, and peers hopefully into the night in the direction of riotous sound. Where are you, she wonders, but her eyes detect no movement on the prairie below, even in the moonlight. Ahh, well, maybe tomorrow they'll come closer. The concert stops abruptly.

Disappointed, Bonnie vaguely recalls a childhood song she learned from some cowboy record. Her mind struggles, then succeeds in recapturing the elusive refrain of a cattle-driver's lullaby to his herd: "...the coyote's nothin' skeery, just singin' to his dear DearIE." Humming under her breath, Bonnie returns slowly, ponderously, to bed. Soon, very soon, she will sing her own lullabies. She hugs her swollen belly, drifts at last to sleep.

down under

For Ed Wonsawski this Sunday, life can't get much better. While Rita and the kids sleep in, he creeps from the warm bed, dresses quietly, then heads out for an early round of golf. SouthRidge, his favorite course, is a straight shot east down Harmony Road to Lemay. Ed has learned that, though the popular course is always crowded at peak times, if he shows up early as a single he can usually get on fairly quickly even on weekends. He doesn't mind the chill air or the damp grass or playing with strangers. In fact, he enjoys being anonymous so he can concentrate on his strokes. On such occasions he doesn't even keep score, except for a running tally he keeps in his head.

This tally, though informal, is far from inaccurate. Years of calculating prices for the chemicals he sells at various markups to various customers have had their effect. Today, Ed has succeeded in accumulating a respectable par-plus-something. When his putting doesn't suck, he thinks happily, he can really hold his own.

On the way home he stops at Gib's—voted Fort Collins' best for the umpteenth time—for a bag of fresh bagels, then returns like a triumphant adventurer to his clamoring kids. ("Didja get any *raspberry*, Dad?" "Ugh, who wants raspberry? How 'bout *onion*, Dad?") But Ed takes the bickering stoically. It wouldn't be Planet Earth if ten-year-old Gregory and six-year-old Laura weren't at odds.

Ever the optimist, Ed in no way equates the perpetual discord that seems to run in his young family with failure to carry out his fatherly duties. In typical Ed-style, he roughens the hair of his two tow-headed offspring and placates everyone. "I got something for everybody, guys." He slices the bagels, sets out the cream cheese and jelly, and lets the mayhem begin.

Rita, contentedly sipping the latté he has brought for her, smiles sleepily over the morning paper. Her long brown hair hangs in thick hanks around her somewhat pudgy but clear-skinned face. Though it is May, she still wears the thick gray fleece robe and slippers Ed gave her one Christmas for winter wear. The outfit makes her resemble one of the stuffed animals Laura has strewn all over her room. Though the thought has several times occurred to Ed that, were his wife ever to get up and move a little bit—like, say, get breakfast for *him* once in a while on weekends instead of vice versa— she wouldn't need such heavy clothing so late in the season, he never says anything. She is capable of moving finely on occasion, and that's good enough for him. Ever the optimist.

After Ed cleans up the breakfast mess, he clomps upstairs to his bedroom to change. Rita is already done. She is now attired in a lime-and-forest-green spandex outfit that drives Ed nuts every time he sees it. Clad in that thing, she looks nothing short of naked, but green. Her leotard ends in a thong that separates her sizeable haunches enticingly. "Mmmm, honey, why dontcha commere," he coaxes, now sprawled in his boxers on their still unmade king-size bed.

Rita smiles that smile and wiggles her hips at him. "Uh-uh, Ed, you know I have exercise class now."

Ed groans. "I'll give you a workout, honey."

Rita waggles a finger at him. "Maybe later, sweetie. I gotta go." She sashays from the room, wiggling for all she is worth. Ed grins at her retreating fanny.

Rita's drive to their health club, The New Pulse, takes less than fifteen minutes. Today her latté has revved her up for the torture of her aerobics class. Though she began her formal exercise program three years ago, Rita never subscribed to the "no pain, no gain" philosophy embraced by the pencil-women who frequent the advanced classes. To her, they are a sorry-looking bunch with no laps on which to place their babies or boobs with which to suckle them. Such foolishness.

Rita believes her presence thrice weekly in the low-impact beginners' class should guarantee her place among Fort Collins' super-fit without subjecting her to the pain that adjective usually entails. She does not regard this approach as sneaky, but smart. Thirty-nine years of age, she has never needed knee surgery or even treatment for a muscle sprain, and she intends to keep it that way.

She marches her robust green body into the gym with head held high and takes her place with no apologies to anyone. When Tracy begins to call the routine to the mind-numbing bam-bam-bam of the music, she falls resignedly into step. Thirty minutes of numbness is the only way she can get through this ordeal, which she endures just for Ed, anyway. At least he appreciates the results.

Pulling into the driveway after class is over, Rita sees that the grass has been freshly cut. Ed is on the driveway next to her, monkeying with the lawn mower. Rita swears that, next to his golf clubs, the mower is her husband's favorite toy.

Ed is originally from Chicago. Though he grew up in a ranch-style home in the suburbs, he spent many a childhood hour at his grandparents' small bungalow in the city. There, he often helped maintain the tiny plot of lawn that was his grandfather's pride and joy. At his grandfather's side, Ed learned that a house surrounded by lush green turf could create envy among neighbors regardless of their income or position in the community. Green, green grass was a status symbol that shouted: *"Hey! You might be richer, but we have a stronger work ethic than you!"*

The fact that, in those days, a strong work ethic seemed to carry greater value than it does now does not bother Ed. He only knows that on Sunday afternoons men of his grandfather's generation, rich and poor, tall and short, fat and thin alike, rolled up their collective shirtsleeves and attended to the serious business of making those small patches of green around their homes greener still. Afterwards, well satisfied with their efforts, they'd sit around on the back porch nursing a glass of beer and a stogy. Over the radio would come the voice of the announcer calling the plays of the Wonsawskis' favorite baseball team, the Chicago Cubs.

As clearly as if it were yesterday, Ed can remember the summer of '69. He had been ten years old and the Cubs, who hadn't won a pennant since '45, were finally turning things around. With the big-nosed Leo Durocher managing, Adolpho Phillips (what a great name!) in center field, crowd-pleasing Billy Williams in left, and Ron Santo at third base, the team had steamrolled its way to first place. Hopes that they'd go on to take the pennant were as high as the young boy's hopes for his own future.

Then, along about September, everything fell apart at once. Ed's beloved grandfather, who had struggled with diabetes all his adult life, entered the hospital and never came out. At virtually the same time, the Mets came from behind to overtake the Cubs and win the pennant.

Afterwards, the double letdowns of losing his grandfather and the Cubs losing the series seemed to Ed to be two events forever intertwined. But he never forgot the warm sense of accomplishment and camaraderie those Sunday afternoons with his grandfather had entailed. Even now, much to Rita's disgust, he allows himself an occasional moment of nostalgia by lighting his own fat cigar. Funny how, to Ed, the aroma of those cigars always seems to be combined with the fragrance of freshly cut grass. Ed remains loyal to the memory of those times in one other way as well.

By and large, the lawn-care services listed on five pages in the local phonebook take care of most of the yards in his neighborhood. One could perhaps deduce that old dreams do die hard from the names of such services (Vista *Green*, Tru*Green*, nitro-*green*, Ever*green*, *Green*ing-Up, *Green*works, to name a few). However, Ed knows that none of those idealistically named services would care for his lawn like he does. High-efficiency operations whose employees are trained to zoom in and zoom out of "zones" as fast as possible, the services allow no time for digging the stray dandelion or thistle. If the chemicals they apply five times a year won't take care of a weed, nothing will.

And try readjusting a scheduled "enrichment" to suit the vagaries of Colorado weather (fertilization during times of drought can burn grass badly) when 899 other customers are waiting in line as well. This is service at its streamlined best, and the 899 other customers are well satisfied, thank you very much. Does Ed care to sign on, or does he not?

Ed does not. Hiring a service would betray not only the memory of his grandfather, but his thriving relationship with his lawn as well. He cannot see himself doing either of those things until he is too decrepit to push the mower. As a hearty forty-one-year-old six-foot-two Colorado Polack, he does not anticipate such demise for a long time to come. For Ed, summer Sundays are a compilation of Gs: golf, then grass, then Grandma's. It is a good combination that suits him just fine.

Now, however, Ed looks up from his mower and frowns. "Hi, babe," he greets Rita. "Say, did you call the city like I asked you to do last week? Those damn rats are working their way closer to the property line, and I want to know what the city's gonna do about them. They carry plague, you know."

Ed's unfenced backyard abuts the Cathy Fromme Prairie, a one-thousand-acre natural area purchased in chunks by the city of Fort Collins for a little less than two million dollars. The wide-open spaces and rolling terrain of the prairie typify how Fort Collins looked before it was settled, and they afford the Wonsawskis a great view, but Ed considers them a mixed blessing nonetheless. The "rats" he abhors are a small colony of black-tailed prairie dogs.

Rita's manicured hand flies to her mouth. "Oh, honey, I forgot. But I'll do it tomorrow, I promise, okay?" She neatly changes the subject. "Are you coming in to get cleaned up for Mom's now?"

"Sure." It is only May, but Ed has already finished cutting the grass for maybe the fifth time. Because he likes to get what he calls "all that winter crap" off the grass before it really starts growing, he is always the first in the neighborhood to be seen with lawn mower up and running. Ed doesn't realize he shares this habit with his nemesis. Because their first line of defense against predators is a clear field of vision, black-tailed prairie dogs, too, keep the turf around their colonies well clipped. Momentarily striking a pose to survey his own turf before pushing the mower back into the packed garage, Ed looks more like a sentinel prairie dog standing tall on his own estate than he would care to know.

An hour later, the Wonsawskis' minivan pulls into Rita's mother's driveway. Only minutes away from their house by car, Grandma's house is located high up on Coyote Ridge, which overlooks the Cathy Fromme Prairie. From her spacious patio you can also see the Wonsawskis' backyard, which Ed teasingly refers to as "down under." But the kids don't care about the relative position of their families' houses. They clamber out of the vehicle, charge up to the screen door, and let themselves inside. Ed and Rita follow more sedately, admitting themselves to the familiar scene of Laura throwing herself at her Grandma as if it has been years, not one week, since she has last seen her, while boy-trying-to-be-a-man Gregory looks on with masculine disdain for these histrionics. Rita's mumbled greeting does not include a kiss or hug for her mother, though Ed fondly pecks the older woman's soft cheek. "Hey, it's good to see you, Pat," he says.

"You too!" Pat concurs. "How have you been?" she asks as she shoos her tribe into the family room adjoining her kitchen, from which tantalizing smells are already making Ed's mouth water. He'd bet on roast pork with caraway seed today.

"Fine, fine." Big Ed is still in his satisfied Sunday mode. He knows things will only improve with the fine dinner Pat always has waiting. Rita is already settled comfortably in a corner chair. She leafs through a magazine while the kids dig enthusiastically through a large basket of kid stuff Pat keeps next to the fireplace. The kids think it magical that odd changes occur in the basket's contents between visits, so they can never be quite certain what they will discover. Now Laura utters a high-pitched squeal.

"A Poochi Dog!" she shrieks.

Rita looks reprovingly at her mother and tsk-tsks her. "Really, Mother, you spoil them rotten."

Pat grins. "I know, I know, but I don't have to live with the consequences, you do!" she teases her daughter as the family room quickly fills with the sound of the barking dog, one of those electronic wonders that performs more the more the children interact with it.

"Thanks a lot." Rita rolls her large brown eyes, the picture of martyrdom.

Ed, who has settled his large frame on the sofa, tactfully intervenes. "So how's your lawn-care service treating you these days?" he inquires.

"Oh, you know, it's never the same as when we did it ourselves," replies Pat. "I really don't know any of them. They whiz in and out of here in about twenty minutes, it seems to me, and I just get the bill in the mail. I wouldn't call them detail-oriented, exactly, but I guess they get the job done," she concludes.

"Well, if you ever need anything, let me know," Ed offers sincerely. He knows that Pat, trying hard to adjust to widowhood, is a proud woman who will not ask favors lightly. In this way she is very different from his own family, most of whom are still back in Chicago. The

Wonsawskis were always calling each other up for help with one thing or another, and nobody thought any the less of anybody for doing so. It was simply understood that family was there to help you when you needed them. If you didn't ask, the more fool you.

"Why thank you, Ed." Pat jumps up to go do her magic in the kitchen. Rita does not get up to join her, but from her easy chair, inquires whether her mother needs a hand.

"Oh, no, honey, you just relax." Pat waves away her daughter's offer. Ed has witnessed this scene before. Pat and Hal had begun inviting the Wonsawskis for Sunday dinner immediately after the kids were born. Ed recalls how, in the beginning, Pat insisted it was her pleasure to host these gatherings as a way to keep the families close. And it was true that, when the kids were babies, Rita did have her hands full tending to them. But now the kids were older and Rita frequently had free time on her hands. She could do more to help her mother, thinks Ed. Rita is just one of those people who never seemed quite aware of the work a good home-cooked meal entailed, perhaps because she never made them. At home, their diet consists chiefly of processed or frozen entrees that make their way from box to microwave to mouth in a matter of minutes.

"Time to eat," Pat calls from the kitchen. They all help bring the steaming dishes to the dining room table and are just about to seat themselves when Gregory interrupts.

"Can I please have a soda?" he asks, looking from his mom to his grandmother with what he hopes is an innocent expression on his face. One thing Rita insists on at home is adequate dairy intake. Milk is always the beverage of choice at the table, period. But once in a while Rita does let her son partake of the forbidden fruit Grandma keeps stashed in the extra refrigerator in her garage.

Pat knows better than to say anything, leaving this little power play up to her daughter. "Oh, I guess so," Rita gives in. She can't *always* be the bad guy. Gregory jumps up and heads down the hallway to the garage.

A moment later he is back, can of soda in one hand, perplexed expression on his face. "Where's Grandpa's car, Grandma?"

Pat hastily arranges a relieved expression on her face and in her voice. "Oh, I finally got rid of that old thing," she claims, waving her hand airily in a dismissive gesture.

Rita's eyebrows rise perceptibly, while her lower jaw drops. "What do you mean, Mother? You didn't really get rid of Daddy's car, did you?" She speaks in an I-can't-believe-you're-telling-me-this tone.

"Well, you know, Rita, I can't keep all his stuff around here forever. I got an offer I couldn't refuse," Pat parries. "Some fellow down the road had his eye on it and met my asking price so, I sold it," she confesses.

"What fellow down the road?" pries the irritated Rita. "I hope you know that car was a *collector's item,* Mother. Surely you didn't let it go for peanuts, did you?"

Now it is Pat's turn to be exasperated. "I'm not an idiot, Rita. I told you, he gave me what I asked, and that was that."

"But I didn't even know you had advertised it for sale." Rita does not like feeling out of the loop.

"It was sort of a spur-of-the-moment thing," explains Pat. "I was washing it out in the driveway when he came by, took an interest, one thing led to another and pretty soon that was that."

Rita shakes her head. "Well, I hope you got what it was worth." She tries again to coax more info out of her mother, but Pat doesn't even sniff the bait.

"As I said, I'm well satisfied." End of conversation, for Pat at least, but on the way home Rita pursues the subject.

"I can't believe she sold Daddy's car without telling me," she complains to Ed.

"She just did," counters Ed. Then, in an attempt to mollify his wife, he adds, "Remember she said it was a spontaneous thing, babe. You can't blame her for taking advantage of an opportunity like that. You know, without the right buyer, a car like that could sit in someone's garage for a long time. I can't blame her for wanting to get it out of there, can you?"

Rita utters an insulted "hmph" and turns her face stonily toward the window. When their van bumps along the corrugated washboard that serves for road in Coyote Cañon, her petulance is further irritated. "Why don't they fix this damn thing?" she complains.

"Did you read that last letter from the Homeowners' Association?" asks Ed. "The road's the main item on the agenda tonight. I'm going because I want to hear about it myself."

bumps in the road

Seven-thirty that same evening, Tammy Berry, a hard-working Fort Collins realtor who is also secretary of the Coyote Cañon Homeowners' Association (HOA), surveys the packed first-grade classroom that is their meeting place with satisfaction. For once, a quorum is present! Normally, only the beleaguered board members and a few people who can't stand blanks in their Day-Timers show up.

"Hey, Ed, how's it going?" The questioner is a man who not only lives down the street, but is also the purchasing agent for the Ford, Lincoln and Mercury dealership that belonged to Ed's father-in-law when he was alive. The dealership is still one of Ed's best customers.

Squeezing his large frame behind a ridiculously small desk, Ed nods. "It'd be better if I can convince you to seal your floors." The PA's laughter is cut short when Bob Bower, HOA (and local bank) prez, bangs his gavel.

"Will this meeting please come to order." Without the rising inflection necessary to make his words a request, they become a command. Bob wears his rank here as comfortably as the three-piece suit he wore to church that morning. His demeanor bespeaks board-, not back-, rooms, but Ed respects him because he works the crowd as easily as Ed works the controls of his lawn mower.

"I see we've finally figured out how to entice you to meetings." Bower pauses, shakes his head. "If I had the name recognition Rex Vanderkliest has with you right now, next election I wouldn't even have to give campaign finance a thought, would I?" Knowing laughter acknowledges the fact that Vanderkliest, here to represent the county on the road issue, is indeed the night's main attraction. "Weell," drawls Bower, "even Rex can't override the rules of Parliamentary Procedure, so you'll have to be patient." There are groans of objection, but Bower holds up a placating hand.

"We'll pass around an attendance sheet in lieu of taking roll, which would be difficult in view of the fact that I've never seen half of you before. Then we'll read and approve the minutes from last meeting, hear brief reports from the officers and committees, and conquer unfinished business. Following that, we can get to the matter uppermost on our minds."

True to his word, Bower carries out the necessary steps with dispatch. Less than half an hour passes before he announces, "And now, ladies and gentlemen, the moment—or I should say, the man—you've all been waiting for: Rex Vanderkliest, county road engineer extraordinaire."

Patient to this point, when Vanderkliest steps to the podium, the audience promptly forgets its manners. Audible boos accompany the balding engineer to his post, but Vanderkliest maintains an unruffled demeanor. Unfortunately, he is a veteran of hostile meetings; fortunately, his personality and manner alone go a long way toward defusing such occasions. A slight smile plays about his mouth as he waits for the noise to subside. When it does, he speaks in a mild tone that indicates he does not take the crowd's ill will personally.

"Hi, folks. I'd like to say 'Good evening,' but, seeing as the condition of your road and my title make it unlikely things'll turn out that way, how about I start by giving you a little background on roads like yours, and then answer some of your questions." Before he can continue with what he has to say, the engineer is rudely interrupted.

"Yeah, like why's the damn thing going to hell and why aren't you fixing it?" An obnoxious man in the back of the room nevertheless gets nods of support from a good portion of the audience who, though they may have phrased the question differently, want an answer all the same.

Vanderkliest nods. "Okay, I'll skip the sugar-coating and cut to the chase." He pauses, gathering his thoughts.

"I inspected your road last Wednesday, folks, and I'm sorry to tell you that, in my judgment, it's in need not just of repair, but total replacement. The unevenness of the surface is so advanced that the short-term benefits you'd get from any stop-gap repair measures wouldn't be worth it. Basically, your road's in such bad shape only pulverization and removal of the present surface followed by reconstruction from the ground up will get you what you want." This statement is met by exclamations of approval from the audience, but Vanderkliest holds up a warning hand.

"Now for the hard part," he continues. "Unfortunately, you should also know that the county road budget doesn't even come close to covering the costs of all roads in need of repair. Therefore, eighteen months ago, we were forced to begin charging property owners in housing developments like yours the cost of their own road replacement."

This statement is met by loud cries of objection from most of the audience. Ed is among those who cannot believe what they have just heard. "Are you telling us we're going to have to pay for replacing our road *ourselves?*" he asks, just to make sure.

Vanderkliest nods. "I'm afraid so. Because the population in our area has been increasing so dramatically, the increase in single-family homes—or housing developments needing roads—has grown disproportionately larger than the county budget can stand. Passing the cost on to homeowners is about our only recourse."

Ed is not finished. "I can understand informing homeowners in new developments that they'll have to bear the burden of their own road costs, but you guys built our road, what, about eight years ago?" Ed looks around the room for confirmation, but Vanderkliest responds.

"Close. Actually, your road is eighty-seven months old."

"Uh-huh. But doesn't the county have to sign off on completed construction, and isn't it a fact that our road is failing because it was improperly underlaid in the first place?" Though Ed is no expert on road construction, he has done his homework. Before Vanderkliest can respond, other voices from the classroom chime in.

"You're damn right. Pay attention when you're driving, and you'll see that the dips in the road correspond to every place they laid a culvert beneath it."

"So if the road wasn't built properly in the first place, and you guys signed off on it, shouldn't the county have to pay for it?" The room quiets.

Vanderkliest scratches his bare pate. "Well, I can understand that's the way you'd think it should be," he agrees. "But the county attorney has informed me there's a seven-year statute of limitations on accountability for roads, which unfortunately has just expired. So, legally, you still have to bear replacement costs yourselves."

"Shit." The man in the back of the room has not fallen asleep. The next comment is more practical.

"Well, how many people is that?"

For this question, Vanderkliest has come prepared. "Liability falls only upon those property owners whose land actually abuts the road. This includes those whose property lies along the cul-de-sacs that are offshoots of the road as well, which brings it to a grand total of— let me see—" he consults some paperwork "seventy-two households."

"Only seventy-two?" The voice asking the question is incredulous. "That's diddly squat in terms of finance. So how much are you estimating per household?"

Vanderkliest turns more pages but doesn't dodge the question. "Each household would have ten years to pay off seventeen-thousand dollars per property. If you sold your house in the interlude, the unpaid balance would be affixed as a lien against your property. I might add that, the longer you wait, the cost for road replacement will only increase."

Ed is stunned by Vanderkliest's pronouncement. Rita likes to spend money, and she'll have a fit when she finds out about this. Ed is already strapped for cash at the end of each month, and right now seventeen grand worth of additional mortgage sounds damn near impossible to take on. Though the meeting drones on, at this point Ed tunes it out. How in the hell will he make ends meet?

Ed lays the news on Rita as they're getting ready for bed. Rita's sense of outrage causes her limited self-control to evaporate. "You mean we have to pay to replace our fucking road *ourselves?*"

Ed nods grimly.

"Well then, let's just pack our bags and move. I'm not married to this joint, are you?"

"I already checked, and there's disclosure laws. We can't sell without notifying buyers in writing of the road situation. Who'd knowingly take that on when they could just as well buy somewhere else without the additional cost of the road?"

"Bird lovers?" suggests Rita, but she recognizes a lost cause when she sees one. "Shit, Ed. Shit. Shit. Shit."

a competitive spirit

It is precisely 4:30 A.M. when the muted beeping of his alarm watch wakes Richard Blackburn from sound sleep in his hotel room in Toronto, but the intrusion does not cause Richard to groan with objection. Instead, he rises from bed in a single practiced motion, hits the bathroom in bare feet. A splash of cold water on the face, a brief pause to regard that face speculatively in the mirror, and Richard is already yanking on a sweat-suit that has been draped over the room's lone chair and stuffing his feet into the running shoes that sit beneath it. When a hasty search to locate his key card pinpoints it atop the nightstand, he pockets the slim piece of plastic, leaves the room quietly.

Outside, though the night sky is paling, Richard does not stop to ponder the mysticism of another dawn. He breaks immediately into a smooth jog that will carry him in a large eight-mile loop around his hotel. He plotted this course yesterday and knows exactly where he is bound. As he runs, he reflects excitedly on his progress. He is in the second of an eighteen-week marathon-training program. When he completes it, he will finally be ready for his first marathon, which will take place in Boulder in September. Richard hasn't yet told Bonnie about this plan, but he knows she'll be okay with it. The baby will be two months old by then, and he thinks Bonnie will be thankful for the little getaway the race will entail. It'll be a great stress reliever for both of them.

Meanwhile, he is actually ahead of schedule in his training! Anxious to progress as rapidly as possible, Richard does not stick to the bare-bones mileage increases stipulated in his training manual. Though the manual clearly spells out the dangers of increasing weekly mileage by more than ten percent, he figures those warnings are for novices, not people like himself who've been jogging since college. Though he has done little distance training per se, he is an experienced—even veteran—jogger. In fact, Richard has lengthened his runs by forbidden increments several times already without suffering pulled muscles, shin splints, or blisters. This proves his theory that the training manual is really for the uninitiated.

Technically, today should only be a six-miler according to the manual, but Richard feels so strong he knows he can run eight this morning. That way, come January he'll be way past running what he thinks of as a subsistence marathon, for which the only lowly goal is completion. Training harder will give him the competitive edge to actually finish well up in the pack—maybe even *place*—in his age group. Wouldn't *that* be something! Just thinking about this possibility brings an idiotic grin to his face as Richard puffs determinedly, rhythmically down the sleepy streets of downtown Toronto.

Back at the hotel after his run, Richard checks his watch, not for the time, but for elapsed time. Then, to the dismay of the night desk clerk still on duty, he commences stretching in the middle of the lobby. "What's it to ya, man?" thinks Richard. He hates stretching in the confines of a hotel room, and nobody is up and about yet, anyway. Working methodically, he carefully stretches his calves, hamstrings, quads, groin and hip flexors without trying to rush the process. He holds each position for a full thirty to sixty seconds, enjoying the feeling of his muscles flexing and extending luxuriously. Stretching is crucial to injury prevention for serious runners, and he will not shirk this part of his workout even if he is in Toronto. "One, one-thousand" he intones softly. When finished, he crosses the lobby, says seriously to the still-frowning clerk: "Works wonders for my lower back, ya know?" before disappearing into the elevator.

By nine o'clock, a shaved, showered, and professionally attired Richard is on duty himself. Richard is a sales rep for Fort Collins' fast growing Advanced Technical University. ATU culls its course offerings from over fifty of the top engineering schools around the country, then offers those courses via internet or satellite to students from around the globe chasing any of eighteen different masters' degrees in engineering. It is distance learning for the tech-savvy made, if not easy, at least darn convenient, thinks Richard.

And ATU has fashioned a wide net for capturing the interest of prospective students. First, the school persuades high-tech giants like HP, AT&T, Lucent, IBM, and others to come on board as "membership companies." These companies, which are forever hosting educational fairs to promote the continuing education of their work force, then welcome ATU to those fairs like a maiden to the marriage bed. That's when Richard shows up.

Manning his booth with just the right amount of swagger, Richard has the art of making an impressive presentation about ATU down pat. His pitch on course offerings and degrees is polished and to the point. He can read the interest level of the candidates who stroll by at this AT&T Canada fair with the skill of a carny weight-guesser, and he makes no apologies for the similarity. His job is to get more people to sign on the dotted line to take courses from ATU, and he likes it.

Now he has his eye on an approaching long-haired blond. She has already passed his station twice before without talking; this time, Richard plans to reel her in. He meets her gaze directly and gives her a friendly nod and smile. "Thinking about upgrading?" His opening gambit is brief although, giving her the once-over, he doesn't think she needs much in the way of upgrading.

But she smiles and nods ruefully. "Yeah." A sexy toss of that long mane. "You know you just can't stay static in this business, no matter how good your credentials are."

"Don't I know it," agrees Richard who, though he can fake the lingo well enough to pitch graduate programs to prospective students, is no engineer himself. Computers and electronics have never been his bent: he is a people-person who likes trying to persuade complete strangers to come around to his point of view. "So what do you do?" he inquires gamely.

"I'm a software engineer," she responds. Then, "But, you know, sometimes it feels like we're a dime a dozen these days."

Richard nods sympathetically. "Sure. Any field where the money is eventually gets overcrowded. Then it gets harder and harder to distinguish yourself. Do you have your master's?" he pries.

She shakes her head no. "And I know I need it," she confesses. "It's just so hard, once you're working full time, to figure out how to go back."

"Ahh, but that's the beauty of a school like ATU," Richard purrs. "It can't *get* any more convenient than we make it. This is graduate education at your doorstep, you know."

The blond purses her lips thoughtfully. "I have heard about you," she admits.

For a fraction of a second, because he is wearing his nametag and because he is vain, Richard thinks she means him, personally. "You have?" he asks with pleased surprise, wondering if she is a runner, too. Her legs are encased in knee-high leather boots, so it's hard to tell. He is about to comment on a race he ran in Vancouver a year ago when she sets him straight.

"You import courses from the best U.S. universities, then tie them together in grad programs you offer via the internet, right?"

"Or satellite." Richard takes his disappointment in stride.

"Well, do you have any literature?" she asks, nervously flipping her hair off her neck.

"But of course, madam," responds Richard with a slight bow. He loads her with a catalog, course offerings, and registration material just as three more looky-lous close in on his table. "You know, if you have time, I could tell you a lot more about what we have to offer over lunch than I can here," he offers. "What's your name?"

"Starre."

Richard grins. He hates eating alone in strange cities. "Call me on my cell," he instructs, thrusting his card at her. She rewards him with a shy smile before strolling off. Richard turns brightly to the waiting newcomers. "Hi there!"

a family affair

Lying in the warm sun just outside the den, Kaia nudges her firstborn away. The nudge is gentle, but firm. Banks is a scrappy little guy who would come to the well of her own body to drink forever if she let him. And she has no intention of letting him. She has nursed him for nearly two whole months already; now he must learn a tougher reality. The next time he approaches, she reflects, she'll have to resort to a nip. Sighing to herself, she repeats the refrain of weary mothers the world over: "Just what don't you understand about the word 'no'?"

Meanwhile, she watches her three pups gamboling about the entrance to their den, located a short way up a rocky ravine that feeds down to the prairie below. Little do her children know their playful leaps and pounces herald the beginning of a far more serious game they must learn all too quickly to survive. Even for a versatile coyote who will eat just about anything, Kaia knows, this small prairie is not a cornucopia. Finding enough food to stay well fed requires constant hard work. There is no guarantee of plenty—ever.

Kaia suspects her mate of two years and the pups' father, Marcus, is probably holed up somewhere in the shade, sleeping the afternoon away in perfect peace. Even at night, she sees far less of him now that the pups are here than she did during breeding season. "So what else is new?" Kaia chuckles softly to herself, then nips the recalcitrant Banks firmly on his ear. Yipping in pain, he retreats once more to his sisters' company. Thank goodness neither Leila nor Liza resist weaning like Banks. At the moment, one stubborn pup is more than enough.

acting up

Returning from what, primarily because of his duster, had turned into a hot, sweaty walk on the nature trail, Davin enters his house through the back doors that lead into the downstairs family room. The large room is blessedly cool and, compared to the glare outside, so dim it takes his eyes a moment to adjust. When they do, Davin puts a CD by The Cure on, then wanders over to the burgundy-covered pool table and picks up his cue. He habitually shoots a few rounds to unwind after an intense session on the trail. The trail is where Davin, unarguably the most talented actor at Poudre High School, works the traits of whatever character he will next assume on stage well into his own mind. He uses a self-taught blend of imagination and visualization that somehow enables him to *become* whomever he wants to portray on stage.

While his classmates think him a lucky devil to whom acting comes as easily as walking, only Davin knows the extent to which each characterization drains him. His present cause for sweat is the character of Jean-Paul Marat in Peter Weiss' brilliant play, *The Persecution and Assassination of Jean-Paul Marat as Performed by the Inmates of the Asylum of Charenton Under the Direction of Monsieur de Sade*, or for short, *Marat/Sade*. Davin finds this ambitious production, slated to open the end of the school year just before graduation, the perfect vehicle for the capstone of his high-school acting career.

The play takes place in 1808. The infamous Marquis de Sade, imprisoned in a mental asylum for siding against the aristocracy, argues the merits of the French revolution with one Jean-Paul Marat. Marat is a thin forty-nine-year-old who, for relief from a skin disease, spends his time shrouded in a white cloth, sitting in a bathtub. He is at once a figment of Sade's vivid imagination and, simultaneously, Sade's political alter ego. Suffering "revolutionary burnout," Sade still sympathizes with the goals of the revolution while regarding its bloody reality with detached distaste. But Marat regards the rebellion as so noble a cause its advancement is worth any cost.

Davin understands that attitude. His assumption of a Gothic persona early freshman year was an act of rebellion, too, for which he's paid the painful price of his father's respect. Thinking about his father takes the pleasure out of what he is doing, and Davin misses an easy shot. He tosses his cue aside in disgust and goes over to the bar, where he mixes himself a tall rum and Coke, half of which he gulps down as if it were milk. Even though his father has long since let Rosa, their live-in housekeeper, go, Davin swears her ghost still hangs about the place. Rosa would have a fit if she caught him drinking. Davin lifts the remainder of his drink to her in mock salute and swills the other half. Nobody gives a damn what he does now, and he can't decide whether that feels better or worse. He rinses, dries, and replaces his glass on the shelf to conceal the evidence, then heads upstairs.

Though he knows he should start on his math homework (God, how he hates all things related to math or science), Davin again hears the devil whisper in his ear, and he tiptoes into his father's study instead. He is so sick and tired of listening to his father complain about all the money he's lost on the market lately—all the "dot.thises" and "dot.thats" that haven't lived up to his father's earnings' expectations—he thinks maybe he'd better check things out for himself. If things are really as bad as his dad would have him believe, thinks Davin, it's a wonder they aren't living under a bridge.

As he boots up his father's computer and waits for the desktop to appear on the screen, Davin considers the ambiguity of his feelings about his dad's misfortune. Yeah, it'd be a pain to be poor (they've never been broke before), but on the *other* hand, knowing that his father has for once failed at something he's tried to do feels…well, it feels *freeing*. Davin scans the desktop for likely file names and zeroes in on "Investments." He clicks the file open and studies the chart that appears on the monitor. It's a neat summary of all his dad's stock transactions for the past year. His father, a time-management fanatic, keeps everything in his power organized to the nth degree.

There is a whole page of stocks listed, and each has corresponding figures entered under the "buy," "sell," "dates," and "volume" columns, but there is no column for profit or loss. Frowning, Davin pulls out his father's desk chair and sits down. This is going to take longer than he thought. He reaches for the calculator in the top desk drawer, takes up pen and pad, and begins to work. He painstakingly multiplies every "volume" entry times its corresponding "buy" and "sell" figures, then determines the difference between those two products. As he works his way down the page and realizes all the tallies he has so far are negative numbers, Davin begins to sweat. "Holy shit!" he whispers under his breath. He is nowhere near the bottom of the page, but, if these figures are true, he knows his father's losses are far greater than he has imagined. Concentrating hard, he jumps when his father's voice interrupts from the doorway behind him.

"Well, Davin, there's nothing I like better than a snoop in my own house." His father's large frame fills the doorway.

"Hey, Dad, I just wanted to see how bad off we really are," counters Davin. "You've told me we're broke, you know, but no details." He returns his father's accusing glare with one of his own. "If we're really as bad off as you say, I deserve to know too."

"So, now you know," states his father flatly.

"Uh-uh." Davin shakes his head. "I'm not done with the math yet," he confesses.

His father laughs bitterly. "That figures." Davin responds to the insult by tossing aside his pen and stalking from the room. Moments later, his father hears the jingle of keys and the roar of that monstrosity some old lady down the street has bequeathed his son in the name of good will.

Sighing, Gavin David Hassletree III, Fort Collins' eminent cardiac surgeon, reaches over and deletes his "Investments" file from the computer before crumpling Davin's worksheet in his skilled hands, carrying it to the kitchen, and putting it down the garbage disposal. Then he sits wearily at the large kitchen table that boasts seating for eight, but these days rarely accommodates more than a lonely one, and thinks bleak thoughts.

He and Davin just can't seem to get along. Davin's strange mode of dress embarrasses Dr. Hassletree, and he finds the fact that his son wants nothing to do with a career in medicine or the hard sciences bitterly disappointing. Davin could have chosen from a myriad of professions that would have satisfied his father. Chemical engineering, electronics, computer science, hell—even a stupid trainer's degree in sports physiology would be better than the damn theater. But no, *his* boy has to go and pick for his life's work a field straight out of la-la land, where you dress up in goofy clothes and play make-believe for the amusement of the masses.

Try as he might, Dr. Gavin Hassletree cannot stop taking offense at this. He sees Davin's love for the theater as a personal affront he feels in his gut every time his son demonstrates incompetence in subjects the doctor holds most dear. This gut-ache so embitters the doctor he retaliates with stinging remarks that persistently drive Davin away. The irony of the fact that such comments, over time, are slowly eating a hole in Davin's heart, and that an organ so damaged by the corrosion of contempt remains inoperable to even the most skilled of heart surgeons, escapes Dr. Gavin Hassletree, III, entirely.

Davin, meanwhile, determinedly guns the engine of his Lincoln up the incline of County Road 38E. The road winds its steep way up to Horsetooth Reservoir, a 6.5-mile-long manmade lake that for years has provided most of Fort Collins' drinking water. But now the reservoir stands practically empty, so shallow it can barely support the intrepid fish population that still struggles for life within it. Davin considers the event that brought reservoir life as he knew it to its present vegetative state when, a while back, somebody discovered that the northernmost of the construct's four dams was seeping water from underneath itself to the surrounding land.

Davin smiles at the resultant brouhaha. "Seep" is, after all, a relative term that can define anything from a bare trickle to hundreds or even thousands of gallons of water per unit of time. Wouldn't one's perspective of the seriousness of the situation depend on where you were standing relative to the seep, and how long you intended to stand there? Ahh, the perfect math problem, Dad. Davin takes both hands off the steering wheel and pounds it with grim satisfaction at his inventiveness.

Resultant studies indicate that each of the reservoir's dams could use a facelift, so the lake is drained to its lowest level in history, and the reservoir becomes not a shadow, but a sad puddle of its former self. Davin pulls into his favorite parking spot at Skyline Picnic area. He leaves his car and makes his way over to a scarred picnic table upon which he perches to take in the view. The place is deserted, so he pulls a joint from his pocket, lights it, and inhales deeply.

To the east sprawls the entire city of Fort Collins. Above the city, Davin can see the immense congregation of atmospheric pollutants residents refer to as the brown cloud. The cloud really is an ugly yellowish-brown mass that, Davin knows, usually blankets the entire Front Range from Fort Collins seventy miles south to Denver. He is too young to know that people used to come here to breathe the air for its cleanliness. Just as well. Davin does not need to add the woes of the atmosphere to his personal experience with pain.

To the west sits the now defunct Horsetooth Reservoir. Funny, Davin thinks, how, when the reservoir was full, one always imagined that its depths concealed all kinds of mysteries—underwater grottoes, perhaps, that sheltered everything from the coveted lurking bass to the secretive mermaid. A small town once stood on the land now covered by the reservoir, and Davin has even heard it said that the town's lone church steeple will eventually thrust its spooky finger up from the receding water. But the lake has been drained to its lowest point, and nothing more exotic than the rusting body of an old Porsche has appeared. The exposed bottom of the drained inlet across the way reveals itself as nothing more than raw, reddish earth, devoid of even the smallest interesting feature.

Davin considers the harsh landscape across the way. A person could turn out like that, too, he thinks. What if he goes for a career in theater and then finds himself, *inside* himself, lacking? The possibility frightens him, but he already knows he will not use it as an excuse not to try. After rising to leave Davin pauses, briefly searches the ground around him, bends to pick up a chunk of uneven, pinkish stone. Then he does what boys—short and tall, thick and thin—have always done when confronted by a body of water. He whips his arm back and in a single poetic motion, flings the stone as far as he can out toward the liquid that waits to drown it. But the satisfying splash of rock into reservoir is not to be, this evening. Horsetooth water is so low that its encompassing ridges have become formidably high and wide. From where Davin is standing, it would take the arm of a behemoth to heave a rock all the way to the water. The stone Davin hurls clatters impotently onto dry ground far down the side of the same slope atop which he stands. Davin raises both arms in a sardonic salute to the struggle, bows deprecatingly to the disappearing sun across the way, and exits the scene. There is no applause.

a shopping list

Rita Wonsawski is ensconced on the huge chocolate leather couch in her family room. Ed is at work, the kids are at their friends', and Rita watches as the long rays of the afternoon sun highlight a strip of tile on the floor. The favored tiles (large, ceramic squares of mottled rusty-gray) march in a straight line from her patio to her front door. The sunshine turns the tiles into a beckoning pathway, but the absurdity of the idea of coming in the back door and exiting the front does not inspire Rita to move off the couch. She remains seated, thinking.

Rita is worried about her mother. It seems to her that Pat has been doing some strange things lately, like impulsively selling her father's car to a perfect stranger. That car had been Daddy's pride and joy, Rita repeats to herself for the thousandth time, and she still resents the way her mother just dumped it without even asking her. Rita had been hoping her mother would give the car to her. Then she could have sold it and maybe made enough to make a few road payments or get a couple outfits. Ed's so frantic over what that road's going to cost, he's clamped down on spending like a monster vise. Rita hasn't seen a new outfit in weeks.

What hurts the most, though, is that even after she told her mother about the road and how expensive it was going to be, Pat never offered to help. *You probably forgot about that, too*, Rita accuses her absent parent. She wonders if her mother is beginning to show the first signs of Alzheimer's. That'd figure. Since her brother and father died, she was Pat's only living relative except for a third cousin who lived in a nursing home somewhere in Toledo. It'd be just her luck, now that her kids were finally both in school and she had a little time to herself, to have to nurse her mother through Alzheimer's all alone for the next ten years.

Just thinking about it makes Rita tired, so she stretches from a sitting to a reclining position on the couch, then reaches for the cordless phone lying on the coffee table. She checks her breast pocket for a small slip of paper on which she has written a phone number, then dials.

"Senior Services, this is Eileen," a not-so-senior-sounding voice responds to the ring at the other end.

"Uh, hello," says Rita, "I have a question. I wonder if you could tell me anything about how to have someone evaluated for mental incompetency."

Eileen has fielded lots of questions in her two weeks on the job, but this one throws her. "You mean competency, right?" she checks, cracking her gum in Rita's ear.

"No, I don't think so. The person in question is showing signs of, well, you know, losing it."

A moment of silence follows. "Well, all's I know is there's a competency test but I never heard of an incompetency test." Eileen is proud of her developing awareness of senior services.

Exasperated, Rita moves on. "Well, I mean, is there a central testing agency or someplace I could take her to?"

"No-no," Eileen double-negatives. "That's like a very tough thing you're asking, you know?"

Rita is overjoyed to have found a sympathetic listener. "Tell me about it. She's started doing some strange things, and I just kind of wonder. So how would I go about having her tested?" she asks again, critically inspecting the nails of the hand not holding the phone. A couple of nails have serious chips in their lacquered surfaces, because Ed has made Rita forego her weekly manicures. Irritated by what she views as an unfair exchange (why does all the road money have to come out of *her* expenses?), Rita nonetheless has tried to cooperate by doing her nails herself. But she just doesn't have time to give them the attention they really need. At this moment her current shade of polish, Rich Red, looks pathetic. For a second, Rita's mind wanders from the name of her nail polish to just the word "rich," but the voice on the other end of the line brings her back to the present.

"Well, I'd probably start with the family doctor, or somebody," Eileen says dubiously.

"Mmmm," Rita considers. "Is there a certain crylon they go by, or something?" she asks, meaning to sound professional but missing "criterion" by a long shot.

Suddenly Eileen senses she is out of her league. "I really don't know," she confesses to Rita. "I mean, it's like a really hard thing you're asking about, but it's worthwhile, you know? I'd start with the family doctor," she repeats. "I'd make an appointment, and meanwhile I'd keep a list of stuff that bothers you."

Rita thinks a list is a very good idea. "I'll do that," she promises, and presses the "off" button on the phone before momentarily punching in another number from memory.

"F.C. Family Practice," another female voice responds.

"Hi, this is Rita Wonsawski, and I want to make an appointment for my mother, Pat Schreveport," states Rita. She has made this call a million times for herself, Ed, and the kids, and she knows the drill. After arranging the appointment, she makes a third and final call.

"Hi, Ma."

"Rita!" Pat is surprised and pleased to hear from her daughter, who doesn't check in often. "Is everything okay?"

"Everything's fine, Ma. I just called to tell you I've been a little worried about you lately, and I've made an appointment with Dr. Trowbridge for you for next Wednesday at two-thirty. I'll take you."

Pat is dismayed. "What on earth for, honey? I've got bridge that afternoon," she objects, "and besides, I feel fine."

Rita hesitates. This is the tricky part. She decides to turn the tables. "Well, Mother, how long has it been since you've seen a doctor?"

Now it is Pat's turn to hesitate. "Well, I don't remember, exactly," she confesses.

As if she were the predator and her mother, the prey, Rita pounces. "That's what I thought! You really should take better care of yourself, Mother. You have to stay on top of your health now that Daddy's gone, you know." It is a good thing Rita can't see through the phone line, or she would at this point see Pat making a strange face. Pat doesn't like Rita telling her what she has to do "now that Daddy's gone," and she screws up her face and silently lip-syncs her daughter.

"But don't worry, I'm sure he'll probably just want to draw a little blood and ask you a few questions, you know, preventive stuff like that," Rita gushes persuasively. "Now don't forget to put it on your calendar. You can get a sub for bridge," she urges her mother. Puzzled, Pat replaces the receiver and pencils in the appointment on her large desk pad calendar. It is unlike Rita to be so solicitous, she thinks, but she will humor her. Even at this stage Pat would welcome a small dose of caring from her daughter.

At precisely this same moment, however, Rita retrieves a pad and pencil from her own desk and prints in large block letters: "Things Wrong With Mom." She taps the pencil on her teeth a moment, then prints: 1. Forgets things.

She thinks a moment more, then adds "like last time she saw doc." That would do for starters, but she'd better drop in once or twice between now and next Wednesday to come up with more ideas. What a pain.

Ed arrives home at exactly five o'clock. His demeanor as he enters his own home after a long day of work is not beaten down but large and lusty. "I'm home!" he sings out as he barges from the garage into the laundry room, then down the hall, across the family room and into the kitchen. Here, he plants an assured kiss on Rita's lips and disengages himself from his large green lunchbox (really a small cooler), his steel Thermos, and his quart bottle for extra drinking water. Ed fills each of these items appropriately every weekday morning and totes them to work with him. The heavy leather carryall in which he keeps current paperwork, as well as numerous large boxes of samples and novelties through which he regularly paws, remain in his car.

Ed is an industrial chemical salesman. He sells every type of chemical imaginable (and some not so imaginable) for business use. He sells solvents, degreasers, choke-and-carb cleaners, truck-washing systems, and more. He sells hand-cleaners, bowl cleaners, grout cleaners and floor soaps. He sells metal-stripping compounds, waxes, sealers, disinfectants and deodorizers. His customers range from tiny one-man radiator shops to the French-owned international asphalt-and-paving conglomerate known as LaFarge. Ed deals with people in all walks of life all day long. He deals with the rich, the trying-to-be-rich, and the poor. He speaks to people who may have advanced degrees and lousy attitudes, and those with no degrees but great intelligence. He holds his own among all of these because he is expert at what he does, and those who buy his products frequently need his advice as well. Ed dispenses that freely.

Besides Fort Collins, his territory includes the northern Colorado towns of Loveland, Greeley, and Windsor, then stretches northward to take in Cheyenne and finally Laramie, Wyoming. Ed has been selling chemicals in these places for so long he has his timing down to the minute. He knows precisely when to leave from anywhere in his purview in order to get home by five, and he does just that five days a week, fifty-plus weeks a year. This does not indicate that Ed is lazy; rather, he is a man so experienced in his trade that his working days have assumed a rhythm as strong and steady as the heartbeat of a triathlete.

Once divested of the paraphernalia necessary to sustain him throughout his day, Ed bends down and retrieves a container of powdered hand cleaner from the cabinet below the sink. He dumps a generous amount of cream-colored powder onto his left hand, adds tap water, and scrubs his hands robustly. While scrubbing, he looks out their large kitchen bay to the backyard, where Laura and Gregory and maybe a half-dozen other neighborhood kids are taking turns bouncing on their trampoline. "They sure love that thing, don't they?" he asks Rita, who is dumping a couple of cartons of boxed macaroni and cheese into a bowl.

"They spend more time doing that than anything else," she confirms, adding parenthetically, "now all we need is a pool so they can have the ultimate workout."

Ed rolls his eyeballs at her, shakes his head, grabs Rita in a bear-hug and utters his favorite line: "*I'll* give you a workout, honey!"

Rita laughs. "I mean *them*, Ed, *them!*" she clarifies, wiggling out of his hold. "You know, they have more energy than you and I put together these days."

"Ahh, well, I think it's supposed to be that way, isn't it?" Ed asks.

Rita, her back to him once more, shrugs in reply. She is working hard, cooking.

At the table, after grace, neither Ed nor Laura or Gregory complain about the macaroni-and-cheese entrée with canned fruit cocktail on the side that Rita has prepared for dinner. Rita feels she has gone the extra mile by making sure that both kids receive an equal number of maraschino cherries in their salad. What more can one do?

"Oh, by the way, honey," Rita begins but Gregory is excited, and not about macaroni and cheese.

"Dad!!" he exclaims.

Rita frowns at her oldest. "Don't interrupt, Gregory." Then, "I spent some time on the phone with the city this afternoon, Ed," she continues, "and let me tell you, it was a real hassle finding somebody who actually knew something. But I finally got a hold of the guy who actually runs the city's prairie dog department, or whatever it is."

"What'd he say?" Ed is pleased that Rita finally remembered to check into his problem with the rats that are about to invade his backyard.

"He said," said Rita, "they do very little in the way of *removal* anymore." Here she catches Ed's eye and throws significant looks in the way of Laura and Greg. Ed understands that "removal" is a euphemism for "exterminate." He nods in complicity with his wife.

"So what *do* they do?"

"Well, their referred method of control, when someone complains, is to put up what he called 'an artificial visual barrier.'" Rita is proud of her newfound knowledge; she strains to get the terminology right.

"Meaning?" Ed thinks Rita means "*preferred,*" but he is used to his wife's way of expressing herself. He does not correct her.

"The way he explained it, it's a two- or three-foot black vinyl fence. You know, you've seen them in other places like construction sites." Ed nods. "Anyway, that would keep the animals from being able to see over wherever they put the fence, which in our case would be along our back property line, I guess," Rita concludes.

"How would that keep them out, when they could just tunnel under it?" asks Ed curiously.

"Oh, I don't know," Rita is tiring of this topic. "Something about them being able to see all around being their best defense against things wanting to eat them."

"Mmmm, can we have *that* for supper tomorrow night, Mom?" Gregory smacks his lips ghoulishly.

"Yuck!" Laura sticks out a macaroni-and-cheese-coated tongue.

"Stop it, you two," Rita commands. They stop it. "Anyway, they won't live where they can't see."

"Well, I'll be damned if I'm gonna have a three-foot fence of black vinyl back there," Ed states.

"It'd look pretty tacky," Rita agrees.

"*And* ruin our view." Ed is adamant. "I'll think about it," he assures his family. Rita makes no mention of the other phone calls she made that afternoon.

Gregory finally senses an opening. "Dad!" He tries again, with a little less enthusiasm than his first salvo.

"Hmm?" Ed inquires.

"It's Pinewood Derby time! We're gettin' our wood this week; will you help me make the car?"

Ed considers. The last time he agreed to do a father-son project for Cub Scouts had been for the Great Cake Bake, and the memory of that affair makes him cautious now. "Will it be like the Cake Bake?" he asks his son. Ed doesn't care to spell out the details of what he is really asking, which is: Do you remember how we baked and decorated that cake together like we were supposed to, and it was a big sloppy mess but we had a great time doing it, and then when we got to the hall all the other cakes looked professional? Ed couldn't remember the last time he had heard any other father mention cake-decorating as a hobby, but the memory of all those gorgeous cakes staring them in the face, and the humiliation he and Greg had endured when their cake was the last to sell, has not faded.

"Whaddya mean?" Gregory is puzzled by his father's question.

Ed bites the bullet. "Well, son, are they telling you you're really supposed to build this car all by yourself, or are some kids getting a little 'help' on the side—know what I mean?"

"Ahh." The Cake Bake has made Greg older, wiser. "Well, all's I know is I heard Jimmy Aizer bragging about how his dad was gonna take his car over to the wind tunnel at CSU and test it there."

Ed digests this piece of news. "Mmmm—might help to have a physics professor for a father, eh?"

Gregory is not sure what a physics professor is, but he knows enough to nod sagely.

"All right, tell you what." Ed has made up his mind. "Sure I'll help you with the derby car. But this time we're not gonna be as stupid as we were last time. Let me check around a bit and find out more about how this works before we start, okay? I'm for damn sure not gonna build a loser like we did last time!"

"Awesome!" Greg pumps his arm in support, while little Laura suddenly squeals in pain. She puts her hand up to her mouth and spits out a small, brown cherry pit. She holds it up for all to see.

"That hurt, Mommy!"

Rita rolls her eyes. "Give me that!" She takes the pit and flings it into the garbage. "Good thing you don't have your imminent teeth yet."

Laura nods, wide-eyed at her close call.

snakes alive

It is 6:30 A.M. and Bonnie Blackburn is taking her exercise by walking eastward on the Cathy Fromme nature trail. Seven-plus months' pregnant, she is large-bodied but still capable of rhythmic motion if it is not too hot. She takes pleasure in the steady cadence, the soft *swoosh* of her breathing. Do the prairie grasses hear it as she moves among them? In the cool, windless air they stand still, vigilant, but later they will shimmy with the hot afternoon breeze. Bonnie thinks briefly of Richard. She knows that, by this hour, he will already have inhaled (in quick, determined gasps) a thousand times more than she in his pursuit of ultimate fitness, but she tries not to mind this huge imbalance. Richard, she thinks when she is feeling charitable, needs to run like she needs to paint. Besides, he is coming home today; how can she begrudge him anything?

Bonnie reaches into the pocket of her maternity shorts and withdraws a generous handful of trail mix. It has *some* nutrition, she thinks defensively to herself, picking all the M&Ms out of the handful and eating them in one mouthful. Well, when she gets home she'll do the right thing and have oatmeal for breakfast.

Moving steadily along, Bonnie imagines that her baby takes as much pleasure in these early morning forays as she does, for it lies contentedly within her now, not kicking and punching to enlarge the dimensions of its uncomfortable home. Maybe the soft song of her regular breathing is the best lullaby of all. In. Out. In. Out. Bonnie pictures rich, red blood flowing from her body across the placenta, through the umbilical cord and into her baby, who sips from this potent cocktail everything it needs to grow cells of bone and brain, liver and lungs, fingers and feet. What a miracle! The glory of what is happening inside her fills Bonnie with a feeling of largess.

She is happy to be right where she is right this minute. In gentle swells the Cathy Fromme Natural Area rolls pastorally away to the southern horizon. Thinking (for the thousandth time?) of her own baby putting the finishing touches on itself inside her, Bonnie's mind drifts momentarily to the real Cathy Fromme, a Fort Collins' city councilwoman who fought hard to preserve open spaces but died in her thirties from breast cancer. She left behind two young children and the legacy of this place. Billed by the city as "jewel of the high plains," the one-thousand-acre preserve is really just a small chunk of shortgrass prairie, a reminder of how the area looked before Fort Collins grew up and pushed the greater prairie out of its way.

Bonnie has walked the trail that meanders through the natural area so many times she considers herself its intimate. Her artist's eye knows that, for most months of the year, her surroundings would appear brown—even unsightly—to those unfamiliar with the harshness of an arid western landscape. Except for brief flares of spring grandeur, the shortgrass prairie of the high plains is no garden of overcrowded verdure. The dry, alkaline soils characteristic of the region fall far short of nourishing their offspring so generously as Bonnie's body nourishes her baby. Perpetually lacking in nutrients and moisture, these soils rarely support the growth of tree or shrub. Rather, stoic clumps of vegetation stand as tiny islands ringed by surrounding patches of bare, brownish-red dirt.

This morning, Bonnie does not keep a careful eye on the dirt to either side of the trail. Eighteen months ago, when she and Richard first moved to Coyote Ridge, it had been winter. With the advent of summer and her initial sallies onto the footpath that beckoned her to the prairie, she had at first been overly cautious, ever mindful of the signs that warned travelers to "Stay on Trail," "Keep Dogs on Leash," and "Beware of Rattlesnakes." But she had watched for snakes diligently that entire summer and never seen a one, so she had relaxed her vigilance. The city probably had to post the signs to protect itself from liability, even though the risks are small, figures Bonnie.

She approaches the underpass that will allow her to cross safely under Taft Hill Road. The city hired some artist to embellish the rough exterior walls of this tunnel with sculpted artwork showing half a broadly feathered eagle's wing and the sinuous curve of the mythical rattler. With understated finesse, dozens of fork-tailed barn swallows have embellished the texturized interior of the tunnel roof with beautifully constructed, small round nests. Bonnie feels sorry when her intrusion causes a mass exodus of the nesting birds, who swoop swiftly, unerringly out of the close confines of the tunnel into the safety of the blue sky. She wonders, over the course of the day, how often other trail-users cause this same interruption to the poor birds' harried attempts at domesticity.

Exiting the tunnel, Bonnie blinks in the sunshine. She doesn't have far to go now. Rather than walk the entire length of the trail to the raptor observatory just off the Shields' Street parking lot, at this late stage of pregnancy she walks only to the bench the city has installed just east of Taft. One of several viewing spots along the way, this bench overlooks a thriving prairie dog colony. When she reaches the bench, Bonnie sits down heavily, glad to rest before her return trip. She stretches her legs out in front of her, grateful that it is too early in the day for swollen ankles. She munches another handful of trail mix.

The day is warming quickly, and as usual in mild weather, the prairie dogs divert Bonnie from constant preoccupation with her body and her baby. Atop several of the mounds of dirt that surround each burrow entrance, sentinel animals stand as if stationed at little lookout towers to watch for approaching danger. Bonnie is amused by the picture of herself sitting on the bench observing the prairie dogs, vs. the sentinel dogs standing at attention keeping a sharp eye on her. Just who is watching whom? Stretched to full height and standing stock-still, the watch-dogs utter a few sharp calls to alert the colony to her presence, but this must be a warning of the second order, for no animals dive down their burrows. Because this colony is so close to the trail, these animals are probably well conditioned to human presence, thinks Bonnie.

Bonnie regards herself as an amateur naturalist. She has read the brochure the city provides about the Cathy Fromme Prairie, and although she can't remember the scientific name of the black-tailed prairie dog—*Cynomys ludovicianus*—she does remember it's an animal important to the prairie because lots of things eat it. Eagles, coyotes, foxes, and those nonexistent rattlesnakes all supposedly dine on prairie dog, but in spite of all her visits here, Bonnie has never seen anything prey on the furry creatures. That's okay. To her, the little mammals going busily about their day are cute, harmless, don't deserve to be eaten at all—they even greet each other with a heartwarming ritual of teeth- and nose-touching that looks suspiciously like kissing!

Would Bonnie feel so cheerfully disposed toward these creatures if she knew what had happened a few weeks earlier? In April, while the newborn pups were still hidden belowground, their mothers suddenly turned murderous, killing and eating not their own babies, but two out of five of their nieces' or siblings' babes. Were these mothers so desperately hungry they had to resort to cannibalism to survive? No such rampages have been observed among other species in the animal world. Stranger still, when the surviving pups finally appeared aboveground, the adult females nursed not only their own young, but those of their relations as well. It was as if they flipped a switch that transformed them from rabid kid-killers into model moms—a trick pharmaceutical companies would pay dearly to duplicate.

But Bonnie, innocent of such knowledge, continues to watch the colony before her with simple pleasure. Only when the hand that ventures into her pocket comes up empty does she know it's time to go home (desperate hunger is not on her agenda, today). She rises from the bench by twisting and using the bench-back as a railing to pull herself up. Now her crotch aches a little from the baby pushing down on it, but the thought of hot oatmeal with brown sugar, whole milk, and strawberries keeps her feet moving. She does not walk Indian-style, one foot neatly in front of the other, but in a wide-legged gait that accommodates her swollen abdomen. Horsetooth Rock, a molar-shaped chunk of granite that's a local landmark on the western ridgeline, beckons her home.

Eyes fastened on this 7,255-ft promontory, Bonnie does not notice when she passes within inches of a western rattlesnake sunning itself alongside the trail. The snake is not large, and its mottled skin is such perfect camouflage it looks to be nothing more than a weathered stick. Bonnie cannot be blamed for missing it. Were the snake to move—assume the infamous coiled position, say, associated with its famous rattle—and catch her attention, Bonnie might do herself real damage. Her brain would know she is supposed to stop and back slowly away, but chances are her body, empowered by adrenaline, would make a reflexive leap for safety. Such sudden movement would strain Bonnie's already strained tissues as well as prompt the snake to strike.

But Bonnie is lucky today. The snake, still cold from the previous night, is not interested in coiling, rattling, or striking the bare leg of the creature so brazenly invading its space. It lies perfectly still, its reptile blood slowly warming to a higher level of function, and allows that leg to pass unchallenged. It does not take Bonnie's disregard for its presence personally. Bonnie is lucky today.

It is late afternoon by the time Richard returns from his trip to Toronto. He carries his suitcase into the bedroom and finds Bonnie asleep on the bed. She has removed her underwear (too hot) and wears a loose cotton nightgown that allows her swollen body parts to fall where they may. She has placed a towel under her face to catch the drool that seems to accompany these deep naps of late pregnancy, and Richard can see a small puddle glistening under her cheek, but he is not repulsed. He sits on the edge of the bed and places a hand upon her brow. Bonnie stirs, then wakes. Her eyes flutter open. "Hi, honey," says Richard.

Bonnie says nothing, but her eyes fill with tears. She reaches up and encircles Richard with both arms. When Richard draws her to his chest, her body feels like she has been lying in the sun for too long, rather than on a bed in an air-conditioned room. It radiates heat from every pore. "God, you're hot!" exclaims Richard.

Still tucked against his chest, Bonnie laughs tearfully. She has a nearly complete person living inside her, she has hormone storms raging through her body at any given moment, she has a *gargantuan* appetite, and she is fat. "I've been soaking my feet in ice water when I just can't stand it anymore," she confesses.

Richard laughs. "Well, honey, if that helps that's fine. Do you want some now?"

"Uh-uh. I'll just sit here so we can talk while you unpack." Bonnie arranges pillows so her back is comfortable.

Richard nods. "Toronto was good, Bonnie, well worth it," he says with his back toward her as he begins putting his clothes away in the closet. Bonnie grimaces just as Richard turns around.

"No, I mean it," insists Richard. "I'm actually ahead of quota!" Bonnie knows this is not a quota assigned by the school, but one Richard holds over himself as a goal to be met. At the beginning of each month, he checks to see how many sign-ups he'd gotten for ATU for the same month the previous year. Then he adds twelve percent and strives to meet that new number each new month. It is his simple but effective way of guaranteeing improved performance in his job.

"You were gone too long," Bonnie accuses her husband. "You know, just because I'm not due 'til the fourth doesn't mean this guy knows that," she says, patting her middle.

Richard's eyebrows rise at her use of the male word. "Did you?"

"No, we agreed, remember? They know, but I don't want them to tell us. It's more fun not knowing."

Richard tips his head first to one side, then the other. "Just don't be expecting last-minute paint jobs in the nursery, Bonnie," he cautions, not altogether jokingly.

Bonnie looks at the man who will soon become the father of their first child. She wonders, but does not ask, whether he will at least be good for changing diapers. Can you ever know someone well enough to know the answer to a question like that?

Bonnie and Richard celebrate his return by going to a nearby Italian restaurant for dinner. Below a loose black tunic, Bonnie wears a longish print skirt of black background with striking gold and red flowers on it. Leaves of muted green adorn the flowers, with the spaces between interrupted by what appear to be whitish fronds (zebra stripes?). The overall effect is dramatic and appeals to Bonnie's passionate love of color. On her feet are comfortable woven black sandals that seem to expand along with her swelling feet, but because she can no longer reach her toenails, they are bare of the rich, red polish she normally favors. She is not the type to go for a pedicure, and asking Richard to do her toenails would be going too far.

Over healthful pasta primavera and just two glasses of merlot (two glasses of wine won't hurt the baby, in spite of what the doctors say), Bonnie is abloom. She and Richard do not often allow themselves the pleasure of dining out, and her cheeks glow with the pleasure of being served a meal she did not have to prepare on dishes she does not have to wash. She turns her attention fully to the man seated across from her. "So, how's your running going, honey?"

Richard brightens. This is talk he understands. "Great! In fact, I've been meaning to ask you something I've been thinking about for awhile, Bonn."

"What?"

"Well, there's this marathon I'd like to run in Boulder in September. The baby'll be two months old by then, and a break'll do you good. Would you come?"

Bonnie frowns. "Do you mean with or without the baby?"

Richard shrugs. "Either way, I guess. Whatever you think."

Like vapor that, released to the open air, vanishes, Bonnie's feeling of contentment from their luxurious evening likewise evaporates. "How can you do that to me?"

"Do what?"

"Put the whole matter of whether or not to bring the baby on *my* shoulders, like you don't have anything to do with it."

"But I'll be running a *race*," explains Richard.

"So?" Bonnie challenges.

"Well, it's just that, I probably wouldn't be able to help much, so I thought it should be your decision, you know?"

Bonnie stares at Richard. She wants to screech at him, maybe claw his eyes out. Stopping short of making any proclamations she'll regret later, Bonnie throws her napkin down on the table and awkwardly extricates herself from her chair (it's impossible to make a dignified exit when you are almost full term). "I'll wait in the car."

The next morning at 5:00 A.M. Richard is back upon the familiar ground of the nature trail. He has assigned himself ten miles today (even though the manual says eight), and his feet slap the asphalt with their usual determination to get ahead. Bonnie doesn't understand how the discipline of his running bodes well for *both* of them, thinks Richard resentfully, unconsciously sucking in a breath every two strides and then blowing it out to same. Only disciplined people get places in life, and she should be glad he's of that ilk rather than like the guys who're on the golf course every Friday afternoon (and there are plenty of *them*).

Approaching the underpass at Taft Hill Road, Richard's two-beat in- and exhalations make a steady whooshing sound—ii-in, ou-out—until he catches a glimpse of unexpected motion to his left. It's 5:00 A.M., for chrisake, what could be out here now? He slows, then comes to a complete stop as a mother coyote and her three pups emerge from the brushy creek bed to his left and trot purposefully, disdainfully, across the trail in front of him. Richard is not frightened, nor does he feel particularly privileged. As the animals disappear into the cool gray dawn he worries only about picking up his pace to compensate for the interruption.

a simple hello

It is close to the witching hour, but the prairie doesn't sleep. A full moon casts pearl-gray shadows next to every mound of rabbitbrush, and she watches her night creatures play softly with these shadows as if they, too, were ethereal. The glint of moonlight on silver fur is brief before it winks out, but the prairie catches that glint and sighs. She knows this stealthy slipping in and out of shadow is the quiet prelude to an overture that will conclude with screams of death. It is night, and time for night creatures to eat.

Having left the pups back at the den, Marcus and Kaia trot assuredly across their home range, which measures just under ten square kilometers. Abiding by an unwritten law, neither of the pair forages outside this range, just as coyotes that reside on contiguous ranges don't poach off theirs. Nonetheless, Marcus and his family can't call this small chunk of prairie their own; for several seasons they have shared both their territory and friendship with Allegra and Hark, a pair of unmated younger coyotes who live here too. Now Marcus and Kaia top an unimposing hill and join these two as if for a pre-arranged meeting.

First on the agenda is the greeting. Coyote "hellos" entail complex behaviors involving visual, auditory, tactile, and olfactory signals far more complicated than the simple handshake humans perform for this act. Initially, the four animals identify each other's scent without benefit of trademark cologne or shaving cream. (In daylight, their keen vision enables them to recognize each other when they are still several hundred yards apart.) Next, they touch noses or hind ends, greeting one another with low whines. Now fully aware of each other's presence, do the four call it a night and go their separate ways?

Heavens no! At this time, again as if by mysterious pre-arranged signal, they raise their skinny snouts to the moon and erupt in a boisterous chorus of yips and howls that shatter the night like drunken young liberals crashing a party of elderly conservatives. Four sets of canine vocal cords produce four songs that vary from sweet to raucous, from near harmony to utterly blatant discord.

Is Marcus hollering more than just "hello" with his jubilant cries? Is he stating "We are here: Keep out!" to would-be intruders, and do Allegra's plaintive wails reaffirm her status as a maiden in that small group? Does Hark's song strengthen his bonds of friendship with the other three animals?

Human brains might contemplate such questions, but dogs within hearing range of the jubilee waste no time speculating. With one accord, every canine in the neighborhood adds his voice to the evening's songfest. Within seconds, the entire area is under a noisy siege of howls, barks, yips, and growls that claim the night as theirs.

Then, as abruptly as it started, the coyote concert stops. While the dogs (slow to take the hint) continue their excited outcry for some time, Marcus, Kaia, Allegra, and Hark separate quietly and, ghostlike, disperse into the night like the shadows that surround them. Though popular opinion holds that coyotes hunt in packs like their larger brothers, the wolves, this is a misconception. By and large, members of the species *Canis latrans* (literally "barking dog") forage alone. This is demanding work. Empty bellies are always tough taskmasters.

doctor's orders

It is 2 P.M. Wednesday when Rita Wonsawski pulls into her mother's driveway. She exits her vehicle and marches up the walkway to the front door. Rita does not notice that the snow-in-summer that grows next to the walk no longer creeps *onto* it (she is not a yard person, and non-yard people never notice such things). She does not ring the doorbell or tap courteously on her mother's screen door but simply opens the door and marches into the house.

"Hi, Ma. Ready?" she inquires of Pat, who is sitting in her family room waiting for the arrival of her daughter.

"Well, sure, honey." Pat rises from the couch, and Rita is nonplused to see that her mother looks terrific. Her mostly gray hair curls softly around her face, which glows with a light application of powder, rouge, and lipstick. Today, Pat's usually dirty (she *is* a yard person) nails are beautifully polished a soft peach to match her ensemble of loose-fitting crepe slacks and tunic. The tunic has cotton panels inset across the bodice with little black outlines of animal heads: an elephant, a giraffe, a chimpanzee. The effect is light-hearted, young.

"Aren't you a little overdressed?" accuses Rita, who is dressed in snug jeans, sunflower-yellow long-sleeved tee shirt, and matching fleece vest with gray trim. In this outfit Rita looks like a woman of substance—yellow substance, perhaps, but substance.

"Oh, I know, honey, but if this doesn't take too long I can still catch the tail end of bridge this afternoon. I hate to miss seeing the girls, you know?" says Pat a little wistfully. She has belonged to this bridge group for seventeen years; its members are her friends, her therapists, her confidantes.

"I doubt we'll make it. This *is* all the way across town, you know." Rita wonders if her mother has forgotten where the doctor's office is.

Pat laughs. "Of course I know, honey—I've been going to that clinic since you and Steven were born! But," she adds victoriously, settling into the car, "bridge is at Jane's house today, and she lives just off Lemay right down the pike from the doctor, so there's still hope!"

Rita, catching a whiff of Pat's exquisite perfume, rolls her eyes in exasperation. "Whatever." Then, "But how'll you get home?"

"Irene'll be there; she'll give me a ride." Pat has worked this all out in advance. Rita is silent, and Pat looks disconsolately out the window. She doesn't know why it's so hard to get along with her daughter. Years ago, yes, she'd admit she frequently criticized when she shouldn't have (Rita had been *such* a difficult child to raise, compared to Steven). But Pat felt that losing first Steven and then

Hal had, if nothing else, at last taught her to shut up in time to avoid damaging her relationship with her loved ones when things got tense. She worked hard now at being a supportive mother to her only remaining child, and a good grandmother to her grandchildren as well. Would Rita *never* forgive her her past sins and open herself up to the love Pat longed to give?

At the clinic Rita settles her mother in a chair with a magazine, then approaches the admissions desk, where she speaks briefly with the receptionist, who nods understandingly. Rita hands a folded piece of paper to the young woman, who takes it and clips it to Pat's chart. Then Rita settles herself in a chair across from her mother and leafs through a magazine as well. They don't have long to wait. A door opens. "Mrs. Schreveport?" inquires Dr. Trowbridge's nurse.

Pat rises from her chair. "Do you want to come in?" she asks Rita.

Rita purses her lips and shakes her head "no." Before the door closes and cuts off her vision, Rita sees the nurse accompany Pat down a hall with exam rooms off to the side. Her mother is laughing gaily and talking to the nurse as if *she* were an old friend, too, damn it.

The nurse ushers Pat into an exam room and closes the door. "Now, what are we here for today?" she asks brightly.

Pat, seated in a corner chair rather than on the exam table, is flustered. "Well, I really don't know. My daughter said something about a checkup, I guess."

The nurse frowns, consults papers on the clipboard. "Well, blood pressure is always a safe place to start, isn't it?" she concludes brightly. She slides Pat's sleeve up and attaches the blood pressure cuff, pumps it tight and listens carefully, then records the numbers on Pat's chart. "Dr. Trowbridge'll be in shortly, okay?" she reassures on her way out with the clipboard.

Pat nods although, now that she is here, she feels nothing short of foolish. Why on earth did she let Rita drag her here, anyway? She leafs nervously through another magazine while the minutes tick by. Nearly half an hour passes; Pat fidgets, wondering at the medical community's definition of "shortly," when a recipe in the magazine she is reading catches her attention. Hmmm. "Apple Mousse with Apple-Raspberry Sauce." That sounds good, thinks Pat. She is always on the lookout for new ideas to serve at bridge club. After seventeen years, it's hard not to repeat yourself.

Pat squirms, checks the clock. She has been in here thirty-three minutes. Dare she cut out that stupid recipe, or will the doctor walk in when she is right in the middle of the act? Murphy's Law, Pat chides herself: of *course* he'll walk in. Now the clock shows that thirty-four minutes have elapsed. On the other hand, the girls would probably *love* this!

The temptation proving too much to resist, Pat, perspiring now from the adrenaline coursing through her, reaches down to the floor for her purse and lifts it smoothly to her lap. She opens the top flap of the purse and removes a small pair of scissors from a side pocket (does Pat steal recipes *regularly?*). Then she spreads the scissors open and using one of the pointy ends, quickly scores the page with the recipe all along its bound edge. She does this not once, but three times (scoring is faster than cutting and quieter than tearing) before she hears the ominous rustle outside her door that indicates the doctor is looking at her chart. Mercilessly now, Pat yanks the page from its binding and stuffs it brutally into her purse just as Dr. Trowbridge enters the room.

"Well, hi, Pat, good to see you," says the good doctor. "I apologize for running so late," he adds as he settles himself on a small stool and consults the clipboard with her chart that has a small paper attached.

"Oh, no harm done, doctor," gushes Pat, patting her hair coyly. "I was late myself, and I was so nervous about getting here on time, I've worked up a sweat." She fans herself briskly with the magazine. The doctor looks up at her over his reading glasses and smiles. He sees a good-looking elderly woman with face aglow.

"Did you drive yourself?" he inquires.

"Oh, no, Rita brought me, but she was a little late picking me up. Kids never change, do they?" The doctor shakes his head.

"So how have you been feeling, Pat? It's been over three *years* since you've been in here, you know," he accuses.

"Well, I didn't know, but I feel fine, actually," confesses Pat confusedly. "I didn't think I needed to come in even now, but I guess Rita thought I should get some kind of checkup, or something. Didn't she talk to you?"

"Actually, no, but I guess she consulted with the ladies up front, who may know as much as I do some days," he joked.

Pat shrugs. "Well, I don't want to waste your time," she apologizes, starting to rise from her chair.

"Oh no you don't, not so fast now that I've got you in here, Pat," contradicts the doctor. He rises, gives Pat a hand, and leads her over to the exam table. "Hop up here and just let me check a few things." Pat rolls her eyes but complies with his wishes.

While doctor listens to Pat's heart and lungs, checks her reflexes, palpates her belly, and does whatever else is on his list, he keeps up running small talk. "So how'd you like those Rockies yesterday?"

Pat smiles. She and Hal used to attend games of the Denver baseball team all the time when he was alive; now, she no longer goes but still pays close attention to the results. "Four-zip and they're on a roll!" she exclaims. "Do you think they have a shot at it this year?"

Dr. Trowbridge shrugs. "Baseball expert I ain't," he confesses. "How's the arthritis treating you these days?"

Pat shrugs. "I take that supplement with the long name—I forget what it is— that's supposed to help so much, and most days I get around all right."

"And what about vitamins?" probes the doctor.

Pat is happy to tell the truth. "I take vitamins *and* calcium," she boasts.

"*Every* day?"

"Oh, nearly. Once in a while I let it go."

"Do you have trouble remembering things?"

Pat looks at the man like he's nuts. "I'm sixty-eight years old, Dr. Trowbridge. What do you think?"

The doctor laughs. "I hear you. But what I mean is, do you have so much trouble that it's interfering with your ability to function?"

Now Pat looks at him like he's from another planet. "Well, I don't know if I'd be the best judge of that. Of course I forget things once in awhile," she admits. "But I'm also still living in my own home, all by myself, and so far nobody's reported me to the Homeowners' Association as a crazy old woman. I cook, clean, balance my checkbook, and pay my taxes. I drive wherever I need to go and usually get there on time, too. Now what's this really all about?" asks Pat.

But Dr. Trowbridge waves a dismissive hand. "Nothing, but you know, Pat, I want you to get some basic blood work done. Take this over to Express Labs anytime it's convenient," he says, handing her an order. "Also, when's the last time you had a mammogram and gynecological checkup?"

"Oh, that I keep up with," Pat lies.

Dr. Trowbridge takes her at her word. "All right. The only other problem here is your blood pressure, which is borderline high. I want you to buy one of those cuffs and check your BP a few times a day for a week—or if you want you can drop by and nurses'll take it, whichever's easier for you. Fax me the results so I can put you on medication if necessary. I don't want to jump the gun and prescribe on the basis of one check in three *years,*" he adds accusingly.

Pat feigns concern. "I'll do that, and thanks, Dr. Trowbridge," she says.

The doctor nods and leaves the room, but not before crumpling and tossing a small piece of paper that was attached to Pat's chart into the wastebasket.

While Pat settles her bill at the front desk, Dr. Trowbridge's nurse signals Rita into the hallway. "Dr. wants to see you for a minute." She escorts Rita into the doctor's office, where he is seated behind a desk with his reading glasses on.

"Hello, Rita." He looks up over his half glasses.

"Hi. How is she?" It is Rita's turn to feign concern.

"I'm glad to say, for all practical purposes, fine. She has AAMI, or what we call Age-Associated Memory Impairment, which is normal for her age, but there's no sign of any gross dysfunction. None whatsoever." Rita thinks the doctor is looking at her a little strangely.

"Well, what about saying the same things over again, like I had on the list?"

"You mean she repeats herself?" The doctor, with one smooth edit, makes Rita feel like a kid again, like when she'd come in this darn place for a shot and they'd try to fool her into thinking it wouldn't hurt with a Band-Aid that had pictures on it. The stupid Band-Aid never helped the hurt of those shots, recalls Rita, who had been good at prolonged crying fits.

Dr. Trowbridge shakes his head. "Again, perfectly normal. But be sure to call me if things change." Rita has been dismissed.

As Rita and her mother exit the waiting room, Pat, too, crumples a small piece of paper and tosses it into the circular file. Blood work, schmud work. She feels fine.

in memoriam

It is Saturday afternoon, and Old Town Square hosts the usual mix of shoppers, strollers and business people searching for bargains, sauntering leisurely or zigzagging purposefully through the crowd in pursuit of another day's profit (empty bellies are always tough taskmasters). Younger members of this group move about at ease, unconscious of their own significance, but people who have frequented the square for years truly appreciate the lively scene before them. They easily recall the time—not so long ago at all, really—when downtown Fort Collins could read the writing on its own epitaph. Back then, the old district's rundown buildings and gone-to-seed air attracted shoppers about as effectively as an inner city calling to suburbanites. Why patronize the defunct downtown when the glitzy glamour of Foothills Fashion Mall was just ten minutes away?

Area merchants who weren't ready to roll over and stick their feet in the air put their heads together. With strong support from the city and cooperative developers, they began a series of renovations. The aged buildings that had been the district's biggest detraction were carefully restored, the beautiful old architectural features that made these edifices historic treasures, lovingly preserved. Though it took countless hours and millions of dollars, Fort Collins' dying downtown was transformed into a hub that once again featured trendy restaurants, businesses, a brewpub, and best of all, *people*.

Today, a crowd of about a hundred, many of them hoisting crude hand-lettered signs, gathers near the fountain. It is Freedom to Marry Day, a celebration in support of families, marriage, and equal rights for same-sex couples. A CSU student from the Student Organization for Gays, Lesbians and Bisexuals introduces speakers.

Pat stands on the outskirts of the crowd. She is pleased to see that, though she is in the minority, a couple of other gray heads sticking out here and there mean she is not the only senior citizen at this event. Because the day is chilly her hands are jammed in her pockets, but they are still cold. Though she wears a windjacket and beret, she has forgotten her gloves. Pat's nose is red; occasionally, a small droplet appears at the end of it. Sometimes Pat catches the droplet impatiently in a tissue, but sometimes she just doesn't seem to feel its presence. When this happens, the droplet just hangs at the tip of her nose, waiting to hitchhike on the wind.

Though she carries no sign, Pat listens closely to the speaker, who says there are currently 1,049 federal laws that apply to heterosexual but not gay or lesbian couples, who still cannot legally marry in Colorado. Neither may same-sex couples make medical decisions for one another or enjoy family health coverage, taxation and inheritance rights. The crowd boos; signs wave: "Marriage is about LOVE, not GENDER." "If marriage is an institution, OPEN the DOORS." "A RIGHT ENJOYED BY MARRIED COUPLES: TO CHOOSE A FINAL RESTING PLACE FOR A DECEASED PARTNER."

When the speaker says something about love being tolerant and nonjudgmental toward all, Pat's eyes fill. She blinks to clear away the tears, but the blink sends tiny tsunamis coursing through the oceans in her blue eyes. The oceans flood her lower rims and form little rivers of salt water that flow crookedly down the deltas of her wrinkled cheeks. Pat feels in her pocket for the single tissue she has used before, the only one she has. When she finally finds it, it's nothing but a scrap, crushed and torn, but she raises it to her face anyway and with trembling hands, blots her tears.

When the rally ends, those in attendance walk over to Avogadro's Number, a nearby restaurant providing wedding cake and music for the occasion. Pat, who has never been to Avo's, is glad to get inside, out of the wind, but she is surprised by the restaurant's interior. A half wall separates those standing in line for cake from the dining area. Above the wall hang oversized panels of macramé that cause Pat to recall a house bedecked with strands of coarse jute spilling from works-in-progress, Hal clearing a spot on the couch to ask plaintively, "Just how many plant hangers do you intend to *make*, Patty?"

That was back in the seventies, when tying alternating reverse double half hitches, popcorn and butterfly knots into intricate combinations made her feel like she'd accomplished something wonderful. Multicolored pots suspended by macramé plant hangers had trailed yards of spider plants, wandering Jew, and ivy every place there was even a spot of sunlight in her house.

That house had *breathed* green, thinks Pat happily. Her memories float hazily, intertwining with the fantastic mural that covers the walls of this place. Floor to ceiling, they are painted with pictures of lush jungle plants that sport bold blossoms and whimsical faces peeping out here and there. The effect is exactly like she is trying to get in her backyard, thinks Pat. She inches forward in line, looking forward to some hot coffee, when a voice from behind addresses her. "Hey, Pat, what're *you* doing here?"

Startled, Pat turns. She has attended this rally before and never met anyone she's known, but now she recognizes Davin standing two positions back. "Davin!" Davin has stopped by her house several times since Pat gave him the car, and they have begun to develop a friendship of sorts. Now, however, Pat doesn't know what to say. Well, she knows what to say, but she doesn't want to say it across two strangers. Her hand flies to her heart. Then "You go ahead," she says to the intervening people, and she steps back to Davin's place in line. He seems to be with the young man next to him, who wears an earring but, unlike Gavin, is not dressed in black.

"Uh, Pat, this is my friend Zach." Davin doesn't add that, in spite of his success on the stage, he finds it difficult to make what he would call real friends. Zach's one of the few who even come close.

"It's nice to meet you, Zach, I'm Pat." Pat extends her hand cordially with no hint of awkwardness. Zach shakes it briefly, but their conversation ends because they've finally reached the cake. They busy themselves taking their servings.

"Oh, I don't know if there'll be any seats left," worries Pat out loud as she follows Davin down the line. She hates to try to eat standing up.

"We'll get us some seats, just follow me," he assures Pat, and Pat, cake in one hand, coffee in the other, suddenly feels a gush of affection for the tall young man in the black duster leading the way through the crowd in front of her. When he locates a small table near the wall with three empty seats, she sinks gratefully into a chair and cups her hands (they are still cold) around her steaming coffee.

Now there *is* a moment of awkwardness. The three are still in their coats, looking at each other across the small table. Pat sips her coffee, smiles, takes a small forkful of cake. Davin breaks the ice. "This is the lady I told you about who gave me the car," he informs Zach.

Zach grins. "Got any more you wanna get rid of?" he joshes Pat.

Now it's Pat's turn to grin. The caffeine and sugar begin to work their magic; her mood lightens considerably. "Oh, sorry, I'm afraid that was all I had in stock."

Zach shakes his head. "Just my luck."

"So, what *are* you doing here, Pat?" Davin returns to his original question. "Are you a member of the church that's sponsoring this, or something?"

"What church?" Pat is unaware the rally had a religious affiliation.

"I think it's the Unitarian Church that's behind this, isn't it?" Davin checks with Zach, who nods.

"Think so."

"No, that's not it," explains Pat to the curious twosome across from her. "If that was the reason, I'd probably know more people here, but I don't." The two young men remain quiet, waiting. Pat senses bemusement on their part. Do they think she is some kind of nutso old lady activist or something? She wipes her mouth on her napkin, looks steadily at her youthful companions. "I'm here for Steven," she says quietly, calmly.

Davin, whose unnaturally black hair makes his pale face seem even paler, lets his expressive features ask the next question.

"He was my son. Nine years ago, he died in my arms from AIDS."

At this statement, audible talk at their small table ceases. What is there to say? But just as abruptly, the language of the heart—mysterious, complex—intervenes. Davin, heart hurting from his father's contempt, feels intense compassion for this old lady whose heart still bleeds from losing her son. He rises, extends his hand to help Pat rise too. As the three make their way out of Avogadro's, a long arm sheathed in a black duster curls protectively around the shoulders of a small woman in a blue wind jacket. When hearts speak, there is no need for words.

an achy, breaky heart

Dr. Gavin David Hassletree, III, presses his knee against the control that turns the water on at a sink in the hospital scrub room, then vigorously scrubs his arms and hands with a small scrub brush and a mixture of water and iodine. He scrubs for a full five minutes preparatory to this morning's surgery, a quadruple coronary bypass on some farmer fellow from the boonies, Ned what's-his-name, whose one-and-a-half-pack-per-day habit has finally landed him smack in the middle of Poudre Valley Hospital's OR. While he scrubs, Dr. Hassletree's mind drifts back in time.

It is 7 A.M., and Gavin's wife, Julia, holds her young son high in the air. "Wheeee!" Julia's mood is as high as her baby. She bubbles with exuberance as she sits on their large four-poster bed, still in her exquisitely embroidered nightgown purchased on their pre-baby "continuing education" trip to Hawaii. Gavin is already shaved, showered, fully dressed for work. "Oh, honey," gushes Julia to Gavin, "isn't he wonderful? Don't you just hate having to leave him every day?"

Gavin smiles tolerantly. Twelve years younger than he, Julia is still not well versed in the reality of a busy surgeon's schedule. Though she's had time to learn differently, she still wants to believe her husband's responsibilities begin and end with the hours he spends at the office seeing his patients. She conveniently forgets the additional long hours he spends in surgery, not to mention the endless rounds of partner meetings, hospital department meetings, insurance provider meetings, and so on. Then, because Gavin practices with only two other doctors, he is on call every third weekend, when he may be summoned to the hospital at all hours. Meanwhile, there are dictations and reams of paperwork waiting for his attention. On average, Gavin works more than sixty hours a week.

"Will you be home for dinner?" Julia asks plaintively.

"No, I have a late surgery. I'll just grab a bite at the hospital."

Julia pouts prettily. Kissing her goodbye, Gavin wonders whether she realizes that being able to lounge around in her nightgown and play with Davin for as long as she wishes is the tradeoff for his absence. Then he pushes the thought from his head and leaves for the office.

Scrubbing over, Dr. Hassletree's mind returns to today's surgery. He does not feel a great deal of empathy for Ned. This is not because he looks harshly on people whose own behaviors have caused their hearts' demise. Truth be told, Dr. Hassletree's small paunch attests that he himself commits some of the same sins that keep his business steady.

Ahh, those Sins of the Heart—a bite of butter-laden Danish here, a marbled beefsteak there, an elevator rather than a stair—fleshly indulgences people snatch (in quick grabbing motions ranging from the covert to the overt) to help them hobble, step, stride, leap along their life paths. Yet aren't such crimes but simple misdemeanors: what's a chocoholic compared to an axe murderer?

Even so, Gavin David Hassletree, III, knows full well that Sins of the Heart exact their own karma-like consequences. Luscious bites of lipid that slide silkily over the tongue are then broken down by the digestive system into an assortment of microscopic bits, including cholesterol. While some of the fatty bits will be put to good use fueling somebody's marathon, others will stick themselves to the interior walls of another body's arteries. Weeks, months, years will pass while these arterial deposits continue to accumulate. Eventually, the sludge will thicken to the point where it impedes blood flow through the arteries. When this condition, called atherosclerosis, occurs in the arteries that supply the heart muscles with blood (the coronary arteries), the heart may become so starved for oxygen a fatal heart attack can result.

Is there no hope for Ned, then? Ned is sixty-three years old. Though lifestyle changes are not impossible for any human at any age, astute observers will note that the likelihood of people making them effectively begins to drop precipitously from birth. The cold fact is that Ned *likes* his cigarettes. The act of smoking them regularly does not make him feel guilty, it makes him feel goddamn good. Furthermore, last week when a well-meaning nutritionist tried to persuade him to convert to vegetarianism, Ned got up and stomped out of the room. Having spent his entire life raising beef cattle, he can't stomach the thought of *Salad* being What's for Dinner. Shee-it.

Poor Ned. Supine, sedated, his long body lies passively upon the narrow OR table, arms lightly Velcroed in position so they won't flop around annoyingly during his heart surgery. The other people in the cool, brightly lit OR include the perfusionist (Joyce, who runs the heart-lung machine), the circulator (Fred, whose job is to have everything ready and keep the team working together during Ned's operation), the anesthesiologist (Dr. Crumbach), and nurses (First Assist Carol Lynn, Angie, and scrub nurse Ginger). These people do not accord Ned undue respect, in spite of his troubles. A radio plays in the background, while Fred is up to his typical mischief. "Didja hear about the lifeguard?" he asks the relatively new Angie.

"Uh-uh." Angie is not sure how to take Fred.

"Well, there was this lifeguard named Wesley who wasn't buff like the other guards. Kinda scrawny, really, a few zits, never any luck with the girls, ya know?"

Angie's hands are busy but she is listening to Fred.

"Anyway, one day Wesley gets sick of all the action around the other guards, so he decides to ask for help.

"'You wanna know how to get girls, Wes? That's easy,' says the other guard. 'Just take a potato, and stick it down your swim trunks.'

"So Wesley goes home, next day he's back at work with a potato in his trunks. He walks around all day with the potato in his trunks but still doesn't get any action. Finally he complains to the other guard: 'This damn potato isn't helping at all.'

"The other guard looks Wesley up and down. 'Aww, jeez,' he says. 'It goes in the *front*, Wes, the *front!*'"

Angie is still giggling when Dr. Gavin David Hassletree, III, enters the OR, arms raised and dripping from his scrub. Immediately, all jocularity ceases; no one notices the twin splotches of dampness darkening the underarm fabric of the doctor's shirt. While she helps Hassletree into his gown and gloves, Angie's spine stiffens; she feels the need for an antacid. Hassletree assumes immediate control of the small group around him. He is Alpha Dog, and his presence commands respect from all but the stuporous Ned, who perhaps knows more than he lets on *(why so nervous today, doc?)*.

If Hassletree is aware of his sobering effect on the others' moods, he makes no sign. Or perhaps the fact that he attacks Ned's chest with a saw is sign enough. In short order Hassletree opens the chest, inserts a mammary retractor to hold the sternum up, then isolates a goodly chunk of Ned's left IMA—internal mammary artery—which he leaves clamped but still attached to the larger subclavian from which it stems. Later, Hassletree will sever the isolated segment of IMA and use it to form the first of Ned's bypass grafts. (As the name implies, bypass grafts are alternative pipelines that bridge a patient's diseased coronary arteries, thereby allowing fresh blood to flow to his weakened heart. Four such grafts will go a long way toward negating the ill effects of Ned's lifestyle without requiring that he become someone he isn't.)

Meanwhile, Angie has been harvesting a portion of the saphenous vein of Ned's leg, which Hassletree will eventually use to construct the second, third, and fourth bypasses. At the moment, however, he is busy opening the pericardium, the tough sac that encases the heart. After Hassletree's invasive fingers finally expose Ned's heart, Dr. Crumbach administers the heparin that will thin his blood. Then Hassletree quickly puts a couple of purse string sutures in the aorta and the right atrium. The sutures serve as the attachment sites for the cannulas, or pieces of tubing that allow blood drained from Ned's right atrium to flow to the heart-lung machine, where it is oxygenated before being pumped back into Ned's aorta and then on to the rest of his body.

All of this is detailed, complicated work. Anyone looking through a magnifying lens over Hassletree's tense shoulders would be amazed at his accomplishment. The pieces of blood vessel that are Hassletree's raw materials for bypasses are not easy to suture precisely in place on patients' hearts without hitting any veins. (Angie thinks the little she can see looks like sewing earthworms to chicken gizzards—two slimy messes that must be joined with stitches so fine they'd make any quilter proud.)

But no one looks over Hassletree's shoulders (who would dare?), and he finishes the quadruple bypasses in amazingly short order. (Highly regarded as a cardiac surgeon, Hassletree has a reputation for speed that is growing larger with every operation, it seems.) He throws down his instruments and straightens up, having made almost no conversation the entire surgery other than the barking of commands to his subservients. Hassletree exits the OR as grandly as he entered, leaving the conscientious Dr. Crumbach disposed to a little yak-yak, himself, now that he is in command.

"Say, Angie," says Dr. Crumbach seriously.

Angie is at his side in an instant. "Yes, doctor?"

"Did you hear the one about that poor lifeguard, Wes?"

Perhaps Carol Lynn is only imagining things, but it seems to her that even the corners of Ned's mouth turn slightly up as he is wheeled to Recovery.

a super model

Ed Wonsawski is making his rounds in Loveland and having a good morning. He has sold a parts washer he didn't expect to sell, and having that much extra volume in the bag this early takes a bit of the pressure off. Not that he'll spend the afternoon on the golf course, or anything (he'd have to sell three, maybe four washers to be that far ahead of the game), but at least he can take some time to BS with his customers now. And he knows exactly what he wants to BS about. Making a sharp right, he pulls into the parking lot of Smoke-Free, a company he's been calling on for several years.

Before getting out of his white Subaru, Ed reaches back to rummage with one hand in the boxes crammed onto the back seat and floor of his small vehicle. There are boxes filled with cans and bottles of various samples, boxes filled with catalogs and literature specific to some of his products, boxes filled with accordion files of customer transaction sheets (all filed by location: *north Greeley, south Greeley*, and so forth), boxes filled with the small novelties he distributes to his customers each time he calls. Because Ed religiously keeps the boxes in the same place all the time, he hardly even has to turn his head to see what his hand is doing. It returns to the front filled to capacity with small penlights and screwdrivers (though his novelties change from time to time, the fact that Ed's customers expect a handout whenever they see him does not).

Ed doesn't resent the fact that the cost of the thousands of novelties he gives away every year comes out of his own pocket. He is realist enough to know that handing somebody a little something for free is often a better method of persuasion than anything he says. The silly fact is that people *like* freebies, and Ed, a gifted salesman, likes handing them out as well. They put a small touch of bright in what, for many of the hardworking men and women who are his clients, may be an otherwise long day.

Now Ed stuffs the novelties deep in his pockets (it's important they get to the right people; if his little gifts are *too* visible, they'll be gone before he makes it past the front desk) and enters the front office of Smoke-Free.

"Hey, Ed!" Charlene, the big-busted, blue-jean clad receptionist, is glad of an interruption.

"Hi, Charlene, how's it going?" Ed asks sincerely, leaning his tall body sociably against the counter. He never patronizes receptionists. Often they alone determine whether or not he can gain access to key people he wants to meet or see again.

"Aww, not so bad, I guess. But Mandy's having her wisdom teeth out on Friday and *that* might make for a bad weekend. She's kind of a baby about stuff like that."

Ed nods sympathetically. "You can't exactly take her out dancin' with you to take her mind off it, either, can you?" He knows Charlene, a single mom, is a big country-western fan who hits the bars regularly on weekends.

Now Charlene tips her head of dyed red hair back and laughs boisterously. "The competition's bad enough without adding *her* to it, too!" she confides frankly. Mandy, seventeen, has won several local beauty pageants.

Ed smiles, nods, and shrugs as he makes his way toward the door leading into the back. "The boss in?" he inquires with a tilt of his head.

Charlene rolls her eyes. "I do believe he *sleeps* here!"

Ed laughs before vanishing into the back.

Once in back, it takes Ed only a moment to locate Ross, the owner, who is deep in discussion with an employee. Ed makes sure Ross sees him, then hangs out without intruding. When Ross notices him and lifts a hand in greeting, Ed is reassured. Sometimes guys— especially guys who own their own business—really *don't* have time to see him. But Ross is a nice guy who won't leave him dangling like the bored purchasing agents who delight in making salesmen wait just to pull pathetic power plays.

Though Ross lacks even a high-school diploma, Ed considers him to be one of the most brilliant people he has ever met. Besides being the founder and sole owner of Smoke-Free, Ross holds the patent to one of the company's primary products, a portable smoke-ejector fan. He invented the fan's cast-aluminum blade, which, because it is lighter, allows for faster spinning with less wear on the motor. Fire departments from far and wide use the fan, available in electric or gas models with little lawnmower engines on them, to suck the smoke out of fire-damaged buildings.

Ed knows that by now, however, Ross has taken his company way beyond the production of powder-coated red fans. Now, Ross heads a team of employees in four buildings that does everything from component assembly to the production of custom-made fire trucks. Ed thinks Ross' accomplishments amazing, and he holds the man in the highest regard. Now he brightens as, conversation finished, the unassuming Ross wanders his way and sticks out his hand.

"'Lo, Ed."

"Hey, Ross, how's it going?"

"Can't complain."

Ed laughs at the perfect cue. "That means you're going through my chemicals at warp speed, right?"

Astute businessman himself, Ross grins at Ed's quickness. "I guess we could use a few things," he admits. He ushers Ed into his office, where the two quickly come to terms on an order of chemicals. Then Ed changes the subject. "Have you got a minute, Ross? I need your advice."

"What's up?" Ross has time today.

Quickly, Ed tells Ross about the scouts' Pinewood Derby. He takes the little car he and Greg have already cut from pine out of his carryall and shows it to Ross. "So the idea is, all the kids build these little racecars, and then they race them to see whose is the fastest, all right?"

Ross nods. "But," continues Ed, "it's not as simple as it sounds. What really happens in *this* town is that a lot of well-educated dads start messing with their kids' cars in ways I don't even understand."

"Such as?" Ross, a high-tech guy himself, is curious.

"Oh, let's see, Greg told me about a physics guy who takes his car over to the wind tunnel at CSU and runs tests on it," replies Ed.

Ross whistles. "That's pretty sophisticated stuff for Cub Scouts," he agrees.

"Yeah. And it beats guys like me out of the competition just like that." Ed snaps his fingers. "And you know, I wouldn't mind so much if this race was supposed to be dads against dads. But they tell the kids it's for them, and then the smart guys pull all this shit and they win every damn time. That's not right.

"So, anyway, I was wondering if you had any ideas about how I could make this thing faster," concludes Ed, gesturing with Greg's unpainted car.

Ross reaches for the car, turns it over in his hands. "Where're the wheels?"

Ed takes four tiny gray plastic wheels, still unattached to the car, from his case and hands them to Ross, who looks them over carefully.

"C'mon," Ross commands Ed, rising from his chair. "We'll show those SOBs." Ross doesn't like to sugarcoat things. He leads Ed out of the office and over to another building, talking as he goes. "What your car needs first," he explains to Ed, "is perfectly round wheels." Ed knows enough to shut up.

"*These* wheels," continues Ross, waving the hand holding the derby car's small wheels, "may look round but, actually, they're not. They've got microscopic pits and pimples all over 'em that'll interfere with fast, smooth performance on the track."

Ross precedes Ed inside the other building, looking over his shoulder to see if Ed is following the conversation. Ed nods, but keeps his commentary brief: "Makes sense."

"Now," says Ross, approaching a large piece of equipment sitting against the wall, "this'll take care of that."

"What is it?" Ed is not afraid to show he is in over his head now. He's a chemical salesman, not a mechanical engineer.

"This?" Ross grins proudly. "This bad boy's a quarter-million dollar lathe that'll take all those pits and pimples off your wheels in no time."

Ed whistles appreciatively. "That oughta do the trick!"

"Partially." Ross loves a challenge. "But even if the wheels're perfectly smooth, if you let 'em rest on their entire surface width, they'll still generate too much friction."

"What do you mean?"

"Well, picture a runner sled, and picture the difference in speed between one that has its runners and one that doesn't. The second doesn't have a chance compared to the first, right?" Ed nods.

"Well, because these wheels sit on their whole width the way they are now," says Ross, "they're just like a sled without its runners, and they'll generate way too much friction to be fast. But after I take the pits and pimples off, I can use this machine to file the wheels down, too, so they'll rest on just a narrow ridge of surface material. That way, they'll generate minimum friction as they roll, and less friction equals greater speed, see? Can you leave 'em here a week or so to give me a chance to work on 'em?"

That sounds like game, set, and match to Ed, whose smile is huge. "Did you say you needed a fifty-five gallon drum of solvent or anything, Ross?"

"Don't worry about it." Ross claps Ed on the shoulder. "Can you find your own way out while I play around with these?"

"You bet." Ed stops several times on his way out of the building to greet people and hand out his screwdrivers and penlights. Crossing the parking lot back to his car, he thinks about what just happened. Ed has come across the presence of genius before but never when it was combined with equal parts kindness in the same body. He feels lucky to know a man like Ross. He can't wait to tell Greg about Ross and his wheels!

living and learning

Kaia has taken the three pups out for an excursion on the prairie, but her attention wanders away from her children. Her sensitive ears pick up the tantalizing rustle of a small creature in the grass nearby; reflexively, she begins to stalk it. She crouches, moves forward stealthily. It takes patience and skill to catch a deer mouse or meadow vole, and Kaia's entire being is focused on the whispering grass in front of her.

As usual, Banks doesn't hesitate to seize an opportunity for freedom when he sees it. Nonchalantly, he meanders away from Kaia, relishing the chance to explore on his own. Leila and Liza are momentarily confused. They know they should watch and learn from their mother's hunting, but they are young and easily tempted, too. There is a whole prairie to investigate! They shift direction to follow their wayward brother.

Eyes and ears telling her she is close enough now, Kaia leaps into the air with the suddenness of a jack released from its box, comes full-bodied back to earth on the spot that should hold a tasty morsel. But her paws come up empty just as her senses inform her that she has missed her prey by millimeters. Never mind. There is the rustling, off to the left now but still well within range. Kaia crouches, begins the whole process over again.

Banks, Leila, and Liza, by this time some distance away, have found their own source of amusement. Together, they encircle an oddly shaped thing that lies on the ground before them. The thing does not smell like anything they know, nor does it move like anything they have seen before. Its mouth opens and its tongue sticks out while its head sways on its long neck, but the rest of the thing stays put on the ground. Only Banks, who is behind it, notices this thing's tail moves in conjunction with a noise that also seems to come from it. Intrigued, he lunges playfully at the noise. Wait 'til Mother sees what *he* catches! Taking their cue from Banks, Leila and Liza also move in to attack.

Kaia, meanwhile, tries for the third time to catch whatever has been eluding her. She leaps, pounces, captures her prey at the exact instant a yip of pain from one of her children reminds her of motherhood. Vindicated, Kaia downs the tiny creature she has killed in one swift swallow, trots hurriedly off in the direction of sound she could swear was Leila. What kind of mischief has Banks got his sister into now?

It takes just seconds for Kaia to locate her offspring, seconds more for her to assess the situation. Banks is proudly shaking the long form of a snake back and forth like a toy between his teeth (see what *I* caught, Ma?). Kaia can see that the snake, inert, poses no more threat as Liza dances around the two excitedly. Leila—where *is* Leila? Kaia searches anxiously, locates Leila about twenty feet away from the others. She is lying still but lifts her small head, whimpers pitifully as Kaia approaches. Kaia sees that Leila's head is misshapen, badly swollen just below her left eye. The eye itself is almost swollen shut.

Kaia settles onto the ground beside her daughter for a deathwatch as Banks, unconcerned, wanders innocently away.

close encounters

"Davin, where the hell are you going, dressed like that?"

Davin had hoped to escape unnoticed, but now he stops on his way out the door. The tension between him and his father has been simmering for so long he's almost relieved at the chance for it to erupt. "Dad. We've been over this before. Why do you always act like it's the first time you've seen me like this?" Beneath his duster, Davin is dressed in a white silk shirt with ruffles down the front and fitted black pants tucked into black riding boots. Though his face is free of white makeup (there is a fine line between being Gothic or punk), its natural pallor combined with the outfit give Davin a look of foreignness from yesteryear.

It's Saturday evening and Dr. Gavin David Hassletree, III, is relaxing in his living room. Now he carefully sets his drink on the table beside him and tosses his paper aside in disgust. "Well, maybe I just can't get used to my son walking around looking like some asshole from Hollywood. Maybe I keep hoping he'll clean up his act and fly right, for a change."

"Yeah, Dad, and 'right' would mean only one way, *yours,* wouldn't it?" accuses Davin. "Why can't you just accept the fact that I'm not you?"

Hassletree tips his head back to release an ugly laugh. "You can say that again."

"But here's what you don't get, Dad: I don't *want* to be you! What makes you think you're so wonderful, anyway?" challenges Davin. The young man paces back and forth in the front hall, continues before Hassletree can interrupt. "I mean, Mom leaves you umpteen years ago and you sue for custody of me to spite her, and this is where we end up." Davin looks around, spreads his arms. "Here's an equation for you: Dr. Gavin David Hassletree, III," he pronounces mockingly, "equals big house with nobody in it except a son you despise. Big fucking deal, Dad." Davin's arms drop to his sides; he has no more to say.

Dr. Hassletree is enraged. He rises from his chair, points a shaking finger at his son. "Don't you dare talk to me like that, Davin! I'm the one who's raised you all these years, prov—"

Davin interrupts with a bark of dismay. "You were never even here, Dad! Rosa raised me, and you know it. And I'm sure you're sorry she's gone, because now the only source for my 'quality time' is you—do you think you're up to it?" Davin challenges his father. "Wanna come downtown to listen to some metal?"

Dr. Hassletree crosses the room in swift strides, puts his big hands on his son's shoulders and shakes him once, hard. Davin's head snaps back, then forward again, but he does not raise his arms in his own defense. "Don't you think I *tried* to get through to you, Davin? But you kept getting weirder and weirder as you got older, until pretty soon I didn't even know who you were. Do you do this just to torment me?" He waves his hands to indicate Davin's clothes, then just stands there, breathing heavily. There is a moment of strained silence.

As he heads for the front door, Davin turns briefly back toward his father. "What makes you think you'd be worth the effort?" The door shuts firmly on Hassletree's angry reply.

"Shit."

Dr. Gavin David Hassletree re-crosses the living room, reaches for his drink—his third Chivas and water—and downs it in one gulp. Then he stomps into the study, boots up his computer and accesses his investment records, which he's camouflaged under "Correspondence." The entries are the same ones he caught Davin snooping at awhile back. They still don't have profit or loss columns, but Hassletree doesn't need these. The sum total of his dot.com losses are seared into his brain as permanently as the old med-school acronym for cranial nerves, "On Old Olympus' Towering Top, A Finn And German Viewed Some Hops." The light-hearted jingle waltzes around in the doctor's head with its glitzy seven-figure partner, the number 2,723,683. Two million, seven hundred twenty-three thousand, six hundred eighty-three fucking dollars. Gone, thinks Hassletree, just like his wife and kid. How in the hell, he asks himself bitterly, has it ever come to this?

Davin, meanwhile, has driven over to his friend Zach's, but instead of parking in the long line of cars already in front of the house, he plays a hunch and parks a couple blocks away, then makes his way to Zach's on foot. Zach has passed the word around that his folks will be gone for the weekend (they are bringing his older sister home from college in Nebraska), and the high-school kids have wasted no time making his place their own. Even with the windows shut Davin can feel the music pulsing through the walls; when he walks in through the front door, sound hits him like a TKO.

Davin doesn't mind. On weekends he works part-time at Hot Topic, a store in the mall that caters to Goths and boasts the sign "Loud Music Sold Here." Usually a loner, Davin seeks company tonight. He wants to forget his father and the pressure of his future hanging over him; Zach's party will help. While he is still standing in the entryway someone passes him a beer and a joint; Davin accepts both, then scans the crowd to see if Madison, the girl who plays his killer Charlotte Corday in *Marat/Sade*, is here.

He spots her elegant form across the room, strolls over. "Hey."

"Hi, Davin." Madison actually looks glad to see him. She steps casually away from the group she is with and over to his side. "What's going on?" Madison can tell Davin is excited because his normally pale cheeks are flushed with color.

"Aww, you know, just another round with my Dad." Davin doesn't want to talk about this now. Madison takes her cue like a pro and changes the subject.

"So, have you heard from Tisch yet?" she shouts over the music. Davin rolls his eyes, shakes his head "no." Tisch is NYU's premiere school of the arts and Davin's dream destination next fall. But getting into Tisch is a complicated process. First, the school is so good applicants must have outstanding high school credentials, and secondly, potential theater majors like Davin have to go there and audition for a "creative review." Because Dr. Hassletree won't spring for any education involving acting, Davin thought he'd never be able to afford even the expensive admissions process at Tisch, much less go there.

But then a surprising thing happened. Davin's Mom, happily remarried away off in Arkansas, got wind of the situation and sent him a check to cover the audition trip. Davin still can't believe he was actually able to go to New York earlier in the year and audition for the school of his dreams. Now he's actually hoping for a scholarship! Contrary to Dr. Hassletree's opinion, Davin is far from stupid. He and Madison are both students in the grueling International Baccalaureate program at PHS. While it is true Davin has taken the subsidiary rather than the high levels of IB math and science, these classes have still enabled him to pull a 1467 on the SATs, which puts him right up there with the competition for some decent money from NYU.

With the noise in Zach's house approaching the level of insanity, Davin and Madison let themselves out onto the back deck. They lean over the railing and sip their beers as they pass their joint back and forth. "What about you?" Davin asks Madison. He knows she is interested in foreign affairs, and to his credit he makes a valiant effort even though it isn't talk that interests him now, it is Madison's eyes. A wonderful limpid brown with glints of the same deep rust colors that shimmer in her hair, her eyes now smile in anticipation of her answer.

But Madison's reply is cut off by a deep male voice bellowing "*Buuust!*"from the house. The cry is followed by high-pitched screams from the girls inside.

Davin doesn't wait to hear more. "Come on," he urges Madison, grabbing her by the hand and leading her quickly down the deck stairs. Davin leads Madison across Zach's backyard to the fence that separates it from the Cathy Fromme Prairie. They scramble over the fence and take off running through the prairie, putting as much distance as they can between themselves and Zach's house. When they top a distant hill, they collapse onto their bellies, laughing and gasping for air.

"Oh, God, *thank* you!" exclaims Madison. "If it wasn't for you, I'd have been caught, and my parents would *kill* me!"

"Where's your car?" asks Davin.

Madison is elated. "I rode with Julie!"

Davin has the situation well under control now. For once in his life, he feels great: he is the *man*. "That's perfect. I thought something like this might happen, so I parked mine so far away they'll think it belongs in this neighborhood. Now all we have to do is lay low 'til the cops leave, then we're home free." In the distance, they can hear a few other kids who made it out the back door in time to escape the cops, but their voices are too far away to be intelligible.

Madison rolls over on her back to look up at the stars; Davin follows suit. "We should have brought our beer," she says.

"Hey, we're lucky we got out of there with our *reputations*," Davin reminds her.

"Mmmm, true, Davin, but we could still mess those up, couldn't we?" Madison turns her head to look at Davin, then rolls on top of him. Davin (a quick study) understands at once that he no longer has the situation under control. Damn. The *man* takes his leave so fast Davin doesn't even have time to say goodbye; in his place appears that old standby, the jittery boy. With Madison flowing all over him as if he were the ice cream and she, the hot fudge, Davin opens his eyes to the heavens and prays audibly for help.

"Oh, God."

Madison takes this as a sign of encouragement. "Not God," she whispers in his ear with beery breath. "M.a.d.i.s.o.n." She punctuates each letter with little flicks of her tongue that finally close the connection between her and Davin. In response, his hands slip effortlessly beneath her shirt. Momentarily, he is transported to an unfamiliar place. This place is so devoid of anger or bitterness, so replete with *yesses* he is taken aback by its possibilities. Now it is Madison's turn to pray. "Oh, God."

When this remark prompts in Davin an insane urge to practice his mimicry ("Not God. D.a.v.i.n"), he is kind enough to refrain, but wise enough to realize that what he and Madison are doing is not something he cares to continue. Davin's hands stop wandering, take firm hold of the girl on top of him, and gently push her off. Madison topples to the side and lies there, looking at him, but the darkness conceals her expression. For a second, Davin's relief at having stopped doing what they were doing wavers.

Then he feels a cool hand on his brow and hears the voice of nurse Charlotte Corday dripping with feigned concern. "Have you a headache, mon cher?"

Davin tips his head back and laughs. He stands, then bends to help Madison to her feet. He tenderly brushes bits of prairie from her hair, then walks her slowly back to his car. They talk nonstop the entire way.

By the time Davin drops Madison off at her house, it is well after midnight. Heading home with the windows open to the cool air, Davin thinks about the night's events. The cops showing up at Zach's were no surprise. There must have been fifty kids there, and they hadn't exactly kept things quiet. Some neighbor must have gotten annoyed and blown the whistle. But from the number of squad cars appearing (he swears he saw five sets of revolving roof lights in front of Zach's house), you'd have thought the entire FCPD had nothing better to do than check out Zach's party. Poor Zach. There'll be hell to pay from his folks, and the folks of the kids who got caught, too. Davin feels lucky to be out of *that* loop.

Then his thoughts turn to M.a.d.i.s.o.n. In spite of what happened out on the prairie, Davin doesn't feel embarrassed. He did what felt right to him at the time, and oddly enough, that rightness carried him through the awkwardness of the moment. In fact, it set a new tone between him and Madison. When he examines that tone in his mind, Davin discovers it's one of hope that, for a change, stems from real interaction with a girl instead of just fantasies. This is vastly different from his usual day-to-day imaginings, in which all kinds of significant exchanges occur between Davin and girls from all walks of life. Those are fun, but kind of counterproductive when it comes to the real thing.

But the happy fact remains: tonight *was* the real thing! Davin takes both hands off the steering wheel, pounds it once in exhilaration. His eyes close in cadence with his single-beat celebration; when he opens them (a millisecond later?), he is horrified to see a large mule deer caught directly in the beam of his headlights. He grabs the steering wheel and yanks it to the left; simultaneously, adrenaline floods his nervous system and he feels a tremendous impact as his car hits the animal in front of him. Davin's seatbelt saves him from being thrown into the windshield by the momentum of the crash. He is shaken by the suddenness of the accident but not hurt. He exits his car, walks slowly forward to see that which he does not want to see.

The deer is a young buck whose antlers are still in velvet. A large wound on the animal's flank leaks rich, red blood into a pool beneath it that enlarges even as Davin approaches, but he is horrified to see that the animal still lives. Its large eyes gaze up at him in mute remonstrance for his crime; its sides heave with the effort of drawing in but numbered lungfuls of sweet night air. In. Out. In. Out. Davin shudders. Is this his punishment for being happy tonight, or for being Gothic and irritating his father for so long? He crouches next to the deer, lays his hand gently, apologetically upon its forehead. When the sheen leaves the animal's eyes and its sides finally stop heaving, Davin still kneels beside it in humble penitence for his sin.

a windfall

Jasper, a robust male coyote, trots rapidly across the prairie until he comes to a fence. The fence, neither barbed wire nor split rail nor chain link, is invisible to the human eye but all too real to Jasper. The barrier he encounters is composed entirely of scent, and it clearly demarcates the home range of Hark, Allegra, Marcus, Kaia and the pups. The urine excreted by this little band of animals transmits information to Jasper as clearly as a billboard.

A few sniffs and he knows without a doubt the other coyotes live here. He knows which are males and which females, and he knows the rules that are supposed to keep him from trespassing on the others' domain. Strangely enough, however, Jasper raises his head and deliberately, nonchalantly crosses the line onto the other coyotes' range, anyway.

Is Jasper looking for trouble? Is he an animal bad guy risking savage attack from Marcus or Hark just to play the coyote version of "rubbing paint"?

The answer is not nearly so sinister. Instead of living sociably within a group, at the moment Jasper simply prefers the company of himself. No villain, he is just a loner, a vagabond, a bum. Two-legged experts who study his species label him a *transient.* As such, Jasper roams an area that overlaps, but may be up to three times larger than, the thirty-six square miles inhabited by Marcus and Kaia. The latter, deemed *resident* coyotes, will share the same territory for as long as they remain mates—a period usually spanning one to three years. Like humans, coyotes change their familial classifications with amazing alacrity. One research project found that of forty-eight animals fitted with radio collars, while sixteen coyotes could be termed residents and seven transients, fully seventeen changed their status from resident to transient or vice versa within the study period.

Thus, Jasper is free to meld into and out of the company of the other coyotes as he sees fit. Tonight, the tantalizing aroma of ungulate draws transient and residents alike to its source, a mule deer that met its fate at another predator's hands and now lies for the taking by the side of the road. The coyotes will neither mourn the deer's passing nor hesitate to feed upon its carcass. To do either would be foolish, wasteful. As always, the animals heed the call of hunger and hasten to the feast.

precipitating events and disqualifiers

The evening of Friday, June 4th, is pleasant. Bonnie has prepared lemongrass tabbouleh, a variation of the traditional bulgur salad enhanced with fresh cilantro, mint, coriander, allspice, and cayenne pepper, for supper. She and Richard both like it because, even though it's sinfully healthful, this salad hits their tongues like mouthfuls of spring. But Richard wants to get a long run in before eating, and Bonnie is too hungry to wait for his return, so he keeps her company while she eats out on the deck. "Mmmm, Bonn, that looks great!" compliments Richard.

Bonnie smiles with pleasure. "Doesn't it? I'm trying *sooo* hard to eat right, you know? We're down to four weeks. Can you believe it, honey?"

"Well, I believe it, but that doesn't mean I'm *ready* for it," confesses Richard. "It's gonna be such a total lifestyle change, I have to admit I'm nervous."

Bonnie appreciates her husband's candor. She nods her head up and down in agreement. "Me, too." The couple chew on this thought a moment, regarding each other silently across the table. Then, "What if we're no good at it?" Bonnie frets. "I mean, I don't know the first thing about being a parent, you know?"

Richard has had enough of self-doubt. "Hey, the little bugger should consider himself blessed to have drawn our number for his old lady and man, Bonn."

Bonnie giggles. "Why?"

"Because," Richard, rising from the table, intones like Tony the Tiger, "We're GRRRRREAT!" He leans over and plants a kiss on his wife's lips, then checks his watch. "If I'm gonna get that twelver in tonight, I better get going, okay, hon?"

Bonnie makes a face. "What if I said no?"

Richard grins as he retreats through the deck door into the house. "What'd you say?"

Bonnie rolls her eyes and remains seated, looking out over the prairie. When she hears their front door open and close a short time later, she rises and peers over the side deck railing, looking between houses toward the street. Richard's running figure appears briefly between the houses. Bonnie notes her husband's smooth stride and for a tiny moment, she is again jealous of his drive, his will, his can't-be-stopped attitude. Then she turns to bear the dishes from the still cluttered table back inside. That done, she grabs her car keys from the hook by the garage door and hurriedly leaves the house.

Safeway has sugar-free Lemon Crème SnackWell's buy-one-get-one-free! In the interests of health *and* budget, Bonnie makes the short drive to the store and debates how many boxes to buy. Well, it'd be stupid to come all this way for just two, and the dinky boxes are only 5.75 ounces so four'd be only, what? A little over a pound, so she decides eight is the perfect number, throws them quickly into her cart, and makes her way to checkout. With eight items, Bonnie qualifies for the express line (nine items or less, please), but six people are in line in front of her.

Bonnie is having a low blood sugar attack, which this minute places her in the category of the Desperately Hungry. The tabbouleh *was* good, but now she longs to rip open one of her cookie boxes and stuff its contents voraciously, King-Henry-the-Eighthily into her salivating mouth. She restrains herself to a single cookie removed discreetly from its package, then, to distract herself, stretches her neck to count the number of items in the basket of the person in front of her. Bonnie hates people who cheat in the express line and indeed, she counts thirteen (*thirteen!*) items.

"*Cheater!*" she wants to rage at the slim young woman in skimpy tank top and tight (size four?) jeans who has a large box of frosted, filled long johns atop the other groceries in her basket. Bonnie can see the creamy yellow filling oozing out of the ends of the pastry as the woman maintains her thin stance in line. (Oh yes, you can stand thinly. People with walnut butts do it all the time.)

Chewing, Bonnie considers: should she say something about the excess items? She knows the clerk won't—they *never* count, which makes Bonnie wonder what good the stupid "nine items or less" sign does. She finishes her cookie, reaches for another, creeps forward a notch. She is about to let fly with a real zinger when she is again distracted, this time by a strange sensation of warm wetness in her crotch. What's going on? It feels like she's gotten her period, but *that* can't be. Shifting her weight uncomfortably, Bonnie wonders whether she has wet herself a little. She knows the muscles that control her bladder are definitely stressed right now, but that's never happened before. Then it dawns on her. "My water's broken," she says in a small voice.

This strange proclamation causes walnut butt to turn around. One look is all it takes for her to shove her cart aside and step instantly to Bonnie's aid. "Let me help you," she offers, taking Bonnie's arm and leading her gently out of the store.

Bonnie looks at her savior with tear-filled eyes. "Oh, thank you. I don't know what to do."

Walnut butt doesn't hesitate. "I think you better call your doctor. Have you got a phone?"

Bonnie nods. "But it's a month early," she objects.

Walnut butt smiles. "Honey, I got four kids, and not a single one of 'em's ever done anything they were supposed to." When they get to her car Bonnie sits sideways on the edge of the back seat (there's more room there) and, shaking, punches in the numbers (thank goodness she knows them by heart). It takes eight rings for the answering service to respond. Waiting, walnut butt roots around in her large leather shoulder bag until she finds a pack of cigarettes. She lights one and is taking a deep drag when Bonnie looks up. For the first time, she sees that the tiny woman before her has crows' feet. Delicate webs of wrinkles radiate outward from each eye like fine etchings, and the evening sunlight glints off strands of silver in her long hair.

The doctor finally comes on the line. Bonnie looks at her watch. "Ten minutes ago," she says. After a moment, she tosses the phone aside, looks mutely at her guardian angel.

"Hospital?" encourages the angel.

Still mute, Bonnie nods. The angel reaches down and helps Bonnie swing her feet into the car. "I'll drive," she offers. Bonnie drops her keys into the woman's outstretched hands and sees nails that are chewed down to the quick, but the hands take the keys and start the car authoritatively. On their way out of the crowded parking lot, the woman coughs once. The sound is phlegmy, even harsh. The cough fills the car with the smell of stale cigarettes, but Bonnie doesn't notice. She remembers the woman's pastries riding gallantly atop her groceries, wonders if they were a Saturday breakfast surprise for four children who will now be disappointed.

Richard, meanwhile, is well into his twelve-mile run. He particularly enjoys this evening's workout because he doesn't have to work tomorrow. He can push himself tonight, sleep late in the morning, and then go at it again later in the weekend. To give himself an extra challenge now, he has decided to run the dirt trails of Pineridge Natural Area. Here, paths carved on a couple of ridges by local mountain bikers are so steep they are unofficially called "the roller coaster." Richard hits the first climb and bears down, pumping his arms to aid his feet in their attempt to bear him uphill at speed. He crests the hill, then negotiates a short but steep downhill before the tallest, westernmost ridge looms above him.

Puffing up this last ridge, he is finally rewarded by the view of Dixon Reservoir lying placidly below him. Dixon is miniscule compared to its big brother, Horsetooth Reservoir, to the west, but it still attracts fishermen and the occasional great blue heron to its muddy shores. Now Richard executes a smooth turn to the north so he can run atop the ridge as long as possible before starting to loop down- and homeward. He finds the view of the city to his right, the reservoir ahead and to his left so pleasant that he is lulled into forgetting to watch his feet.

Momentarily, those feet fall on the shale mixed with Niobrara limestone that is the primary geologic component of this ridge. Richard would find it hard to believe that the dusty land around him once lay covered by an ocean, but the fossilized remains of tiny sea creatures crunching beneath his feet are ample proof. He need only stop, bend over, and peer closely at the weathered bits of limestone to find ancient evidence of its aquatic past.

Stopping, however, is not on Richard's agenda today. (Perhaps later, when the small hand of his child clutches his on Sunday adventures, he will act differently.) Now he is relaxed and running well when his right foot comes down on a rough spot of ground camouflaged by an unobtrusive plant. The plant, called Bell's twinpod (*Physaria bellii*), grows low to the ground and bears silvery light green leaves and small bright yellow flowers. When Richard's assertive foot crushes both of these, he is unaware that he has trampled something rare.

For the world over, Bell's twinpod is known to exist only in Colorado, where it grows in limited colonies on soil with a strong shale component. Rare but not endangered, the species will survive Richard's unconscious assault. Of more immediate concern to Richard is the possibility of injuring *himself*. When his foot lands on that innocuous patch of uneven ground covered by the plant, it slips. It is only a slight slip—did moisture from the crushed petals of the twinpod lubricate the sole of his running shoe, perhaps?—but it throws him off balance nonetheless. Richard's center of gravity shifts to the right, and he stumbles. He does his best to correct his condition, but his foot is unable to follow the forward momentum of his body.

Hot pain scorches Richard's ankle like an iron applied to tender flesh. Crying out, he falls to the ground. Because three mountain bikers come tearing along the ridge directly behind him, he rolls quickly to the side and feels still more pain in his exposed thigh. Glancing down, Richard sees that he has rolled over a prickly pear cactus, the spines of which now protrude from his bare leg. Glancing up, he barely has time to note that the passing cyclists are about twelve years old. Richard opens his mouth to ask for help but, whooping with the Friday-night euphoria of youth, the three pedal furiously off into their own futures. They are gone as quickly as they have come, leaving behind a vacuum of such stillness, even the birds remain silent.

Checking his watch, Richard sees that it is almost eight-thirty. He is barely able to walk, much less run, and he is six long miles from home. When he does get home, Bonnie will be furious. Too late, Richard realizes he should have told her where he'd be. He picks at a few cactus spines in his leg and wincing, rises slowly, keeping his weight on his good foot. He sees his dreams of a marathon go up in smoke as he puts his injured foot on the ground and tries one small, nightmarish step. Sucking in his breath from the pain, Richard gains all of five inches before dropping heavily to his hands and knees. This time, his action grinds the ill-fated Bell's twinpod so thoroughly into the dirt, the little plant becomes an unrecognizable mess of mangled green. While Richard settles down to wait for help, the crushed leaves of the twinpod release a slight scent the injured man finds strangely appealing.

arrivals, early and late

Zoë is fighting those trying to hold her back. She doesn't speak, but she definitely makes her wishes known: she means to go, and she means to go NOW. After all, anyone who knows her knows, too, that she has a lot of catching up to do. As a headstrong Taurus last time, she left too many heads rolling in her wake. But now she has a better sense of balance—things to teach as well as learn—and she is anxious to get on with the process. Fearful for her well-being, her mentors disagree. "Stay a while longer, Zoë. Give yourself more time to prepare," they urge. But ultimately, Zoë's strong will (she hasn't made the transition to Gemini yet) predominates. These people, this time, this place will be just fine for this round, she insists. She bids her guides an unsentimental farewell and determinedly re-enters the work force.

Bonnie lies on the bed in the birthing room at Poudre Valley Hospital. Her walnut-butted angel (whose real name, she has since learned, is Fay), sits on a chair beside the bed, holding Bonnie's hand in her own small ones. To Bonnie, Fay's hands feel much like her cough sounds: rough, even ragged. But Bonnie clings to those hands as if they were made of purest silk. She finds their sandpaper touch conveys amazing comfort, and she is humbled by this stranger's willingness to help her.

Presently, Bonnie takes advantage of the still lengthy interlude between contractions to talk. "Have you tried Richard again, Fay?" she asks fretfully.

Fay doesn't wish to be the bearer of bad news, but she sees she has no choice. She glances at her watch, a cheap Timex. "Just five minutes ago, honey. Still no answer, but I left another message."

"What time *is* it?"

"It's almost nine-thirty, sweetie," responds Fay.

Bonnie lets out an exasperated breath. "Well, I don't know exactly how long it'd take him to run twelve miles, but I just feel like he should be getting back by now, you know?" She looks to Fay for corroboration. Fay complies.

"Probably any minute now, I'll bet. God, I can't imagine running twelve miles!" she adds, shaking her head. "I mean, who'd *want* to?" she asks Bonnie.

The two women look seriously at each other for a moment, then burst out laughing. "Oh I know I know," Bonnie gasps. "Sometimes it seems so stupid to me, too! But it's just something he likes a lot. And I guess there are worse addictions," she adds.

"Oh sweetie, believe me, LOTS worse." Fay speaks with the wisdom of experience etched on her brow.

Bonnie wants to pursue the topic with her new friend, but a contraction forces all talk, small or otherwise, from her mind. Immediately, Fay resumes her role as labor coach. "Breathe," she commands Bonnie sternly, and Bonnie, glad for anything that gives her even a pittance of control over the weird sensations attacking her body, obeys.

The nurse times the length of the contraction. When it's over, she walks over and adjusts the pump on the IV stand. "Time to bump you up a notch," she says.

"Have I graduated to junior high?" asks Bonnie.

"Mmmm, not quite." The nurse, Melissa, dashes her hopes. "You're about fifth grade, I'd say."

Bonnie rolls her eyes. "How long does this *take?*"

"You know, it can vary a lot, but with induced labors we have to be careful," Melissa tells Bonnie. "If we give you too much pitocin too fast, we'll hyperstimulate your uterus and then have to back off and start over."

"Don't you dare." Bonnie hurts too much to sugarcoat it.

"I hear ya, hon, I hear ya."

It is nine-forty-five and dark when Richard, still stuck on top of Pineridge with his injured ankle, hears voices and sees—of all things—a couple of small bobbing lights coming down the trail toward him. What the hell could this be? Though his butt and back hurt from sitting so long, he itches all over from dried sweat and bug bites, and his ankle is killing him, at this moment Richard still struggles to sit up straighter. As the voices come closer, he discerns the jangle of a dog's collar mixed in with them. Because he can't bring himself to yell, "Help!" but wants to advise whomever of his existence, Richard settles for a hearty, "Hey, there." At once, the jangling and voices cease. "I'm over here," Richard elaborates, then, bowing just slightly to circumstance, adds, "could use a little help."

The jangling resumes at a slower pace. "Where?" asks a feminine voice in the dark.

"Here." The next instant, Richard finds his face being licked by a very big dog.

"T. J., stop it." T. J. is either hard of hearing or unaccustomed to this command, for his oral investigation of Richard's face proceeds apace.

"T. J.!" This time, the order is accompanied by a severe yank on the leash that forces the dog, a St. Bernard, to surrender his place to a young man and woman, both of whom are wearing headlamps they tilt curiously down at Richard's upturned face.

"Hi. Richard Blackburn." From his seated position, Richard, blinded, throws one hand up to shield his eyes, extends the other to the couple. *May as well get off on the right foot.*

"Terry Huett. This is Jan. What's up?" The young man—tall and bearded—is not put off by Richard's unexpected presence.

"I was jogging and my foot slipped," explains Richard. "Twisted my ankle and can't walk."

The young woman trains her light on Richard's swollen foot and whistles appreciatively. "That looks pretty bad. Do you think it's broken?"

"Nah. I think it's just the mother of all sprains."

"How long have you been up here?" asks Terry.

"A good hour."

"Damn, we left our cell phone in the car." Terry and Jan confer, then announce their decision. "I'll head down while Jan stays with you," says Terry. "Can you hold out another hour or so?"

Richard, rejuvenated by their presence, is back in form. "You bet."

Terry does an about-face and disappears back down the trail the way he came, while Jan remains behind with T. J., who plops down beside Richard as if he were a thick rug. "So what exactly happened?" she asks.

"Aww, my foot just hit the right spot at the wrong time, I guess."

Jan nods and her headlamp keeps time, yo-yoing its beam up and down the ridge. "Well, I wish I could wrap it or something to make it feel better, but I have nothing with me except this big fella." She jingles the leash.

Richard can see that, like himself, she is clad in nothing but shorts and a tee shirt that says "Reach for the Stars." She's probably a first-grade teacher or something. "Yeah, that was my problem too. I'll never train again without a phone, believe me."

"Once is all it takes," agrees Jan. "You're really lucky it isn't worse, like a broken leg or something."

Worse? This has fucked up my entire training schedule! an irritated Richard wants to yell at this woman, the night, and the big damn dog, but he keeps his response to a disagreeable grunt. After a moment, feeling guilty, he tries again at civility: "So you come up here a lot at night?"

Jan laughs. "Oh, I know we look like a couple of goofballs, don't we? But T. J. here is so big and furry, he gets too hot if we walk him during the day in the summer. So we started this nighttime routine, and now even Terry and I enjoy it. It's cool, it's empty, and it's quiet." Jan clears a spot with her foot, then settles on the ground beside her dog.

"I guess that's really being kind to your animal." Richard thinks the two must be kind of whacko to be so devoted to their pet.

"Oh we just *love* T. J.," Jan gushes. "He's like our kid, you know?" She fondly tousles the dog's oversized head.

Richard doesn't have a clue, but he suspects now is probably a good time to fake it. "Mmmm-hmmm."

For the first time since she decided to return to the work force, Zoë wonders whether she should have listened to her advisors. As waves of painful force assault her body with pressure on all sides, she panics, tries repeatedly to return from whence she came. But this is not to be. Her mentors, growing shadowy and vague as they recede from her presence, refuse to negotiate: "This was your choice, Zoë. Now you must live with it." Though they are compassionate enough not to insert the word "literally" into their statement, Zoë gets the message. No pun intended, she thinks resignedly. Characteristically (she is still a Taurus), she tightens up her muscles, trying to lessen the impact of the next attack.

Bonnie is in agony. It is 10:45 P.M., and she has, after what already feels like hours of labor, just reached what her nurse calls "a nice contraction pattern."

"Oh, God," Bonnie whispers to Fay, "when does this *end?*"

The faithful Fay shrugs. "My first one took twenty-four hours and my last one, ninety minutes," she tells Bonnie.

Another contraction slams through Bonnie. When it passes, she says through clenched teeth, "I think I'll concentrate on the ninety minutes."

Fay and Melissa both laugh. "Whatever helps," says the nurse, who reaches for the nearby phone to give the doctor another update.

Bonnie has eavesdropped on these updates throughout the evening. She knows that, at thirty-six weeks rather than full term, her baby will be considered a preemie. As such, Bonnie understands her child will be at higher risk for respiratory problems than a full-term baby, and she sends simple, silent prayers winging heavenward: "Please let everything be okay with the baby and Richard." In spite of the prayer, she is convinced that something has already happened to Richard, or he would have been here by now, surely. Her amended request reads, "Whatever it is, please let him be all right."

If it could be possible for a man to feel more awkward and elephantine than a woman in labor, Richard is feeling so. Strapped securely into a Stoke's litter manned on either side by three search and rescuers, he has never felt so helpless or embarrassed in his life. The litter, a cleverly designed contraption of wire mesh body supports framed by welded metal rods, has a wheel attached at one end to make the going a little easier. Nonetheless, the Pineridge trail is so narrow the litter takes up its entire width, thus forcing his rescuers to struggle over the rough terrain alongside.

EMTs all, the competent search and rescuers have bound Richard's ankle to immobilize it for the downhill trek, even as his entire leg is immobilized in a separate wire mesh compartment of the litter. This compartmentalization of body parts reduces chance of further injury from jarring or imbalances incurred during a victim's transport back to civilization.

But Richard is unconcerned about the little jouncing he will experience as he is borne down this stupid hill. Rather, his unanswered call home confirms his fears that Bonnie is either out looking for him herself or rousting out paratroopers to do the same. He hopes she's not doing the typical female thing of overreacting to his absence with uncontrolled hysteria. Richard doesn't need that right now.

Rather than easing, Zoë's pain has increased to a frightening degree. She is encased in some kind of a narrow tube being squeezed on all sides by massive waves of pressure that become ever more frequent and intense. In addition, she now finds her head butting up against a hard substance that won't allow her free passage through the tube. Her head and body aching from the resistance they encounter, Zoë (whose Taurus characteristics seem to have abandoned her) longs only to escape this nightmare and find a place of comfort where she can rest.

It is 12:37 A.M. The Pitocin has worked its magic and Bonnie's body has responded by carrying her well into the second, or pushing, stage of her labor. The epidural she received—what? an hour and a half ago? (Bonnie has lost all sense of time. The sensations flooding what used to be the familiar grounds of her own body have made her a stranger unto herself.)—is wearing off. Her cervix is fully dilated to ten centimeters and there is nothing stopping her baby from being born but her own body, which seems not to want to release the infant it has succored for so long. Bonnie feels as if she is caught up in some primeval battle over which the threat of casualty looms large.

She is tiring quickly now. When Fay tells her to, Bonnie obediently drops her chin to her chest and holds her breath while Fay counts out loud to ten. Then she breathes out, inhales deeply, repeats the process twice more and on command, bears down with her muscles in an attempt to push the being inside her *out*. But, as usual, when Bonnie stops pushing, the stubborn creature inside her slips right back up the birth canal to its previous position. The women in the hospital room wearily maintain their positions as the battle rages on.

When Richard is at last wheeled into the emergency room at Poudre Valley Hospital, he feels a vast sense of relief. He has been shunted from Pineridge to a litter to an ambulance to a wheelchair by well-meaning souls with whom he is anxious to part company. He has been out-machoed by the best of the best (not just search and rescue; it turned out the canine-loving Terry and Jan were getting their Ph.Ds. in astrophysics, for chrissake). Richard's ego is more severely bruised than his ankle, and he wants nothing more than to have his injury looked at so he can get the hell out of here and go home. But first he must be admitted.

"Name?" inquires the woman on night shift at the admissions desk.

"Blackburn, just like it sounds. Richard Blackburn," mumbles Richard surlily from his wheelchair.

"B.l.a.c.k.b.u.r.n?" spells out the woman.

Richard smiles sardonically. "Just like it sounds."

Unperturbed at the insult, the woman continues with her prescribed litany. "Address?" she inquires.

"Fifty-seven-o-three Coyote Drive," replies Richard, settling in for the duration. But now the woman's eyebrows lift in surprise. She touches a few keys on her keyboard, nods to herself. "I thought so. Are you by any chance related to a Bonnie Blackburn?" she asks.

Adrenaline courses hotly through Richard's spent body and he is immediately, fully awake. "She's my wife. Why?" Richard leans forward in his wheelchair and slaps the countertop, objecting vehemently to the ugly possibilities that admit themselves to his consciousness. *Has something happened to Bonnie, too? My God, how could that be? She was fine when I left...*

"Just a minute, sir." The woman's tone is less friendly. She punches more keys but is interrupted by the ringing of her desk phone. "This is Admissions. Connie speaking...oh sure, sure...no, that'll be fine...okay..."

As the woman drones into the phone, Richard guiltily recalls how, when he was unable to reach Bonnie, he immediately assumed she'd been out looking for him. *What if she's been in a car wreck?* His imagination kicks into overdrive. *What if, right this minute, his wife is dying somewhere in this very building because he hadn't been home on time?* The question strikes Richard like a hammer blow, the bluntness of which forces him to realize that, no matter how far he can make his legs run, it will never be far enough, because full control is impossible.

This knowledge causes Richard's fists to uncurl and slip impotently from the countertop in front of him. At once older and wiser, he leans back in the wheelchair a different man than he had been moments earlier. With heartless timing, Connie hangs up the phone and looks distractedly at Richard. "Where were we?"

"My *wife!*"

"Oh yes. Hmmm, let me see here...okay, got it." She looks at Richard triumphantly over her half glasses, then reads from her computer screen: "Blackburn, Bonnie A. Admitted through ER to OB at nineteen-thirty hours." The woman thinks about this for a second, then looks back at Richard. "Were you expecting a baby or something?"

Richard stares back at the woman. "Baby?" he echoes stupidly.

The woman smiles sweetly. "Just like it sounds, Mr. Blackburn. Just like it sounds."

At 1:28 A.M. Melissa picks up the phone to tell Bonnie's doctor that her baby is at last ready to be born. As she does so, however, the door to the room bursts open, and Melissa's hand hesitates. Has the doctor decided on a fortuitously timed check of his patient that will eliminate the need for a summons? But through the door come, not the doctor, but a filthy looking young man in short shorts and a wheelchair pushed by an orderly. Melissa is about to object, when *"Bonn!"* exclaims the young man.

At the familiar tone, Bonnie rouses herself from her torment. *"Richard?"* She turns her head, removes her hand from Fay and extends it toward the newcomer, whom the orderly pushes right up, bedside, to take it.

"Not a moment too soon, Dad," intones Melissa dryly as she waits for the doctor to answer his page.

Fay rises. "Well, guess I'll be going then."

"No!" Bonnie's one-word objection is bleated out between a gasp of pain and another order from Melissa.

"Bear down, now, Bonnie, really bear down this time."

Bonnie grits her teeth, gathers her strength, and pushes for all she is worth.

Fay sits down again.

Richard, holding his wife's hand, apologizes. "Bonn, I'm sorry. I twisted my ankle up on the ridge, couldn't get down for hours."

"You almost missed—" her words are cut off by the sudden entry of the doctor, who doesn't like what he sees.

"Bit overcrowded in here, isn't it?" While the orderly takes the hint and disappears into the hallway, the nurse who will be in charge of the baby after it is born scurries briskly back into the room after a short absence.

Fay stands up to leave again, but Bonnie grabs the roughened hand and restrains her. "You have to stay." Fay sits back down.

The doctor rolls his eyes but assumes the baby-catching position along with control of the situation. "You're almost there, Bonnie, almost there," he reassures his patient after palpating her. "Just a couple more good pushes and you three will have yourselves a baby!" he promises the trio in front of him.

Now conversation ceases. All watch carefully as Bonnie pushes once...twice... and on the third try, sure enough, a baby slips so quickly into the doctor's waiting hands, its arrival is almost anticlimactic.

Zoë is horrified. She finally escapes the hellishly narrow tube she was in, only to find herself in a cold open space. Bright light kills her eyes, and loud voices frighten her. Though she instinctively knows she must open her mouth to draw a new substance into her tiny lungs, she simultaneously emits a wail of displeasure at having to do so. Whatever this place is, it's not where she'd like to be.

"Welcome to the world," the doctor announces with the pleasure of one who never tires of his job. "You have a little girl."

"It's Zoë," says Bonnie happily. "Her name is Zoë. That means 'life.'"

in no sense

The evening after Bonnie and Richard rendezvous at Poudre Valley Hospital for the birth of their daughter, Zoë, a sell-out crowd gathers in the auditorium of Poudre High School. This audience is so lively (graduation is tomorrow!) it does not quiet completely even when the lights dim. But the stagehands wisely do not wait for a complete hush. At seven-thirty sharp (this is, after all, a school), a bell rings backstage, the curtain rises, and the still whispering spectators view a scene that is—for lack of a kinder word—nothing short of strange.

Those in the audience who have read their programs know they have been transported back to July 1808, to the bath hall of the French mental asylum known as Charenton. Oddly clad people mill about an area ringed with benches; a bathtub stands stage left. While some of the people wave their arms or nod their heads repeatedly, others appear to be convulsed by spasms or unseemly laughter.

Davin, playing the 49-year-old Jean-Paul Marat, is carried onstage by white-clad hospital workers and placed in the tub. Authorities have sentenced Marat to the asylum not because he is insane, but because he still champions his countrymen's rebellion against the aristocracy. Though soothing baths relieve the skin disease acquired when Marat first escaped capture by hiding out in sewers, they do not dampen his enthusiasm for the rebellion begun fifteen years earlier. To Marat, the rebellion remains so noble a cause, it is worth the price of even countless corpses.

This viewpoint establishes Marat as the alter ego of Monsieur de Sade. Sade, also staying at Charenton, is a man whose original fervor for the war has dwindled into disillusioned cynicism. Thus the play becomes the vehicle for brilliant argument between one man blind to the ambiguities that shade all human conflict, and another weary of the bloody reality such conflicts always produce. This arguing occurs during complex variations of time and place, among characters ranging from fictional to historical figures who indeed played notable roles in the real French Revolution.

Seated by herself in the audience (she didn't think any of her friends would be interested in a high school play), Pat is struck by the power of Davin's performance. The energy he pours into the character of Marat radiates outward and strikes her breast heatedly. If Davin/Marat's goal is to incite, he succeeds beautifully by catching the audience up in exquisite sympathy for his convictions. The dismal lives of the French working class in the late eighteenth century, Marat exhorts his listeners, can be uplifted only through revolution and a redistribution of wealth. The audience sighs. When Marat claims passionately that he, himself, *is* the revolution, they sigh again—not with doubt about the wisdom of the man's proclamations, but only the collective urge to help him achieve his goals.

Pat finds the entire production troubling. Filled with lurid images of executions, whippings, the excessively sexual and the grotesque, the play does not pander to the soft of heart. When the curtain falls to a standing ovation from the appreciative young audience, Pat remains seated. Afterwards, she does not join the long line waiting to congratulate the actors, but slips quietly back out to the parking lot. On the way to her own vehicle she pauses a full minute before the dented front end of Davin's car. *Well, I got what I came for,* she thinks to herself on the way home.

At the post-play party, Davin is still charged full of energy from his performance. Only at such times does he taste the freedom with which extroverts regard the world each day. He grabs his killer Charlotte Corday/M.a.d.i.s.o.n. by the hand and twirls her around, then catches her around the waist. "Ahh, my pretty, I still live, you see!"

Madison laughs, kisses Davin generously on the lips. "That collapsible knife's no match for your tough old rib cage, Marat." The tingling Davin feels from her act is not in his rib cage. For an instant, he hugs her tighter, then releases her. Madison melds into the crowd.

Ninety minutes of partying pass quickly. The cast revels in the glory of having forced their audience to confront the thorny themes of *Marat/Sade*: how, as always, the full-bellied dismiss the need to help the empty-bellied earn larger pieces of the pie of worldly goods, while the empty-bellied, drunk from the heady vapors of their own power, cry for ever larger pieces of that same pie, earned or not.

But no one at the party seems troubled by the contradictions posed by Weiss' play. Why should they be? If the societal mess detailed in the play has endured for centuries in more parts of the world than not, it is not the fault of these young people. Savvy enough to realize that in their youth lies the innocence of those who have done their world no harm, the young people party exuberantly.

Madison approaches Davin. "I have something for us." She opens her hand, reveals two small white tablets of Ecstasy.

Davin nods, swallows the pill with his beer, which he then passes to Madison, who follows suit. "C'mon," he says, leading her up the stairs to the bedroom. Madison follows willingly. Neither she nor Davin view this journey with dismay. Like most young people, they cross the threshold into adulthood eagerly, in no sense mournful for what they leave behind.

It is early morning when Davin finally pulls his dented car into the garage of his own home. Inside the house, he does not go straight to bed but instead heads to the bathroom, where he spends a long time. Only when peach tinges the eastern sky and the birds begin their morning concert does his head at last hit the pillow. No matter. While the rest of his class is graduating today, he doesn't have to be at work 'til noon.

critical reviews

Around five o'clock the next evening, Pat tugs at Jethro's harness. She is taking the dog on an extensive training exercise in the mall. Because he is wearing his school uniform (a "Seeing Eye Dog in Training" harness), Jethro may enter every establishment on the premises. Now Pat sees an unusual store called Hot Topic she hasn't noticed before. She takes a hard right and enters another world.

Immediately, she and Jethro are deafened by loud music blaring from speakers positioned around the store. Although Jethro's skin twitches, he remains calm. Pat is not so put off by the noise as by the merchandise displayed in the place. Weird outfits hanging from the walls and racks in the back corner appear to be from another place and time. Long black and red capes, white shirts with ruffles, net gloves and black leather boots call to mind last night's play or the gentry of the eighteenth century. Wandering about, she next spies a collection of chains and metal paraphernalia. Who on earth would *buy* this stuff? There is a young clerk with his back to her helping another customer, but Pat has had enough. She turns to leave.

"Pat!" The exclamation from behind makes her stop and turn around.

For a moment, Pat is too surprised to say anything. The clerk she had noticed from behind is none other than Davin, but it's a Davin with a whole new look. Hair of a moderate brown color replaces the ultra-black thatch of old, while the dismal black outfit always favored before has been exchanged for ordinary khakis and a light-colored T-shirt. The new clothes accentuate the young man's thin frame.

"Didn't recognize me, didja?" Davin spreads his arms wide to indicate his new self.

Pat smiles. "I must admit, I didn't, Davin. But," she adds quickly, "you look far more cheerful!"

A strange expression crosses the young man's face. "Well, I dunno about *that.*"

"But last night you still had your old hair," Pat muses out loud.

"You came to see the play?" Davin is surprised Pat would do such a thing.

"Not the *play*, Davin, *you.*"

Now Davin is even more surprised. "Why?"

Suddenly the store manager appears from the back of the store. Unhappy with too much talking, too little buying, he interrupts curtly: "Davin, you might as well take your supper break."

Facing Pat, Davin rolls his eyes. Pat giggles. "I could buy one of those," she whispers, pointing to a spike-studded leather belt.

Davin nods. "Hey, it takes all kinds," he says cryptically. Together, they leave the store and with Jethro leading, head for the food court.

"This is my treat, Davin, what'll you have?" asks Pat.

Davin is unused to such solicitousness. "Aww, Subway's fine."

Pat nods. They get their sandwiches and return to the mostly empty seating section.

"Do you bring him here a lot?" As Davin reaches down to pet Jethro, who wags his tail happily, his arm sets Pat's purse (which is hooked over the back of her chair) swinging.

Pat doesn't mention that the dog shouldn't be approached while he's working. "I bring him here at least once a week," she tells Davin. "It's good for him to get all kinds of experiences with people and places, and because I live alone I really have to work at getting him out and about."

"Mmmm." Davin's mouth is full.

"So let's get back to last night," suggests Pat.

"Did you like it?" asks Davin.

"You want the truth?"

Davin, suddenly cautious, looks at her over his sandwich, then nods.

"I *hated* it!" exclaims Pat. Davin pales while Pat holds up one hand, rushes to explain. "I mean, Davin, that's one of the most atrocious pieces of drama I've ever seen!" Then, conscious of the effect her words are having, she amends. "Well, not atrocious in the sense of a poor script or performances—you were *great,*" she emphasizes, "just in the sense of the grotesque, you know what I mean? I can't believe they even let you perform such a thing in high school."

Davin smirks. "We got around that because it's a 'classic.'"

Now it's Pat's turn to roll her eyes. "Even so. I still have my doubts about such a production being good viewing for young people. Everything was so...*graphic*," she concludes.

"But the shock value's half the fun!" insists Davin.

"You mean you like shocking productions?"

"Oh yeah. Besides drawing in the crowds, they're a kick to perform."

"How so?" probes Pat.

"Oh, you know. You get to have fun with the *excess*. Sort of like an extension of being Goth," explains Davin.

"Goth?" Pat is lost.

"You know. Gothic. Like how I looked before."

"Is that what you call that?"

Davin nods.

"What is it, exactly?" asks Pat.

Davin brightens. He wishes his father would ask this same question. His thoughts flash back to late morning, when he was hoping his new look would start a conversation. But his father had remained walled off behind his newspaper, never even looking up to say good-by when Davin left for work. So much for the death of his old self, which Davin had carefully timed to coincide with his last school performance and the murder of Marat.

Now he informs the interested Pat: "Goth's a mind-set." Seeing the blank look on her face, he continues. "You adopt this certain way of dressing and looking—you know, the black and white thing—that spells out something to other people."

"And what does it spell?"

"It's complicated. For me, I'd have to say I was trying to make a statement. When I started high school I wasn't cool enough to be popular—you know what I mean?—and I wasn't messed up enough to fit in with the punk or rock groups. I was just kind of, well, *out* there, by myself."

"And did dressing like that help you gain entrance to a group of your own?"

Davin shrugs. "I guess, eventually maybe. But it wasn't about finding a group so much as, well, Goth is more like a philosophy that gives you a way to perceive the world."

"Which is...?" Pat prompts.

Davin's shoulders sag noticeably and his face falls. "That it's pretty fucked up," he says bluntly.

Pat recoils slightly. Then, looking at the pain on the young face across from her, she leans forward and asks, "What's the matter, Davin?"

Davin laughs derisively. "Oh, the same thing that's always the matter. My old man hates me," he confides.

Instead of responding with immediate protest that no father could hate his own son, Pat leans back in her chair and sighs heavily. "I'm so sorry," she says.

"He thinks I'm some kind of freak because I like acting instead of science," complains Davin bitterly.

Pat nods. Some time ago, she'd finally remembered where she'd seen the name Hassletree. "Your dad's the cardiologist, right?"

"Yeah."

"And he probably wanted you to go to medical school, right?"

"I guess. But I just *couldn't*, you know what I mean?" objects Davin.

"Sure," agrees Pat. "You gotta be yourself, Davin. And after last night, I'd guess that self wants—no, *needs*" she corrects—"to be an actor, right?"

Davin nods, grateful for the support.

Pat wishes she could give him more. "All I can tell you, Davin, is that you shouldn't give up your own dreams, but, at the same time, understand that parents' dreams for their kids die hard…real hard," she adds sadly.

Davin looks at the old woman who has been so kind to him, decides to ask something he has been wondering about for a long time. "Was it hard for you when…" he trails off, too embarrassed to continue.

It is Pat's turn to be blunt. "When we found out Steven was gay?" Davin nods.

"Until he died," responds Pat, "I thought it was the most awful time of my life. It wasn't so hard for me—I'd suspected for a long time—but Hal just couldn't accept it. My husband owned a *car* dealership, you know what I'm saying, Davin?"

"'Ford tough.'" Davin bleakly echoes the old commercial.

"Exactly. And when he found out his son would never even come close to fitting in with that—" Pat pauses, visibly upset at the memory—"that stupid, narrow-minded, two-word description of how things ought to be, well, he just about—" she stops again, sips her drink once, looks at Davin with a face as pained as his own, draws a shaky breath and finishes: "He just about destroyed his relationship with his only son."

For a moment the two sit silently.

"What happened?" Davin, reluctant, finally asks.

Pat's hand goes to her chest. "It took Steven dying for Hal to come to his senses."

Shocked, Davin says nothing.

Pat nods. "Like I told you, parents' dreams for their kids die hard. But just because your dad's a blockhead doesn't mean he doesn't love, you, Davin."

Davin is amused (no one's ever referred to Dr. Hassletree as a *blockhead* before), then scornful. "Yeah, right."

Pat shakes her head insistently. "I mean it, Davin. Even though he might not show it, your dad loves you and needs you."

"Uh-uh. He only took custody of me to spite my mom," Davin states flatly.

Pat shakes her head again. "Don't you believe it, and don't stop giving him a chance."

"*Him* a chance??" Incredulous now, Davin looks at his watch. "Hey, I gotta get back to work."

She nods ruefully, dissatisfied with the way this conversation has gone. They both rise. "Can we walk you back?" Pat points her chin at Jethro.

"Sure," says Davin curtly.

"What I'm trying to tell you, Davin," continues Pat, "is that sometimes parents are weaker than their kids in, oh, it could be lots of different ways. Some struggle with alcohol or drugs, some are lousy communicators, some spend their whole lives trying to fulfill their own needs at the expense of their kids, some just don't get how to be good parents."

Davin looks contemptuous. "Check all of the above."

Pat nods. "Okay. What I'm telling you is, if that's the hand you've been dealt and you know it, you've gotta use your own strength to give your dad a hand. Maybe you're an old soul who's gone a lot more rounds than he has. Maybe it's your job to teach him a better way," she offers, half jokingly, half not.

Because the IB program at PHS included broad study of world religions, Davin doesn't find Pat's suggestion of reincarnation troubling. Nonetheless, he balks at the idea of assuming any responsibility for his father. "I don't think so. Just a couple more months and hopefully, I'm outta here." They have reached Hot Topic, and he turns to go inside.

Pat has to throw one last curve ball. "I just want to know one more thing, young man." Davin pauses, looks down at her with eyebrows raised, lips pursed in the best *"now what?"* expression she has ever seen.

"What the *hell,"* Pat intones forcefully, "did you do to that car?"

Davin's expression turns to chagrin. "I collided with a mule deer." He turns again to leave.

"Take it to the dealership," Pat instructs Davin's retreating back. "I'll arrange it so they'll fix it without charging you the deductible," she offers. Davin doesn't turn around but nods his acknowledgment, raises one hand over his shoulder in backwards farewell before vanishing into Loud-Music-Sold-Here-Land.

Pat, who is running out of dog food for Jethro, means to stop at the store on her way home from the mall. But her mind is churning with thoughts of her Steven mixed up with thoughts of Davin and once outside, she realizes she has forgotten where she parked her car. She and Jethro march around the hot parking lot a good quarter of an hour before locating her vehicle. Once re-ensconced in her car, a sweaty, frazzled Pat drives right past the store entrance without a second thought. Only when she is halfway home does she remember the dog food. "Damn!" she exclaims in disgust. She pulls an illegal U-turn in the middle of the road, causing nearby drivers to swerve, honk, and raise their middle fingers at the lunatic. This upsets Pat further. For an instant she takes both hands off the wheel and gives *double* middle-finger salutes back to those who've judged her.

When she at last reaches the same supermarket where Bonnie's water broke, Pat looks over the back seat at Jethro. "Don't you *dare* tell Rita," she orders her furry friend, shaking her index finger at him. Jethro has heard that tone of voice before. He looks at his mistress knowingly, wags his tail once. "I know. All you care about is supper," sighs Pat, picking up her pet's harness and letting him out of the car. "Well, lead me to it, then," she commands, and Jethro steps out like a pro.

When she has the dog food in her possession at last, Pat makes her way to the checkout counter. She wedges Jethro's harness handle between the bars of the shopping cart and roots around in her handbag for her billfold—she likes to have her cash in hand before it is her turn to pay. She locates her billfold, opens the compartment where she keeps her paper money, and frowns. *That's odd. I thought I had five twenties in here, not two,* thinks Pat. *Am I going batty, or what? Oh my God, if Rita finds out I can't even keep track of what's in my wallet, she'll flip.* Pat maneuvers her cart and her dog forward in line. Well aware she is beginning to sound senile, she looks down at Jethro and for the second time in fifteen minutes, repeats, "Don't you *dare* tell Rita." This time, her voice is fraught with such pleading even Jethro knows better than to wag his tail.

In the small hours of the morning, Pat wakes from restless sleep. Something is bothering her, but as usual, she can't quite identify whatever it is that niggles at the back of her brain like an itch she can't scratch. Irritated, she throws aside her covers, then trudges to the bathroom to down a couple of aspirin. She and aspirin are good friends. Pat takes the small white tablets for any and all ailments, including head colds. Whether it is the little pills themselves or her faith in them that effects the countless cures she has experienced over the years, she doesn't ask.

Back in bed a quarter of an hour later, true to form, the aspirin provides the reason for Pat's insomnia. Her thoughts flash back to the supermarket and her feeling that she should have had more cash in her wallet. Then, with a rare moment of perfect clarity, she recalls opening her wallet to get her tithe out for church that morning and noting that she had exactly one hundred dollars left. Quickly now, her thoughts accelerate, taking her back through the events of the day. Nothing out of the ordinary—the kids over for Sunday dinner, then her late afternoon trip to the mall with Jethro, her surprise encounter with Davin. Here her mind hesitates, unwilling to consider what it must: *Could Davin have taken her money?*

Struggling to recreate the events of their meeting, Pat visualizes bumping into Davin in that strange store—no, she was wearing her purse by its shoulder strap, securely tucked under one arm. There was no way he could have gotten into it. Then, later, when they had supper at the food court, she had hung her bag over the back of the chair. Could he have somehow reached in and taken money from her wallet while they had been eating? That doesn't seem likely...still,

Davin had reached down to pet Jethro. Had he managed to snake his hand into her purse at the same time?

Depressed by this chain of thought, Pat takes refuge in doing what her daughter is forever accusing her of: losing it. Her thoughts flutter and skip about, touching briefly on trivia. How flaky had been the crust of her apple pie at dinner (Ed, bless his heart, had had seconds!), how her butterfly bushes needed dead-heading, how she hasn't seen Bonnie this weekend and must run over some cookies tomorrow...

against all odds

Early in the evening of the following Saturday, Ed, Rita, Greg, and Laura Wonsawski pile into their mini-van. It is Pinewood Derby Day, and the Wonsawskis are excited. "Do ya really think it'll work, Dad?" Greg asks for the bazillionth time, turning the little car over and over in his hot, sweaty hands.

Ed is not annoyed. Not only does the Cake-Bake fiasco still chafe, but last week at the pre-race trials, their car with the perfect wheels had performed dismally. Ed recalls the scene. "What's the matter with it, Dad?" a disappointed Greg had asked after their car finished last in its heat.

"Oh, Greg, we forgot about the *weight*," Ed had explained. All derby entries had to fall within an official weight range. At the weigh-in, the Wonsawskis learned that their car was just a fraction of an ounce above the required minimum.

"The heavier cars go faster, no matter what kind of wheels they have, huh?" Greg had observed sadly.

Ed had been forced to agree. But that night, after Greg had gone to bed, he had hit upon a solution. "I know how to fix our car, Greg," he had announced the next morning.

"How?" The question was posed in a tone just bordering on snotty. But after all the hype about the wheels, Ed couldn't really blame Greg for being unconvinced.

"Look, the only thing wrong with our car is that it's a little on the light side, right?" Ed had persisted. Greg had nodded. "Sooooo," continued salesman-turned-derby-car-expert-Ed, "all's we have to do is drill some holes, stick in some weights and TA-DAHH! We'll haf ein fast car!" he promised.

As good as his word, that evening Ed and Greg had calculated how much additional weight their car could legally carry. Then they had rummaged through Ed's tackle box to find four little lead sinkers that together weighed that same amount. Next, they had drilled four small holes into the car body, one above each wheel. They inserted a sinker into each hole, plugged the holes with wood putty, then painted over them. When they were finished, they had a car with perfect wheels *and* the maximum allowable weight.

"This baby," Ed had promised his son, "is gonna *fly!*" But by that time, there were no more trial races scheduled. The Wonsawskis had to wait until actual Derby Day to find out if Ed's promise would hold true.

Now, after a week that seemed like a year to Greg, race day has finally arrived. Thanks to Ross fine-tuning their wheels on his expensive lathe, Ed feels he has a good chance to finally prove himself a *winner* in his son's eyes. "Well, I guess we'll find out shortly, eh?" Ed responds to Greg's original question, but his eyes catch Rita's. She smiles back, as tickled as he with their improved prospects. Neither she nor Ed appreciates the irony that, in turning Greg's car over to Ross, they have joined ranks with the smart-aleck parents who sacrifice their sons' involvement with their derby cars for a better shot at *winning.*

"Can I hold it?" Laura, next to Greg in the back seat, asks.

"*No!* You'll mess up the paint job," objects Gregory, clutching the car possessively to his chest. Because the Wonsawskis decided early on to focus on speed and not bother with artistic merit or the "show" competition, Greg was allowed to paint his car himself. Though the vehicle's surface is now hideously decorated with crooked racing stripes in blotched colors, Greg sees only superb artistry. "We shoulda entered the paint competition, too," he says regretfully. "We'da blown 'em out of the water in *everything!*"

"No you wouldn't of, that's *ugly.*" Laura, pointing to the small wooden vehicle, exercises her right to hurt her brother back.

"It is not!" Gregory manages to shout before Rita turns around.

"Do you two want to go, or do you not?" she threatens. Cowed for the moment, both kids shut up.

When they reach the elementary school hosting the derby, Ed finds the parking lot overflowing with life-sized vehicles. "Where do they expect us to go?" he grumbles.

"You could park down there and we could walk," suggests Greg, pointing down a cross street.

"Oh, honey, I'd never make it in these shoes," objects Rita. She is clad in a new outfit: white capri pants topped by a spaghetti-strapped Lycra top that is violet with white polka dots. On her feet are woven straw sandals with three-inch heels but no heel straps. Her finger- and toenails are painted purple but they do not have racing stripes.

Briefly wondering where Rita got the money for her ensemble (he has learned the hard way to give his wife a weekly allowance for household expenses and no more), Ed nonetheless sympathizes. How sexily dressed women manage to do anything when they wear getups like his wife's amazes him. "I'll drop you here," he offers, pulling up by the door. "The kids and I'll hoof it." Rita exits and the van pulls away.

Minutes later, Ed, Greg and Laura enter a gym bursting with people. Small groups of neckerchiefed Cub Scouts dash frenetically in and out among standing pillars of adults. One of the groups slows briefly to engulf Gregory in a giant-sized act of phagocytosis before resuming its unchecked movement around the room. The temperature and noise level in the gym are not conducive to meditative moments. Ed catches sight of Rita and dispatches Laura to her care before proceeding over to the track.

The Pinewood Derby track is a sight to behold. Constructed of well-varnished wood, the highest segment of track stands about four feet above the table on which it rests. Six lanes wide, the track descends steeply before rising into a couple of hills along its forty-foot length. Built-in legs hold the end of the track just up off the floor. Though the race has not officially begun, excited fathers and their cubs are already holding informal test runs with their derby cars.

"Can we run ours?" Greg begs Ed.

Ed shakes his head negatively. "No sense giving 'em a preview of what they have to beat," he whispers, winking conspiratorially.

Greg draws air into his mouth in a silent "ohhhh" of understanding, then backs coolly away from the track.

"Say, Ed, could you be a judge?" somebody hollers across the din. Ed can't identify the asker, but butts his broad shoulders cooperatively through the crowd toward the end of the track, where the judges will record the order in which the little cars cross the finish line.

Rita, meanwhile, has clustered with other moms from Greg's pack. She thinks she looks terrific, and she is happy to give these gals an eyeful while they simultaneously give her an earful. The moms talk about strep throat that's going around. They talk about Jerry and Eve Grundig's not-so-amiable divorce. They talk about their latest trips to Mexico (nobody goes to *Iowa* anymore), and what they think of the latest in Fort Collins' never-ending string of new restaurants. They munch cookies and drink sugary punch while complaining they haven't lost an ounce. The moms are having fun!

When deep-voiced shouts from the other end of the room indicate the derby is finally under way, no mothers move in that direction. A moment later, however, when Brett's mom appears with new blond highlights in her hair, the women erupt in a flurry of their own. "When did you *do* that?!—You look fan*tas*tic!—Who's your *hair*dresser?!" Her mouth full of sugar cookie, Rita's hand drifts up to her own hair, arranges it behind one ear. She stops tracking the conversation. Would *she* look good streaked? There is an annoying tug at her side.

"Can we go home now, Mommy? I don't like it here," whines Laura.

"Oh, sweetie, we just got here. Why don't you get yourself some cookies and punch and see if you can find Jamie?" suggests Rita.

"I'm not hungry, and she's not here," protests Laura, whose cheeks are flushed from the heat.

"How do you know?" argues Rita. Just this once, she wants to enact with women her own age. Is *that* too much to ask?

"I saw her mom, and her mom said," pronounces Laura defiantly. "So let's go, okay?"

"Laura, honey, we have to cheer for Gregory." When all else fails, take shovel: apply moral authority thickly.

Even at six, Laura knows her mother is really saying she's not ready to go and they won't leave until she is. Her young face clouds visibly, only to brighten a moment later when Andrea (Cooper's mom) intervenes.

"Why don't you let her come out to the playground with us?" she offers kindly, gesturing with the hand holding that of Cooper's four-year-old sister, Megan.

Rita considers. She has never had much use for Andrea Clearmont, a bespectacled plain Jane whose long gray-streaked hair is tied up in a sloppy bun. Andrea wears a baggy tee shirt over cut-offs and ugly leather sandals that look all too comfortable (Rita's own feet have begun to protest their remarkable elevation). And she makes Rita feel guilty because she is always the first to volunteer for every filthy, buggy campout or cookout the Cub Scouts have. *Yuuckkkk. Maybe just this once, though.* "Well, I guess that'd be okay. Don't let her get too hot, though," Rita cautions Andrea, relinquishing Laura with the necessary show of concern.

Andrea smiles sweetly. "We'll be careful." On the way outside, she lets the two girls stop at the water fountain to fill a small, brightly colored canteen. The girls are taking turns sipping from the canteen and chattering like long-time friends before they even reach the door.

Track-side, Ed is busy doing his level best to be a good judge. This is tricky business. The Pinewood Derby begins with six-car heats, and Ed and three other judges have to watch all six cars at once as they cross the finish line. Sometimes Ed is not exactly sure whether one car beats another, but the important thing, he feels, is to trust his gut and speak with authority, or there'll be run-offs all night. Nobody wants that, so all four judges pool their best guesses and come to consensus quickly on close calls. Everybody knows this is all just for fun, anyway.

At the top of the track, where the races begin, there is less room for human error. A starting gate extending across all six lanes ensures that all the cars begin each race at exactly the same time. But the scouting district only owns one racetrack, so every Pinewood Derby draws from a wide area of participating packs. Thus it is that Ed judges a full hours' worth of six-car heats before he spies Greg's car (Laura was right, it *is* ugly) in the starting line-up. Ed's pulse quickens. He glances around, but no one suggests that he withdraw as a judge because of conflict of interest during this heat.

And hey, none of the other judges have said anything about *their* kids' cars coming down the track, Ed rationalizes. He plants his feet, gives himself a "heads up," and watches carefully. Greg, meanwhile, has elbowed himself to a good observation point as well. He signals his dad an excited thumbs up. Ed winks back but murmurs an inaudible *Hail, Mary* just to be on the safe side. The starting gate opens, and the little cars begin their seconds-long quest to establish their owners' positions among the ranks of men. Of the six cars, only the first two will qualify for the next heat. Cars that come in third, fourth, fifth, or sixth are immediately relegated to Loserville. Every father and son in the room knows these odds, and no one objects. This is all just for fun.

As the six cars come whizzing down the track, Ed holds his breath. Greg's car takes the lead, but wobbles a little when it passes over the seams where the track segments are joined together. *Damn!* thinks Ed, recognizing the problem immediately. *That's not the wheels, it's our axles.* Their perfectly smooth wheels, riding on their perfectly honed microscopic ridges, are attached to the small wooden body of their perfectly weighted derby car in a manner anything but perfect. Too late, Ed realizes the nails he and Greg used to attach the wheels to their car have nothing to prevent them from coming loose or even falling out.

"*God, let them hold.*" Ed sends a silent plea upward but keeps his eyes wide open (he is, after all, an official judge). An instant later, his request for a small miracle is granted, for the wheels hold and Greg's car is the clear winner in its heat.

"*Yeah!*" Ed sees Greg holler triumphantly and pump his arm victoriously once, twice, three times.

"*Oh, yeah, this is what it's all about!*" thinks Ed happily.

Hours later, weary but elated, the Wonsawskis finally return home with a trophy for overall third place. "I can't wait 'til next year!" announces Greg shrilly, still hyped from all the excitement.

Ed laughs. Victory *is* sweet. "You know, we just notch those nails a tad like Grant's dad showed us and we'll be unbeatable!" he promises his son as he retrieves Laura, who is asleep in the back seat. Though the night has brought relief from the day's heat, Ed notices her face is still flushed. Probably too much sun.

"So who took first, anyway?" Now that she is home, Rita can admit her ignorance of the day's proceedings.

"Well, that was really weird," replies Ed as he makes his way to Laura's room and deposits her gently on the bed before removing her shoes. "It was some single mom and her kid. You could tell they just did the most basic car possible: hacked a simple wedge out of the wood, jammed the wheels on, painted the thing red and *Va-voom!*

The thing went like hell!" Ed is still shaking his head and marveling as he gently closes the door to his daughter's bedroom and heads down the hall to his own room, where Rita is already in bed.

"You know, hon, I think I'll sit outside awhile, okay?" Ed, too wired to sleep, thinks he deserves one of his rare stogies. When a slight snore from the other side of the bed is the only answer he receives, he tiptoes out of the room.

Outside, Ed leans on his deck railing, savoring his accomplishment at the derby even more than the taste and aroma of his fine cigar. When his eyes adjust to night vision, however, Ed thinks he sees small shadows moving here and there on the outskirts of his yard. *Goddamnit!* The rats seem to be enjoying his backyard as much as he is. Ed stares hard into the night, wishing he was just imagining things, but the furtive movements continue. Swearing softly to himself, Ed crushes his butt in an old ashtray Rita lets him keep hidden in the corner behind their grill, then makes his way around to the back door to his garage and disappears inside.

Moments later, he reappears outside with a bagful of something held under his left arm. In the faint light from nearby yard lights (he hasn't turned his own backyard light on), Ed's hands look ghostly white because they are now clad in cheap latex surgical gloves. He makes his way with his bundle to what he estimates is the center of the prairie dog colony adjoining his backyard. Then his right hand dips into the bag and comes out holding a handful of something he scatters on the ground around him. Moving in concentric circles outward from his central position, Ed continues with this strange behavior until he covers the entire area inhabited by the small rodents he finds so irritating. Then he folds his bag tightly closed and disappears once more inside his garage.

the sixth sense

It is close to the witching hour, but the prairie doesn't sleep. Wide-eyed, she watches Two-Legs stumble about the small home of her Barking Squirrels (not dogs at all, prairie dogs are rodents belonging to the squirrel family), but she cannot discern his intent and once again, sighs softly to herself. The prairie remembers back to the time—not long ago at all, really, just a hundred years or so—when she was vast. Then, she was home to more than five *billion* Barking Squirrels who inhabited more than a hundred million acres of grassland from Canada to Mexico. Then, a single prairie dog town in Texas covered twenty-five thousand square miles and contained almost four hundred million animals! Then, remembers the prairie wistfully, she was grand indeed. Now, she watches Two-Legs carefully and wonders. The prairie has long since learned that what she doesn't know *can* hurt her.

Meanwhile, the tiny colony of *Cynomys ludovicianus* living next to Ed's backyard on the Cathy Fromme Prairie sleeps peacefully, unaware of Ed's nocturnal presence on their home turf. Contrary to Ed's impressions (were his eyes and imagination playing tricks on him in the dark?), black-tailed prairie dogs are diurnal animals that limit their aboveground activity to daylight hours. At nightfall, these small mammals retreat down their cozy burrows, which are complete with sleeping chambers where they can dream the night away in safety and comfort.

When, early Sunday morning, the sun again strikes the little town, small heads peep cautiously from the mounds of dirt surrounding each burrow entrance. Is it safe to emerge? Who will be the first to venture out? Aboveground, the prairie dogs face constant danger. Hawks and eagles threaten from the sky, while coyotes, badgers, red foxes, and rattlesnakes may lie in wait below. Though this dawn comes quietly, with nothing visibly stirring, the older mammals know things are not always as they seem on the prairie.

Indeed, if the prairie dogs could see into the taller grass bordering their town, they might postpone their emergence indefinitely. For there, cleverly camouflaged behind vegetation but still ominously close to the outskirts of the colony, the buff-colored forms of Marcus and Kaia lie patiently, motionlessly in wait. Though these two coyote parents normally forage alone, intense pressure to provide food for their hungry pups has caused them to team up in a partnership that will increase their chances of a successful hunt. This is not remarkable behavior for adult coyotes, amazingly adaptable animals always willing to change their behavior to increase their odds of survival.

If Marcus and Kaia can succeed in catching several of the small rodents, they will return to the den and, in short order, regurgitate a warm meal for their waiting pups. Watching intently, the coyotes see the first signs of movement in the colony before them. Will their long wait pay off? But Kaia suddenly whimpers softly to her mate. Though she cannot identify it, she senses something odd, something not-quite-right to the scene before her. Marcus does not ignore his mate's warning. Coyotes have not gained their reputation as notoriously savvy animals for nothing. By mutual consent, the pair—bellies empty—slink off to other hunting grounds. This day, breakfast for Banks and Liza will be fashionably late.

departures

Dr. Gavin David Hassletree, III, was not present when Ned what's-his-name had picked up his Stetson, jammed it on his head, and told his wife, Helen, he was going out to check on a few things. "Are you sure you'll be all right?" Helen had asked with concern.

"If I sit around here any longer I'm gonna turn into one o' them knickknacks," was Ned's gruff reply as he pointed to the prized figurines Helen had arrayed on every available surface in their living room. Helen had nodded sympathetically. Ned's recuperation from heart surgery had been an ordeal for both of them, simply because Ned, used to long hours of hard work on the ranch, quickly became discontent penned up in the house. Helen was as eager to get her husband up and running again as Ned was. When you'd been married as long as they had, togetherness, while still valued, definitely had its limits.

Ned had walked with his characteristic long strides to the barn, where he'd asked Jim, one of his hands, to saddle his favorite riding horse, Kinky. "Are you sure, boss?" Jim had asked.

"Damnit, just throw a saddle on 'er, will ya?" Ned hated feeling like his every move was being judged in a new way since his surgery. It was bad enough having to use Jim to saddle his mare and give him a leg up. When he was finally mounted, Ned rode with relief toward the north pasture. It had been so long since he'd been up there, he wouldn't have been surprised to see that the creek had cut a new course.

He'd spent an enjoyable morning moseying around his property on horseback, taking simple pleasure in the blue sky, the light breeze, the young mule deer that bounded out of a stand of aspen. Though Ned wasn't given to praying, he was so grateful for another shot at life he'd taken his hat off and waved it jubilantly around the air above his head. "I know you think I'm off my rocker," he'd confided to Kinky, who, except for her ears twitching back to listen, ignored him.

"Well, maybe I am but at least I'm *here*, dear," Ned crooned to his horse, and at that exact moment pain of an intensity he had never known clobbered him in the chest so fiercely that he dropped the reins and slumped over Kinky's coarse mane in agony. Kinky, who was used to Ned talking out loud while he rode, was not used to this motion on her back. It didn't jive with anything she knew, so she stopped to see what would happen next.

This upset Ned's fragile equilibrium. One booted foot came out of its stirrups and dangled by the horse's side, scraping it lightly. This was a touch the horse knew. Reassured, she started forward. Now Ned's loose foot no longer served to anchor him to his horse, so he began to tilt over toward the other side. With both hands clutching at his chest, Ned could not regain his seat in the saddle. In seconds he was on the ground beside his horse, left foot still raised and painfully twisted in its stirrup.

It was at that time that the old cattleman's cracked, blue lips moved and he uttered faint sounds, but Kinky being the only witness to these events, no testimony was ever given as to the nature of their substance. Had Ned finally found his God? Was he, during his last minutes in this earthly realm, praying for release from pain, or just the chance to spend another ordinary day with Helen or (better yet) Kinky? Or had Ned made it to the point where he could honestly feel grateful for the whole grand mess of things: joy *and* sorrow, health *and* sickness, love *and* loss?

Helen did not ponder such questions, but took great comfort in the fact that her husband of forty-four years died doing what he loved. Then, being a woman of practical nature, she ordered an autopsy.

Working in his office several weeks later, Dr. Gavin David Hassletree, III, is irritated when, unannounced, a stranger enters. "Dr. Hassletree?" inquires the stranger, a neatly clad young man who does not extend his hand after Hassletree, peering stonily over his reading glasses (he *hates* to be disturbed), gives an affirmative nod. The stranger merely nods in return and then, still standing, presents Hassletree with a large envelope. "I'm from the law firm of Kirkland, Reyes and Schiller," the man says without introducing himself, "hereby notifying you of a civil suit filed against you by Helen Cantrell."

"Who?" Caught off guard, Hassletree is confused.

"Wife of Ned, whom perhaps you'll remember better. It's all in there." The young man points to the envelope Hassletree is still holding, then leaves abruptly.

"Everything okay? I couldn't stop the guy from coming back here," apologizes the doctor's receptionist as she sticks her head around the door. Hassletree is using a large letter opener to slice open the envelope he has just received. He nods curtly. His employee doesn't notice that the doctor's skilled hands are trembling noticeably as they withdraw documents from the envelope.

tiers of sadness

"Gramma!" The word is half sighed, half cried as little Laura rushes into Pat's house and arms.

"Sweetheart!" Pat is a reassuring haven for her granddaughter. Then she again hears the sound of a car in the driveway and frowns. "Isn't your mother even coming in?"

"Nuh-uh. She said she's late for aerobics," explains Laura, shrugging out of her colorful little backpack.

"Mmmm. And I hear you're sick?" Pat asks, concern in her voice.

Laura nods. "I have strep throat. Mommy says I got it at the Pinewood Derby from Megan's canteen we shared water from."

"Is that right? So Megan is sick, too?" asks Pat.

"Nuh-uh. Mommy called up her Mommy and Megan's fine, but Mommy said she's gonna get it too," Laura informs Pat seriously.

"Ahh." Pat knew kids' germs traveled fast, but she wasn't so certain about the backwards part. Laura was just confused. "So, what do you want to do, honey?"

"Got *books!*" Laura finally escapes the backpack, dumps the contents all over the floor.

For once, Pat doesn't have to pretend to approve. "You went to the library!" she observes.

Laura's hands, busy sorting through the pile, land on what she seeks. "Read *this* one, please, Gramma."

Pat takes the book. "*Oceans of the World.*" Oh, God. Her daughter always did have pretentious aspirations for her children. But they settle on the couch, open the book, and begin.

Fifteen minutes later, Laura is bored and fidgety. Pat shuts the book firmly. "Tell you what, how about just a plain old story?"

"Okay, but can it still be about oceans?"

"You bet," responds Pat. "This," she begins, holding her granddaughter close, "is the story of How the Oceans Came to Be.

"Once upon a time, far away and long ago," she intones in a mysterious voice, "you know there were no oceans at all, Laura. Oh, there were puddles here and there from rain, and small creeks and ponds scattered about for drinking water, but no body of water even half the size of an ocean. And because there were no oceans, there were also no whales, no dolphins—Laura has been to Sea World— not even any of those little shrimp you like to eat so much!"

"Where were they, Gramma?"

Pat's shoulders rise in an exaggerated shrug. "Not here yet, because they didn't have any place to live," she says.

"Were people here?" asks Laura.

"Oh yes. But it was a long time ago, so there weren't many people, and they were all happy," answers Pat.

"All the time?" Laura is suspicious.

"At first," Pat qualifies. "But then, like always, things changed."

"What happened?"

"Well, one day a little boy named Djardin was playing outside when he noticed a strange thing on the ground. The thing looked like an ugly old ball, but when Djardin tried to pick it up, he found it was too heavy to lift. He tried and tried, but he couldn't get the thing off the ground."

"What did it look like?" asks Laura.

"Ugly," repeats Pat. "The outside of it looked like wrinkled, cracked old leather. Parts of it were dirty purple, and other parts a kind of ugly, fuzzy bluish-gray, as if they had mold growing on them. Have you ever seen mold?" Pat checks.

Laura nods. "On bread Mommy forgets we have. It stinks."

"This thing stank too," Pat agrees. "But when the boy crouched down to look closer, he saw that the mold, or whatever the fuzzy stuff was on the round thing, grew in the shape of a face. The thing seemed to have two eyes, a nose, a mouth, two ears and even scraggly old hair and a beard."

"Was it a *head?*" Laura's eyes are wide.

"Well, it was about the size of a head, but Djardin didn't know what it was for sure, so he sat down to keep it company and think for awhile. He sat there for the longest time, just looking at the round thing, which appeared to be looking back at him. Djardin sat beside the thing all afternoon, until finally the sun began to set. And then he finally thought to ask the thing itself. 'What are you?'

"At that, the thing blinked its fuzzy eyes, cleared its fuzzy throat (aHEM), and answered in a hoarse voice, 'Why, I'm a seed of course.'

"At once, Djardin's head filled with visions of a tree loaded with his favorite fruit, called zingleberries. 'Will you grow into a fruit tree?' he asked the seed with great excitement (zingleberries were very hard to find).

"At this point, one of the eyes on the round thing winked slowly. 'I've been waiting here a million years for somebody to find and plant me. You honestly can't think, now that I finally have a chance to grow, that I'm going to spoil the surprise and *tell* you what kind of seed I am, do you? What if you didn't like me?' asked the seed.

"Djardin thought about that for a whole minute, but he couldn't get the idea of a treeful of zingleberries out of his head. 'I bet you're a fruit tree, and you're just saying that to trick me.' But the seed just blinked its eyes and said nothing, which made Djardin just a tiny bit mad.

"'If you won't tell me then I'll just plant you right now and find out for myself!' he threatened.

"'Please do,' said the seed, then it closed its eyes and remained silent.

"Immediately, Djardin ran back to his village. He told about the wonderful seed he had found that would grow enough fruit for everyone in the village to eat, and he rounded up a team of people to help him plant it. The people were happy to help Djardin. Fruit was scarce in their dry land, and a whole treeful of it would be welcome indeed. The people took great care to plant the seed in a sunny spot with good soil and afterwards, they took turns watering it regularly.

"This made Djardin even happier than he had been before. Every day, he went to inspect the seed to see if it had sprouted and just a week after they had planted it, Djardin found a tiny little green shoot sticking its nose out of the soil. 'It's up! It's up!' he ran shouting back to the village. Then the entire village came out and danced around the little green shoot in joyous celebration.

"Once up, the shoot grew so quickly the people were amazed. In no time it was an inch, then two inches, and soon a whole foot tall. After that it grew a foot a week, so that, after just two months, the tree was nine feet tall! It had branches with leaves that made a wonderful circle of shade beneath them, and Djardin used to lie under the tree and dream about zingleberry muffins, zingleberry pie, and zingleberry cake. When the tree burst into a frothy mass of pinkish-white blossoms that, from a distance, made it look as if a great cloud had settled down to earth, Djardin knew it wouldn't be long at all until his dreams came true.

"Sure enough, soon the tree shed its blossoms and showed the first signs of tiny fruit. Because it was unripe, the fruit was green of course, but Djardin knew it would grow and ripen quickly in the hot sun. The villagers were so excited about all the fruit they were going to get that they decided to hold a harvest party.

"Now, although the fruit did ripen as expected, even Djardin had to admit it didn't look like zingleberries. Instead of the rich purple color of zingleberries, the berries on this tree were, of all things, multicolored! There were red berries and orange, blue and pink, green, violet and bright yellow. The tree looked like a gay blend of all the flavors of delicious that there ever were, but the most maddening thing, for Djardin and the other children of the village, was that, even when the wind rose, *not a single berry* fell off that tree. The tree had such smooth bark and was by now so tall not even the older children could climb it, so no one was able to sneak a taste of the beautiful berries. The thought of all that fruit growing just up out of reach nearly drove the children crazy, but they had to wait for the harvest festival like everyone else.

"Finally, the great day arrived. The villagers gathered buckets, baskets and ladders and carried them to the tree. The mayor announced that, once the first basket was filled, they would pass it 'round so everyone could take a handful of berries and eat them right away. Because Djardin was the one who had found the seed for the berry tree, he was given the honor of taking the first handful. He grabbed some berries and crammed them into his mouth. The look of joy on his face at their wondrous taste told all. Quickly, the basket went from person to person until each had had a sample. By then, another basket had been filled, and the process was repeated all over again.

"The villagers ate and ate. They had waited so long for this fruit to be theirs that no one suggested they stop. No mothers said, 'You'll spoil your dinner' to their children—this *was* dinner!—or 'You're going to get a stomachache.' Everyone just ate until they could eat no more. Then, even though many beautiful berries still hung on the tree, the villagers dropped their baskets, left their ladders leaning against the tree and went home to bed stuffed to the gills.

"The next morning when the people awoke, they felt strange. Now, in spite of eating all those berries the day before, no one was sick to his stomach, but everyone agreed they felt different in a way they couldn't understand. Finally a little girl put the feeling into words. 'I am sad today,' she said, and then she started to cry. The villagers gathered 'round and stared. No one had seen sadness or tears before, because they had all been happy. But quickly, like the germs that jump from one to another of us without being seen and leave pain and sickness in their path, the sadness and tears spread from person to person as well. Soon all the villagers were wailing and clinging to one another in despair.

"The mayor was beside himself. What had happened to his happy village? How could he get it back again? Then he heard a voice in the crowd say, 'The *tree!* It has to be the tree that caused this, because it's the only thing that was different yesterday.' The people grumbled among themselves. Could that be true? Could their beautiful berry tree be the cause of their distress?

"Then another voice shouted, 'Let's cut it down!' and the mayor found his voice of authority at last.

"'Grab your axes!' he ordered the people, and the people obeyed. They had experienced an entire morning of sadness and already, they had had enough. They wanted things back the way they had been before, when everyone was happy all the time.

So they marched to the tree, fully intending to chop it to the ground.

"When they arrived at the tree, however, the villagers had another surprise waiting for them. Overnight, all the berries they had left on the tree had disappeared, so that not a one was left. The tree appeared happy. Without the weight of all its berries dragging them down, its branches waved gaily in the breeze. So now the people had second thoughts. They thought about the wonderful, almost magical taste of the berries they had eaten yesterday. They milled around the base of the tree, but no one lifted his axe. What if their sad wasn't from the tree?

"Then the mayor once again took charge. 'Ask it what kind of tree it is,' he ordered Djardin.

"Djardin trembled slightly, but everyone from the village was looking at him so he asked in a squeaky voice, 'Oh tree, what kind of tree are you?' But the tree remained silent while the villagers just stood there, feeling miserable.

"'Ask again!' the mayor commanded Djardin.

This time Djardin, feeling braver—maybe this whole thing had nothing to do with the tree—spoke up quite loudly: 'Tree! What kind of tree are you?'

"And now, from deep within the tree's majestic trunk came a soft moan. Slowly, the moan grew in volume until it became a roar that filled the people's ears with pain. Only then, when they were writhing from the pain in their ears, did the roar separate itself into words that put fear into the hearts of all the villagers. 'I,' roared the tree, 'am the Great Tree of Sadness, and I shall be with you from now until the end of Time.'

"No sooner did a voice from the crowd shout out, 'Not if we cut you down, you won't,' than the tree actually laughed.

"'You fools,' it said to the villagers 'it's too late. In the night my seeds have been carried to all the corners of the earth by my friends the four winds and the birds. From now on, wherever you shall roam, there will I be. Should you cut me down, two more of me will grow in my place. Henceforth, my fruit will be always among you, and none will be able to resist its glorious taste. From now on, all who call themselves the Children of Men will eat from the Tree of Sad.'

"'But *why?*' challenged the mayor, who wanted his happy village back. 'We have done nothing wrong. Why are you doing this to us?'

"At this, the great tree sighed a mighty sigh. 'Because,' he explained slowly, 'you have been as little children with your constant happiness. But now the Great One is lonesome for your company, and you cannot find your way to Him without sadness to guide you.'"

For the first time, Laura interrupts her grandmother. "Does the Great One mean God, Gramma?" she asks.

Pat smiles down at her granddaughter. "I think so," she replies.

"Anyway, from that time on, wherever the people were and wherever they went, there were always reasons to be sad. So—not every day, but often— the people cried great tears that fell onto the thirsty earth and disappeared into the dry ground. Now, as time passed, so many tears fell to the ground that the earth was unable to hold them to herself anymore, so she released them to her surface in the form of a small pond. But people kept crying. Eventually, the pond overflowed her shores and grew into a large lake. Still, though, Laura, people kept crying.

"Now earth again released the tears from their boundaries and turned the lake into a great salty sea but, after many years passed, even that sea wasn't large enough to hold all the tears the people cried. And you know what happened next, don't you, Laura?" Pat asks her granddaughter.

Laura nods. "All the tears together made the oceans, didn't they, Gramma?"

"That they did, sweetheart, that they did," agrees Pat.

There follows a peaceful moment in which grandmother and granddaughter sit quietly together, thinking. Then, outside, someone presses a car horn aggressively twice.

"That'll be your mother," says Pat. Laura scoops up her books and dashes to the door.

"Bye, Gramma!" she says hurriedly on her way out.

"Bye, honey," Pat says to the sound of a car backing out of her driveway.

accounts payable

"Yeah, Dad, when were you gonna tell me, like, on the way out the door as they cart you off to jail?" Davin shouts furiously. It is late on a hot night, and Davin is so angry spittle forms at the corners of his mouth, which itself feels caked with some kind of coating. His tongue, too, feels thick and dry—it is hard to get words out. Davin strides around their living room, continuing to shout. "I can't believe I have to read this in the *paper!*" he accuses his father harshly, waving the *Coloradoan* wildly about. His frantic movements stop briefly while he again looks down at the offensive headlines, which read, "Local Doctor Faces Charges of Fraud, Malpractice, Theft."

Seated in an armchair, Dr. Gavin David Hassletree, III, stares bleakly up at his son. The doctor is dressed but unshaven, a half-empty glass of Scotch on the end table near his elbow. "It's not like they say," protests the doctor, palms down on his thighs.

"*What* isn't like they say?" Davin pounces. "You didn't promise some poor schmuck who's since keeled over four bypasses and deliver two? Or you didn't do two and bill Medicare for four, huh, Dad?" Breathing heavily, Davin flings the paper down on the floor at his father's feet. "Well, whichever it is, it sure beats my snooping in your investment files all to hell, doesn't it?"

"Davin," the doctor tries again, but Davin cuts him off.

"*What*, Dad? Are you gonna tell me your 'victims'—ohhhh, I love that term, it makes it sound like *you* shoulda been wearing black all these months, with maybe a coupla fangs thrown in to get the point across—*don't* include 'the federal government, Medicare, Blue Cross/Blue Shield,' and let's see, 'a number of private insurance companies,' not to mention poor Ned what's-his-name and all the other suckers you gypped when they were out cold in the OR?" Davin recites this list painfully, accurately, from memory.

"Look, I never thought it would come to this, Davin," the doctor says wearily. "I thought it would blow over or be settled quietly out of court."

"That's not exactly saying you didn't *do* this, Dad!" Again, Davin is outraged. "My father, the Cardiac Con. Fuck."

"It's not like that, Davin!" Now Hassletree is angry too. "Hell, this is more complicated than you know."

"Yeah, I'll bet. So complicated there's gonna be headlines for weeks blasting our name all over town. Didn't ya ever stop to think how this would affect *me?* I'm gonna be the laughingstock of—"

"—of what, Davin, your senior class you didn't even bother to go to graduation with because you're such a rebel, a loner nobody can understand, including your own father?" accuses the doctor, latching onto his favorite theme.

"You never get it, do you, Dad? Well, try this: Maybe I didn't march because I was ashamed I'd only have one fucking person there to watch while everybody else had *squads* of family and friends and huge celebrations afterwards. What would we have done, take all two of us out to eat and look at each other lovingly across the table? That'd have been unforgettable. I'd need one of those scrapbooks with the acid-free paper to preserve the memories, Dad."

Davin searches his pocket for his keys, but his words have found their mark, for Dr. Hassletree's face now acquires a look of sheer desperation. "Davin, wait. At least listen to my side of things, okay?" he pleads, rising ponderously from his chair.

Rather than excite in Davin a sense of just desserts, hearing his merciless father at long last beg for mercy on his own behalf prompts only an unwelcome recollection. *"Don't stop giving your father a chance."* Though Pat's advice replays itself uncomfortably in the son's mind, awarding his father another chance is at this moment beyond Davin's capacity. He does not pause at the door but leaves behind a bitter laugh that bounces off the walls and echoes harshly in the large room.

Alone again, Dr. Gavin David Hassletree, III, falls heavily back into his chair. Briefly, his skilled hands cover his face but seconds later reach defiantly for the glass of Scotch. When the living room timer suddenly shuts the lights off, Dr. Hassletree remains seated, staring obstinately into a darkness filled with ghosts.

turnabout

As always, the removal of a single strand of the prairie's intricately woven food web causes consternation among those dependent upon that strand for survival. When Ed poisoned the prairie dog colony behind his house, he forces the raptors, reptiles and mammals that feed there to look elsewhere for their sustenance. Among those scurrying to find additional food sources are Marcus and Kaia. But the clever coyotes are better suited than most for having to make do in a pinch. Appeasing their hunger in new ways is a challenge they face with characteristic boldness. If, on occasion, they throw in a pinch of glee for good measure, wherein lies blame?

This night, the coyotes respond to Ed's act of destruction with a simple counter-move. For the first time, they leave the comfortable, familiar Cathy Fromme Prairie to hunt, instead, a small (seventeen-acre) parcel of open space but a short distance away. The fact that this long, skinny oval of land happens to separate the homes in Phase I of Ed's subdivision (whatever that is) from those in Phase II escapes these animals' knowledge. What the coyotes keenly *do* sense is that the oval is rimmed with the large box-like structures that house Two-Legs as well as his delectable pets. Easy pickin's.

Later, as the heavy-bellied Marcus and Kaia head slowly home, the prairie doesn't know whether to chuckle at the outrageous irony of the show she has witnessed or tear out her foliage in dismay. For the prairie knows that, while the coyotes' prey this night consisted exclusively of domestic cat, domestic cats themselves annually kill hundreds of millions of birds and three times as many small mammals. As small, abundant, *un*natural predators, domestic cats instinctively hunt and capture prey in backyards, open spaces, fields and forests the world over. They do this regardless of whether they are well fed, yet ordinarily do not survive without direct or indirect support from Two-Legs.

Oh dear. The interchanges among her living things are so complex, the prairie at times feels overwhelmed. Thankful she doesn't have to write a job description, watching Marcus and Kaia feed their pups, then hole up for a well-earned rest nevertheless prompts a pang of jealousy in her breast. Would that she could close *her* eyes for once!

small prey

Worry perforating his composure like a corrosive, Davin drives the dark, empty streets of Fort Collins until the eastern sky silvers slightly. But the coming of daylight does not inspire him with hope. Rather, the destruction his father has wrought in the name of profit astounds and sickens him. Looking at it in one sense, he thinks, you could even say his father killed somebody. Could he be charged with *murder?* Stomach churning with this new possibility, Davin finally pulls into a tiny lot off south Shields Street. The lot, about two miles due east of Davin's home on Coyote Ridge, provides parking for users of the Cathy Fromme Prairie. There he dons his old black duster as protection against the early morning chill and on foot, heads west (backwards from his usual direction) along the nature trail.

Though he hasn't been out here since *Marat/Sade* and he presently has nothing to rehearse, from habit, Davin automatically clears his mind as he settles into stride down the familiar path. In so doing, he calms somewhat, and for the prairie, this is enough. The chance to insinuate her own presence into this young man's overwrought psyche is more than she can resist. So subtly her patient remains unaware that he is receiving treatment, she tiptoes her way into his senses and then, BAM!

As light floods the prairie, she turns the volume of song from her western meadowlarks up, then texturizes the sound with the distinctive chirring of her redwing blackbirds. Filling Davin's ears with this joyous noise, the prairie simultaneously opens his nostrils to the scent of her dew-wet grasses and his eyes to her flowers tucked among them. Then, just for fun, she scatters a half-dozen baby cottontails in the vegetation beside the trail. In truth, to Davin the place seems overrun with bunnies whose reactions to his huge presence seem unpredictable at best.

"Huh!" One of the cooler customers provokes a boyish lunge that, in turn, provokes so quick a change from steady-gazed nibbling to zigzagged flight that Davin (quick-change artist himself) momentarily forgets his troubles and laughs out loud. Unseen, the prairie smiles back. It tickles her to draw these two-legged creatures out of themselves. She may be reduced in size from days of old, but her ability to solace souls remains as powerful as ever.

Walking with a lighter step, Davin eventually approaches the prairie dog colony located just south of the trail and a short way east of the Taft Hill Road underpass. He has passed here many times before with his concentration so focused on some character, the busy rodent establishment claimed attention only from his subconscious. Now, however, free from dramatic demands, Davin settles onto the bench at the overlook in hope that he can for once give the colony his full regard. His mind registers something different about the place, but his impression is not strong enough to articulate itself as thought. Prompted only by a vague feeling of change, he surveys the scene below.

Watching for a quarter of an hour or so, Davin is soon struck by the lack of activity in the colony. He recollects that, even when it impinged only on the periphery of his vision and awareness, the prairie dog town was a busy place. Before, even when he was immersed in a character, the small tan animals always imprinted annoying echoes of yips and shadows of movement on the edges of his brain. But today, even with the sun fully risen, the colony is clothed in eerie stillness. Not a single prairie dog forages in the clipped grass around its burrow or stands self-importantly on its hind feet as sentinel. Not even a half-hearted alarm call warns the furry populace of human presence. *Odd*, thinks Davin, who strolls over to check out a sign that wasn't there before. In large print, the sign says: "Warning: Keep Children, Pets Off Prairie Dog Colony."

Below that, in smaller print, the sign states: "Vandals have used poison to eradicate these animals. Though clean-up efforts have been made, small quantities of strychnine-laced grain may remain. Use extreme caution."

Below that, someone has scrawled in black: "It's not a dog's world, it's ours."

Davin is no environmentalist, but sensitized by his father's rejection, he is nonetheless depressed by the killing grounds before him. As if in payment for his brief respite, worry again seizes his guts like a python squeezing the life out of its dinner. Returning to his bench, Davin mentally reviews the list: *Dad is making headlines and will be tried for negligence and fraud committed doing heart surgery, I haven't heard a damn thing—good or bad—from Tisch, and I'm in way over my head with Madison and don't know how to get out.*

As if in accord with Davin's mood and disheartened by what has happened to her Barking Squirrels, the prairie, too, changes attitude. Momentarily, the benevolent face she has worn all morning transforms itself into a visage ancient and harsh. The benign warmth of the morning sun changes to intense, moisture-sapping heat. The meadowlarks' vocal celebration of the new day is replaced by the abrasive noise of perhaps one-, perhaps a hundred-million insects proclaiming their unseen but powerful presence on this small nugget of unplowed land. Seeking shelter from the blazing sun, the baby bunnies disappear entirely from sight.

While Davin, sweating now (as usual, he refuses to remove his coat for the minor inconvenience of temperature extremes), makes his way disconsolately home, Bonnie Blackburn picks up the infant seat in which tiny Zoë lies peacefully asleep and transfers it gently to the shade beneath their upper level deck. It is still early, but she and Zoë have been up long since for a 5:00 A.M. feeding, after which the baby seems to enjoy her longest, most restful nap of the day. During these few hours of peace, Bonnie (who has finally acquired a touch of Richard's discipline) tries to keep her professional hand in by staying up and working assiduously at her art. Presently, she is doing a watercolor of a large yucca abloom in her backyard.

Though many times larger, the plant's base consists of a cluster of long, narrow leaves that call to Bonnie's still food-conscious mind (nursing makes her hungrier than pregnancy, for pete's sake!) the greenery that tops a pineapple. But each narrow, leathery yucca leaf terminates in a sharp point that can wickedly impale whatever comes in contact with it. Bonnie has found this out the hard way when she bent over to study her subject closely. Now, she maintains a respectful distance when she approaches.

Scepter-like, a tall spike emerges from the center of the plant's foliage. On this fine summer morning, the spike bears so large a panicle of white, bell-shaped, drooping flowers that it, too, impresses the viewer with a sense of royalty. Because Bonnie has heard (she does not know for certain) that the plant blooms only once every ten years, she feels twice motivated to capture the beauty of its showy blossoms. These (she does know for certain) are pollinated exclusively by the small white yucca moth, which renders the plant a necessary service while the plant, in turn, provides the moth with necessary sustenance and shelter. A sweet exchange, indeed, thinks amateur-naturalist Bonnie.

Catching movement on the nature trail below them, Bonnie notices the creep who always wears the black coat out on the prairie again (what *does* he do out there?), but, today, she gives him short shrift. A busy mother now, she has no time for conjecture about complete strangers. Carefully, she lays a wash of palest white along her blossom line. But her effort is interrupted by Richard who, still favoring his injured ankle, limps to the deck railing and calls below. "Bonn." His voice has a slightly peeved tone Bonnie is not sure derives from his inability to run or the presence of their new daughter in their lives.

"Have you seen the blue geometric tie that goes with my gray suit? I'm meeting with an important lead today and want to look nice."

Sighing, Bonnie returns her brush to her water even as she tries what she knows will be a fruitless suggestion. "Try the batch that just came back from the cleaners," she offers, even as she starts to make her way indoors to help her helpless husband.

"Have. It's not there," protests Richard.

"I'm on my way, honey." Reassuring herself that Zoë still sleeps comfortably in the deep shade, Bonnie bends over, rearranges the pink blanket, and kisses her daughter lovingly on her little forehead before disappearing through the downstairs door.

Upstairs, while Richard showers, Bonnie rummages through their walk-in closet, searching for the tie. She wonders whether Richard knows these are some of the most precious minutes of her day, during which she feels free to do what *she* wants. *Does he even realize what a struggle it is the rest of the time?*

Probably not. How could he when he's gone so much? Knowing that Richard sometimes drapes his ties over the inside of his shirt hangers, she is pulling every shirt that could possibly go with that tie out, unbuttoning it and looking inside. *Not here, or here, or here...AHA!* Triumphantly, Bonnie retrieves the tie from beneath a white shirt. "I found it!" she sings out to Richard. She tries to sneak back outside, but Richard is too quick for her.

He exits the bathroom clad only in a towel. "You got it? Oh, good. But tell me if you think this would look better," he pleads over his shoulder as he enters their closet.

Bonnie rolls her eyes, but there is nothing to betray her act except the mirror on their dresser.

Richard exits the closet holding up two more shirt/tie combinations. "What do you think?" he asks his wife innocently.

Bonnie is fast getting to the teeth-gritting stage, but she reins herself in. "I really do like that geometric on you, Richard."

Richard nods. "That's what I thought. Thanks, Bonn." He nods, dismissing her.

Gratefully, Bonnie hurries back downstairs. Will the light still be right for her picture? Stepping outside, she glances at the sky and is relieved to see that the light looks unchanged. Good. Then she turns again toward her little angel, Zoë. *Did you miss me, sweetcakes?*

This innocent thought—this simple question asked by a caring mother of her newborn child—is, in the instant it is formulated, immediately absorbed by (and perfectly recorded in) the energy of the universe itself. But no sooner is the thought formulated than the mind that created it moves on. For when Bonnie turns her loving eyes toward her precious child, she sees not her baby girl sleeping peacefully in her infant seat, but an infant seat alone. Cruelly, horribly empty of life, the seat rocks gently to what Bonnie suspects is a wind from hell.

"RICHARD!" Forgetting her distress at his childlike inability to dress himself, she screams her husband's name even as she gazes wildly, frantically about. But Bonnie's searching eyes see no movement, nothing at all except a glimpse of black duster as its wearer disappears over the last of the many stairs leading from the prairie to the top of Coyote Ridge. *Could that guy have Zoë under his coat?* One part of Bonnie wants to tear after him but she stands rooted in place, helpless to leave the spot where she last saw Zoë.

"RICHARD!" She screams again from under the deck. Countless, slow seconds pass before the beautifully dressed father of her child peers anxiously over the deck railing.

"What is it, Bonn?" At this instant, there is no trace of peeve in Richard's voice. Indeed, his face is sheathed in nothing but concern for the fact that his wife is standing outside their house, screaming loud enough to wake the neighborhood.

"Zoë's gone!" Bonnie half yells, half cries. Her panic-stricken face gazes up at Richard imploringly.

"What?" Richard cannot believe he has heard his wife correctly.

"She's just gone, Richard, GONE!" Bonnie screams, waving her hands and turning wildly about in a small circle. "I came back downstairs and she wasn't in her seat and—"

Even with his limp, Richard makes it down the deck stairs in record time. He takes in the empty infant seat with one glance, grabs Bonnie's wild hands in both of his and draws her gently but firmly out from under the deck. "Bonnie, come upstairs. I'll call the police."

"NO! Richard, I can't leave here!" resists Bonnie. "Maybe whoever has her will bring her back!" she tries desperately.

"Bonnie." Richard considers, does not say to his wife that people who take babies don't bring them back. "Come. We need to call the police. Did you see anyone around?" he asks.

Tearfully, Bonnie nods as Richard leads her upstairs. "This guy who hangs out on the trail—he always wears black—was out there this morning, and I saw him at the top of the stairs when I went back outside."

"Does he live around here?" Richard is persistent.

"I don't know. Maybe," admits Bonnie.

Overwhelmed, Bonnie crumbles miserably to a chair in the kitchen, but Richard won't have it. He hands her the phone.

"Bonnie, call the police. I'll take the car, see if I can find that guy." Richard, keys in hand, doesn't have to tell his wife that seconds count now. As Bonnie punches 911 in on the phone, Richard is out the door and gone to see if he can find his daughter.

big prayers

With Richard still out driving the neighborhood, Bonnie sits forlornly on the couch by the front window, watching for the police. She doesn't know what else to do except torture herself with a single question. Why oh why hadn't she simply bent down, picked Zoë up and brought her inside when Richard called, instead of leaving her outside, alone and unprotected? Each of the three possible answers that occurs to Bonnie (she was too lazy, in too much of a hurry, or too busy doing what *she* wanted than to think about the welfare of her own baby) is equally devastating.

With no one to contradict these self-incriminating explanations for her behavior with the absurdly logical (not wanting to disturb Zoë while she was sleeping so soundly), Bonnie readily convinces herself of her own guilt in her daughter's disappearance. Distraught, she puts her face down in a pillow and sobs. She doesn't hear the sound of a car pulling into the driveway, nor see the uniformed young officer who, viewing her distress when he stands at the screen door, hesitates to ring the bell.

"Mrs. Blackburn?" the young man finally asks as he knocks softly at the door. Startled, Bonnie lifts her tear-streaked face, staring in wordless misery. "May I come in?" Still speechless, Bonnie nods.

Letting himself in, the man walks over to the couch and extends his hand. "Art Sanderson from the Sheriff's Department." Because the city of Fort Collins has not incorporated Coyote Ridge, it falls under the jurisdiction of the county sheriff rather than the city police.

Without realizing she is doing so, Bonnie grabs the proffered hand in both of hers and hangs on. "You have to help us. My baby's been taken." The words she utters sound strange and unreal to Bonnie, whose life has changed in a way she could never have imagined just thirty minutes ago.

"That's what you said in your phone call," states Sanderson. As the nearest officer on patrol and therefore, first on scene, he's responsible for initial assessment of this incident. Though he is fully aware dispatch used the phrase "possible baby kidnapping" when relaying Bonnie's 911 call, Sanderson remains cool. He's never heard of a bona fide kidnapping in Fort Collins; more likely, this is a simple case of parents getting their wires crossed over who's got the kid. ("But I thought she went to *Grandma's* on Tuesdays. No, Grandma gets her on Thursdays, you idiot. No wonder I divorced you, you can't even keep track of your own kid.") But Sanderson keeps these suspicions to himself. Taking a seat across from Bonnie, he opens his notebook, says simply, "Tell me what happened."

"I don't *know* what happened," laments Bonnie, hugging the pillow to her chest in a move pathetically reminiscent of holding a baby. "We were outside, I was painting, Zoë—that's her name, Zoë—was sound asleep in her infant seat. I went inside for a couple minutes and when I came out she was just...she was *gone.*" Bonnie's white face contradicts the unbelievability of her words and suggests to Sanderson that she, at least, believes them to be true.

Sanderson takes a moment to digest what he has just heard. Apart from her shock, Bonnie seems coherent and not under the influence of drugs or alcohol. Still, her tale is nothing short of bizarre. A *baby* kidnapping, here in "the Choice City," U.S.A? Silently, Sanderson evaluates Bonnie's mental health, but he concludes it's too early to ask her about it point blank. His next question is inoffensive. "Is your husband home, Mrs. Blackburn?"

"He was still home when it happened, but now he's out looking for a guy I saw on the trail," says Bonnie.

"Mmmm." So the parents are not estranged. Moreover, it's common knowledge among law enforcers that citizens who attempt their own crime investigations often cause more problems than they solve. On the other hand, thinks Sanderson, if it had been *his* kid who'd gone missing, he knows he'd be out doing exactly the same thing. This thought—a mere second's worth of identifying with the unknown Richard Blackburn—prompts a chain reaction the young officer has never before experienced.

Suddenly, the cool detachment on which he prides himself flies out the screen door, to be replaced by a feeling of unease that roils through his gut like salmonella. Surprised at the speed with which his impression of events at the Blackburn house changes, Officer Sanderson does not delay. Trusting his gut as he would no other human, he excuses himself, walks out to his car and radios for help.

Minutes later, a second car from the sheriff's department pulls into Bonnie's driveway and two men emerge. Sanderson briefs both, then conducts them into the house. One—early forties, with reassuring touches of gray at his temples—introduces himself as Tom Selby. The second, younger man is Scott McCarthy. Investigating Officer (sheriff's department lingo for "detective") Selby quickly gets down to business. "Why don't you show us where you were when this happened, Mrs. Blackburn," he suggests with quiet urgency.

Bonnie, grateful to do anything, rises immediately. "It's shorter this way," she offers, leading the men through the house to their back deck door. Selby glances around during their passage, but sees nothing out of the ordinary. The open morning paper, a half cup of cold coffee and a half-eaten bagel are on the kitchen table. "My husband's breakfast," explains Bonnie. "He was just about to leave for work," she says tearfully, remembering with pain what *normal* used to feel like, and knowing she won't be feeling it again until she has Zoë safely back in her arms.

Seconds later, she and the men stand in the backyard, where Bonnie's unfinished painting stands interrupted on its easel. The officers note that her brushes, open palette, and water containers, though strewn across a small table by its side, do not appear to be in disarray. Turning away from her artwork, however, Bonnie heads instead toward the shade beneath the deck. At the last second McCarthy reaches out, catches her elbow and stops her from proceeding any further. "This is close enough, ma'am."

Bonnie stops, staring at her daughter's forlorn little infant seat, which makes an inaudible but powerful statement of its own. She has her tears under control now, but the hand that covers her mouth and prevents all but a low whimper from escaping trembles visibly. "Is this exactly where you had her, Mrs. Blackburn?" asks Selby gently. With her hand still covering her mouth, Bonnie nods. "Have you moved or touched the seat since you found it empty?" Another nod— this time negative.

"You were painting," he gestures over to the easel, "and you went inside. Why?" Selby looks up from his pad for this answer, which he hasn't heard yet.

Bonnie takes a deep breath. "Just to find a tie. My husband couldn't find the tie he wanted, so I went in to help him."

At this point Sanderson's radio crackles, summoning him to other duty. Then McCarthy pops the question she has feared. "Why didn't you take the baby in with you?"

Bonnie draws another shaky breath. "I don't know. I mean, I'm not sure I even thought about it." She looks to the two men for support, but none is forthcoming. They look back at her, waiting. "She was sound asleep," continues Bonnie. "She usually sleeps for almost two hours after her morning feeding—and I guess maybe I figured I'd only be gone a minute or two, and it seemed so harmless to leave her here, you know? I never thought about it being unsafe back here," admits Bonnie. "It was all so quiet," she remembers, "so...*ordinary*." She looks bleakly about, caught up in her memories. Neither officer comments while Selby scribbles in his book.

Then McCarthy fires another round that goes straight to Bonnie's heart. "Was she strapped in?" As Selby looks up from his notebook, pen waiting, Bonnie's eyes fill with more pain. She shakes her head negatively but remains silent. What is there to say of these small sins mothers commit against their children day in, day out, that pale to nothing compared to the big stuff like abuse?

But Selby is not paid to philosophize. "How old is Zoë, what does she weigh, and what was she wearing? Was she wrapped in a blanket?"

"Oh, God." Bonnie's two hands fold together as she prays audibly for strength. "She's just five weeks old. She came a little early, so she's small, still just under seven pounds. She had on a pale green terry jumpsuit and she was wrapped in a pink blanket." While Selby writes all this down, McCarthy keeps the ball rolling.

"You mentioned you saw someone when you came back outside, Mrs. Blackburn?"

"There's this guy," replies Bonnie, who doesn't want to think that what she is saying has anything to do with her baby's disappearance. "He dresses all in black—he wears this big black overcoat— and hangs out on the nature trail a lot. I'd seen him down on the trail earlier (she gestures down toward the prairie), and when I came out he was over there, just at the top of the steps to the Ridge."

"Do you know his name or where he lives?"

"No. I've never spoken to him."

Hearing the deck door open upstairs, the three walk back out into the sunshine to find Richard peering down at them. His first words are for Bonnie. "No luck," he says sadly. "I never even saw the guy."

"All right," says Selby, closing his book and taking control. "Let's talk more inside, shall we?" Bonnie, whose breasts are beginning to hurt because it's almost time to feed Zoë again, heads upstairs at once. She doesn't hear Selby tell Scott to start processing the area as a crime scene.

The morning that has become a nightmare in the Blackburn house drags on. Outside, Scott combs the area for evidence. Inside, Selby, explaining that he's just trying to gather every piece of the puzzle that he can, pries deeply into the couple's lives. "Wheredoyouworkhowisyourrelationshiphaveeitherofyoueverhad anymentalhealthproblemsdidyoureallywantthisbaby?" and so on.

Aghast at the force of this interrogation, Bonnie excuses herself to pump her breasts. Richard is about to use the interlude to make a statement of his own to Selby when the doorbell rings again. It is Pat from next door.

"Hi, I'm just checking to see if you're all okay," the older woman says through the screen door.

"Hey, Pat." Richard returns the greeting, rises to admit his neighbor. "You know, we're not okay, and I think Bonnie could really use a friend right now. Why don't you go and see her in the bedroom," he suggests. Pat takes the hall to the master bedroom and knocks gently on the doorframe.

Bonnie, sitting on the bed with her head in her hands, looks up. "Oh, Pat, somebody's taken Zoë," she cries.

Pat gasps. "What do you mean?" She crosses the bedroom, plunks down beside Bonnie and curls a protective arm around her.

"I left her outside for a minute and when I went back out, she was *gone*." Bonnie still trembles at hearing the words she must speak. "I went in to find a stupid tie for Richard, and when I came out, she just—she just wasn't there," Bonnie repeats the fact of Zoë's disappearance for what feels like the hundredth time, but the words have become no easier to say.

"Oh, sweetheart." Pat takes Bonnie in both arms now and hugs her close. She strokes Bonnie's hair as Bonnie sobs miserably. She does not say, "It will be okay."

After Bonnie calms down, Pat rises and draws Bonnie to her feet. "Do you want to come over to my house for awhile, just to get out of here?"

"No." Bonnie sniffles. "I need to stay with Richard."

Pat nods. "I'll be going then, Bonnie, but you know you'll be in my thoughts and prayers." Bonnie manages a small smile of thanks.

As Pat crosses over to the front door, Selby breaks his discussion with Richard to intervene. "Excuse me, Mrs.—?"

"Schreveport. Pat Schreveport," replies Pat.

"You're the Blackburns' neighbor?"

"Yep. Live right there." Pat points.

"Tom Selby. Nice to meet you." Officer Selby has risen and extended his hand to Pat, who shakes it briefly. "You know, we'll be canvassing the neighborhood later, but as long as you're here, I wondered whether maybe you could help us out."

Pat looks surprised. "Well, of course. What can I do for you?"

"I'm just curious if you happen to know anything about a fellow the Blackburns have seen on the nature trail frequently. I'm told he always dresses in black."

Delighted recognition shows on Pat's face. "Why, yes, I *do* know that young man! We're good friends," she admits cheerfully.

"Do you know his name and address?" asks Selby.

"Why, you're talking about Davin Hassletree, you know, the cardiologist's son," offers Pat. "They live right down the block."

"The doctor who's in trouble for fraud?" Selby isn't sure where this is going.

Pat nods. "I'm afraid so. But his son is a *wonderful* young man— a really talented actor—he saved my dog's life. What's he got to do with this?" Pat is getting confused.

"We're not sure." Selby guides Pat out the door.

hands out

Affected more than she lets on by the happenings next door, Pat is glad to get home. She feels that the strange circumstances surrounding Zoë's disappearance (who takes *babies* to good end?) make it unlikely that the little girl will survive. Life has taught Pat two things: (1) wishing it were otherwise makes no matter. Sooner or later, you get clobbered by loss and (2) when it happens, you're better off making the emotion triggered by that experience a friend rather than an enemy.

Much as she knows the shoulds, however, Pat knows even better that the hows are another story. To make friends with something you have to embrace it, and you can't embrace loss without adding your own jars, buckets, or drums full of tears to an ocean not hungry but thirsty, ever thirsty for more. Should Bonnie and Richard really lose Zoë, thinks Pat, the odds for the young couple to survive their huge hurt will be long indeed.

But Pat is nothing if not a veteran. Granted, she may never have scored outright victory against long odds, but years of practice made her, if not master, at least a devotee of the well-placed kick. The world over, her heroes were the remarkable people who—in unremarkable locations from board- to bedrooms, dining rooms to dens—excelled at taking precise aim, swinging their figurative legs back, and *wham!,* delivering powerful kicks in the butt to whatever would destroy them.

The destroyers come in so many guises besides grief and loss—hunger and cold, poverty and sickness, addiction and despair—Pat thinks of them as an army of quick-change artists, against whom the little guy stands virtually no chance. But when the little guy joins forces with his own kind—when a bunch of little guys line up to help each other withstand the enemy, no matter his costume—well, that's a different story. When that happens, so can miracles.

Over her years, Pat has seen too many such miracles to think them rare. Always, they grew out of an accord that blossomed when somebody stretched out a hand to help somebody else. From that accord she has seen sickness transformed into health, poverty into well-being, despair into hope, sorrow into joy. It took her longer than she cares to admit, now, but she finally figured out that the force powering her heroes' well-placed kicks was not enmity toward the enemy, but love for one another. *Duh!*

Once she made that realization, it was easy to see that her kick-imagery was all wrong. People who came up victors over the bad guys weren't lashing out at them with legs and feet, they were linking arms and forming a combined front of love. Hands reaching out to help others spun silken strands of love that stretched from heart to heart, making what Pat calls not spider- but spirit-webs. When her Hal and Steven died, she clearly recalls, the spirit web spun for her by others formed a gossamer bandage around her heart. To this day, Pat believes that delicate Band-Aid woven from others' love the only thing on earth that stopped her hemorrhaging heart from bleeding out.

But today, the tables have turned. Today, it is poor Bonnie's heart in danger of bleeding to death and Pat who must spin. Pat is not dismayed by this knowledge. Rather, she quickly picks up the phone and cancels her bridge date for that afternoon. Then she heads straight for her kitchen, which, this day, will be her spindle.

An hour later and a block down the road, Davin, refreshed by a shower after his long night, hears the doorbell ring. Except for the occasional Brownie selling her cookies or Jehovah's Witness selling his version of God, this is an odd occurrence at his house. Hair still wet and tousled, he opens the door curiously.

"Davin Hassletree?" Two serious men stand on the stoop and look Davin over carefully. They see a tall, thin young man dressed in shorts and a T-shirt, neither of which is black.

Wary, Davin (who is not in the mood to be proselytized) keeps his reply brief. "Yeah." It doesn't occur to him to wonder how these two know his name.

"I'm Officer Tom Selby, and this is Scott McCarthy from the Larimer County Sheriff's Office. Could we talk to you a minute?"

Frowning, Davin hesitates. "If this is about my dad, you'd better talk with his attorney." He begins to close the door.

"Actually, this concerns *you,*" the McCarthy guy informs Davin.

"Me?" Davin's face registers complete surprise as the men nod and repeat their request to talk.

"Well, sure, I guess." Davin admits the men, who take seats in the living room.

"We understand you were out on the nature trail early this morning, is that right?" asks Selby, taking notes in a full-sized notebook he has brought with him. "Could you tell us approximately what time?"

"Yeah." Davin is puzzled. He wonders if some of the signs along the trail were vandalized and he's a suspect, or something. "I guess it must have been about six to eight or so."

The officers continue without an explanation. "What were you wearing?"

"Pants, shirt, my old duster," responds Davin.

"What color?" asks Selby.

"Blue shirt, black pants, black coat. What's this about?"

"Do you use the nature trail often?" McCarthy ignores Davin's question.

Davin shrugs. "When I'm learning a part."

Thanks to Pat, Davin's reputation has preceded him. "And are you working on a part now?" McCarthy probes.

"Uh-uh."

"So, this morning you were on the trail for...exercise?" suggests Selby.

Davin laughs. "Not my style," he replies. Because the men just sit quietly, apparently waiting for more, he adds, "I guess you could say I go out there to think."

Now it is Selby's turn to be surprised. "*Think?* How old are you?"

"Almost eighteen, why?" says Davin defensively. "You think the age precludes the process?" He is insulted and running out of patience "Look, what's this really about? What's me being out on the trail this morning and what I was wearing got to do with anything?"

McCarthy holds up a placating hand. "Whoa, take it easy. We were eighteen, what, about a hundred years ago?" he looks at Selby, who nods, for confirmation. "I'm not sure I had the thinking thing down pat by then, though." His attempt at humor falls flat.

"Well, did you see anyone else or notice anything unusual while you were out there?" Selby is all business.

Davin shakes his head. "Just the usual. A couple of joggers. A ton of baby rabbits." He smiles slightly, amused by his recollection.

"Okay." Selby rises; McCarthy follows suit. "Thanks, Davin. Call us if you think of anything." The older man hands Davin a card as he makes his way toward the door. "If we need to talk to you again, we'll call you." His tone, as he utters the last sentence, sounds slightly threatening.

In the car on the way back to the office, Selby and McCarthy analyze their impressions of their interview with Davin.

"What'd you think?" Selby asks McCarthy.

"Kind of a smart aleck, wouldn't you say?" responds McCarthy.

"Oh, I don't know. I've seen worse at his age."

"'Do you think the age precludes the process?'" mimics the younger officer. "Shit, I'll give him a process."

"Okay, maybe a little smart-alecky, but don't you think that's normal for that age? Hell, you were eighteen, what, a hundred years ago?" Selby pokes fun at his partner.

"Today it feels longer," confesses McCarthy. "Who in God's name would take a *five*-week-old? But, you know," he muses, changing the subject back to Davin, "the fact that he was freshly showered bothers me."

"Not to mention the fact that he's practically a professional actor," agrees Selby. "Did you catch that surprised look on his face when we told him this was about him and not his father?"

"Mm-hmm."

"I'd give a week's salary to know if that was real or faked." There is a brief pause in the conversation, then Selby resumes. "Well, if what they're alleging about the dad's professional ethics is even half true, this could be one sick kid. Did you find anything on site that could tie him to the baby?"

McCarthy shrugs. "Nada except for prints on the baby seat that are probably the mother's—hell, the guy didn't even have to touch the damn thing to snatch the kid—and one hair that's probably the mother's, too. I wish there'd been dirt instead of gravel under that deck, then we might've at least had a footprint."

Selby nods. "All right, Scott, you'd better run that hair down to CBI this afternoon. The media's going to hit this like vultures to a roadkill, so let's tell them about the prints but sit on the hair, you know what I mean? If it does come from whoever took her, I'd rather they don't know we have it. That'll give CBI time to do the DNA without hassle from the press."

McCarthy knows what Selby means. While Larimer County has a state-of-the art crime lab for processing evidence from fingerprints or blood, it does not do hair or fiber analysis. For scientific examination and/or DNA analysis, the hair from Zoë's infant seat must consequently be routed seventy-five miles south to the Colorado Bureau of Investigation crime lab in Denver. Because it's a long way from New York to Denver in more ways than one, both men are confident that the kidnapping of baby Zoë will merit immediate attention even at the state level.

"While you're doing that," continues Selby, planning out loud, "I'll organize the neighborhood canvass and get LCSR going on a grid search of the prairie."

McCarthy looks grimly at his partner. The reality of having Larimer County Search and Rescue comb the Cathy Fromme Prairie for what might be the remains of the Blackburns' infant daughter weighs heavily on both men. All too aware that *their* age does not preclude the process, the deputies continue on in thought-laden silence.

By four o'clock that afternoon, the Blackburn household is under siege. Reporters from the local news, the local paper, and all Denver newspapers, radio, and television stations have rolled their vans and cams to the top of Coyote Ridge. Bonnie and Richard make a brief appearance, begging the public for help in finding their daughter, before they retreat back into their house. From their deck, they helplessly watch the search and rescue people and additional volunteers begin their geometrically aligned search of the prairie below.

To Bonnie, the day's events have taken on tones of the surreal. The scheduled arrival of her parents later in the evening offers no comfort, because she feels as if she has entered a dimension so filled with pain there is no room for anything else. Bonnie sees the strangers in her house speak without hearing what they are saying, and she hears telephones ring without moving to pick them up. Bonnie stays close by Richard's side. When Richard's hand reaches out periodically to touch her throughout the day, Bonnie grabs it and hangs on until he gently withdraws.

When Pat shows up at the door again, her arms laden with some kind of parcels, Bonnie walks with her through the house to the kitchen. Pat deposits her bundles, leaves momentarily only to return a few minutes later with another load. Then she seats Bonnie at her own kitchen table and asks, "Can you eat something?"

Bonnie, whose tears have stopped, nonetheless shakes her head no. Even the sight of food makes her feel nauseous. Pat sighs. "All right, honey, I understand. But Richard needs to eat, doesn't he?" Silently, Bonnie nods yes. "Okay, then, I brought a few things to tide you over 'til things calm down. There's some taco soup, a big pan of burritos with green chili you can either eat or pop in your freezer for later, and some garnishes and a little dessert. Are your mom and dad coming, sweetheart?"

"Tonight." Bonnie manages a one-word reply.

"Then I'll put this stuff in the fridge. Now, do you want me to stay with you, dear," asks Pat, putting her hands on Bonnie's tense shoulders and kneading them, "or shall I go?" When her kindness causes Bonnie to start crying again, Pat draws a chair next to the younger woman and enfolds her in her arms. The two sit there like that for a long time. Eventually, her head on Pat's shoulder, Bonnie calms, seems almost to sleep. She doesn't notice that the tremors that have finally left her own body seem suddenly to have invaded Pat, whose tired hands now tremble visibly as they stroke their neighbor's unkempt hair.

on the road again

Jasper is leaving the Cathy Fromme Prairie. Keeping to the edge of the foothills west of town, the young coyote ambles southward. Whether he is on the move because he hankers for the taste of prairie dog again or is simply sick of too much company—human or canid—he doesn't say. He just meanders along, stopping to sniff at whatever interests him. Once, he gives playful chase to a rabbit he flushes from beneath some rabbitbrush. When this happens, the rabbit uses everything it has to make good its escape, while Jasper cavorts behind it with the exaggerated movements of a coyote clown. When he tires of this game Jasper continues on his way, but the rabbit, whose heartbeat accelerated to dangerously high levels during the chase, remains frozen in place for long minutes. He knows better than to jeopardize his hard-won survival with more movement. Nothing but the twitch of his long whiskers betrays his position.

voice dreams

It is so late when the airport shuttle finally disgorges Bonnie's parents at the Blackburns', the reporters have packed it in. Darkness has put a stop even to the painstaking efforts of the LCSR team, but its members will return at first light to expand their search. Meanwhile, as lights in houses up and down the street gradually wink off, Bonnie and Richard's house remains stubbornly illuminated. Leading her parents out onto the deck for a few minutes' recuperation after their journey from rural Michigan, Bonnie and Richard speak haltingly of the day's events.

When Bonnie—tears again streaming down her face—once more blames herself for leaving Zoë alone, Richard impatiently cuts her off. He slaps both hands down on the arms of his chair and leans forward earnestly. "Bonn, you *have* to stop looking at it that way. Leaving her asleep out there was the logical thing to do given the circumstances. You didn't do anything differently than a million other people would have done."

Bonnie knows Richard means to be supportive, but she is more than put off, she is deeply offended by his use of the word "logical." With her emotional state of shock now bordering on the physical, she stares bleakly at her husband and the father of her missing baby as if he has betrayed her. "Oh my God, Richard, how can you ever again think of things in terms of logic," she challenges, "when the very worst that you could ever imagine has actually happened to us, *against all odds?* Tell me where the logic is to that!" she concludes shrilly.

Richard, hurt by this attack, abruptly pushes his chair out from the table, unfolds his lanky body and limps to the far end of the deck, where he stares out at nothing.

Aching for both young people but embarrassed for Richard's sake by her daughter's outburst, Bonnie's mother Trish tries to back her son-in-law and mollify Bonnie at the same time. "No, Richard's right, Bonnie," she chides gently, "you didn't do anything different than any other mother would have done. I can't tell you how many times I left *you* outside while I ran in to grab another basketful of laundry, or ran back to the garage to get my garden shears," she reminisces wistfully. As she speaks, she nervously fingers the small gold locket she has worn around her neck for as long as Bonnie can remember.

Unappeased, Bonnie, who at this moment looks older than her mother, now points a trembling finger at her. "But you got away with it, didn't you? You got to be *my* mother for twenty-nine years. I've only had Zoë for thirty-five *days*. How could God be so unfair?"

Bonnie's father George, a retired postman and giver of the locket, who has been quietly sucking at his pipe, now plunks that item down on the table. "Bonnie, talk like that isn't going to get anyone anywhere. We're all tired, so let's try to get some sleep. We'll talk more in the morning." Feelings weighing oppressively on all of them, they retire to their rooms.

Bonnie and Richard prepare for bed in stiff silence. Once there, rather than gravitate to Richard's arms, Bonnie lies board-like on her own side of the bed. Every muscle and nerve in her body is so taut she aches, yet her mind, roiling with thoughts of her baby, refuses to let her body relax into the healing realm of sleep.

Richard, feeling unfairly wronged, is about as far from offering his wife comfort as King Tut from panhandling. He'll be damned if, just because she's hurting, he lets Bonnie label *him* the bad guy in all this. Maybe he wouldn't have been the greatest father in the world, Richard admits guiltily to himself, but he'd been willing to give it the old college try. What more could a guy do?

Bonnie, miserably wondering whether things would have been different if she had just strapped Zoë into her seat, at last falls into a fitful sleep, but some time later (hours? minutes? her sense of time is all out of whack, and her eyes are so swollen from weeping the clock face is blurry) wakes from a vivid dream. She recalls being in Zoë's room, rocking her gently in dim light. She remembers feeling that she should enjoy this rare minute of perfect peace. For one idyllic moment, neither she nor her loved ones are in need of any of the thousand and one things all humans, but especially babies, seem to require every moment of their lives. The joints of the antique wooden rocker (a hand-me-down from Bonnie's grandma) creak softly even on the carpet.

All at once Bonnie understands that, for herself, nurturing, protecting, and guiding this little soul who has been entrusted to her care will be enough. If she can do that well, she knows that she will have done something worthwhile with her life, something, in truth, worth far more than any picture she can ever hope to paint. This knowledge fills her with resolve. I can't promise results, but I do promise to *try,* sweetheart, she vows, holding Zoë tenderly.

It is at this point in the dream that Zoë, so tiny she can't possibly be old enough to talk, opens her eyes and says clearly: "It's okay, Mommy, this wasn't your fault." The figure of Zoë grows shadowy and recedes into darkness now. Though Bonnie can no longer distinguish her baby's precious face, her words continue with perfect clarity. "I'm fine, just taking some time off..."

Sitting up, Bonnie feels the peace and love from her dream course physically through her body with a clarity—an intensity—she has rarely experienced in real life. Simultaneously, she recognizes that, whatever Zoë is now, she is no longer of the earth. Strangely, Bonnie is momentarily able to accept this realization with no distress, but she also knows her respite from grief will be short-lived.

Fearful that movement will destroy this interlude, she sits motionless, looking out the uncurtained window into the night and listening to Richard's light snoring. Though there have been times when she has taken offense at this sound (I'm up: Why aren't *you*?), she does not do so now. Instead, she eventually reaches over and gently strokes the hair of the man who, instead of trotting off on his joyful run, tomorrow must search for the body of his daughter.

Her touch wakes Richard, who turns toward her sleepily. "I'm so sorry, Richard," whispers Bonnie. She is grateful to curl into his arms.

It is still early the next morning when Richard and George join the team re-forming to continue its inch-by-inch inspection of the Cathy Fromme Prairie. Thanks to media coverage of what has come to be called Baby Zoë's Kidnapping, so many volunteers have come forward to aid in this effort that the search can be expanded considerably. But Chris Reid, the man in charge of the ground search, looks upon his new army with a frown. "People!" he hollers, striding up and down the ever-lengthening line.

Braced with hot coffee and donuts donated by a local business, the smiling people—basking in their awareness that they have come to Do Good—stop their chatter and look expectantly at their designated leader. Chris wastes no time. "Good morning," he begins. "Before we get started on procedure, I want to thank you all very much for coming, and that done," he pauses, looks the line over once more, and bluntly adds, "then send about half of you home."

Cries of outrage greet this statement, but Chris raises a placating hand. "Look, I know you all mean well, folks, but you have to understand something. We aren't headed out there to play. We're headed out there to see if we can find anything—and I mean *anything*—that will help locate Zoë Blackburn. This might take a long time. Most certainly, it will take hard work that I can see right off many of you are unprepared for."

Further cries of objection do nothing to deter Chris. "It's not a park out there, ladies and gentlemen," he informs them, gesturing over his shoulder. "The Cathy Fromme Prairie is home to a large population of healthy rattlesnakes and cacti. Because we don't want to include you among her victims, I'll have to ask those of you without long pants and sturdy shoes to please leave now." The forced departure of the scantily shod and clad reduces the number of searchers considerably.

"Along the same lines, thank you for thinking of us, but those of you with children or dogs would be better off spending your time elsewhere today as well," continues Chris. He feels justifiably proud of this last statement, which doesn't even come close to what he really wants to say: *Why in hell would you bring your kids someplace a baby's body might turn up? Damn fools.* Some family groups take their grumbling leave, Fidos at their side.

"Now, the last items on the list are water, hats, and sunscreen. We'll provide plenty of the first for those without, and I'll leave the latter two"—*since you made it this far, you must have some damn sense*—"to your own discretion. Just be advised, you can get a nasty burn out there if you're unprotected for long, but we don't insist you stay all day, either." Finally, Chris feels he can afford to smile at *the few, the proud, the*—*oh, cut it out*, he chides himself. Then he briskly marshals his troops.

About the same time the searchers move out onto the prairie, Angie Creighton, lab tech for the CBI Crime Lab in Denver, carefully tweezes the single evidentiary hair from the Baby Zoë Kidnapping into solution. Detective Scott McCarthy delivered the hair at the close of business hours yesterday, and it is the first item on Angie's list today. Placing the hair in solution is the first step preparatory to viewing it (for coarse analysis only) under the microscope. Once that is done, Angie will initiate the PCR (polymerase chain reaction) method of DNA analysis on the hair.

The PCR process, which will take about ten days from start to finish, unzips the double helical strands of DNA molecules found in the hair (by heating and denaturing them) and then amplifies them by re-annealing the strands with additional nucleotides. In this heartbreaking case of the missing baby girl, Angie wishes she had a magic catalyst that would cut the entire complicated process down to hours instead of days, but she doesn't. Sighing, she places the hair on a slide, slips it under the lens, and slowly adjusts the focus.

It is not yet noon when the searchers on the Cathy Fromme Prairie begin to feel the effects of their work. Not a trace of cloud has appeared in the sky all morning, and the sun's unchecked glare has caused the ambient temperature to climb almost to 90 degrees. Even though his ankle still handicaps him, Richard, accustomed to moving at speed, finds the slow pace of the line's progress mentally exhausting. Sweat trickles down his neck as he inches along with the others. Richard doesn't know whether to hope they find something or to hope they don't. Caught in a flood of bad feelings that erode his confidence as surely as tides wash away sand, he hobbles slowly, painfully forward.

Aware of their identity, searchers on either side of Richard and George limit their conversation to brief exchanges. When someone down the line does, indeed, disturb a healthy rattler, the news provokes no jocularity even among these men and women desperate for distraction. Snake-like itself, the line of searchers slithers along the surface of the prairie until a loud shout, "Over here!" brings it to a halt.

Adrenaline rushes through Richard's body like a jolt of electric current. Breaking the rules, he breaks out of his position in line and limps rapidly toward the location of the shout. While sympathetic eyes watch, no one tries to stop him. Elbowing his way into the cluster of three grouped around whatever they have found, Richard doesn't waste time on preliminaries. "What have you got?" Heart in his dry mouth, he looks down at a plastic flag that has been stuck in the ground to mark the location of something pink lying twisted, dirty, and Richard can see for himself, stained with pathetically small streaks of blood.

"Well," Reid responds gently, "it looks like a piece of fabric that might—"

"That's Zoë's blanket. Or part of it," amends Richard, confirming their suspicions.

Scott McCarthy is already on his fourth interview in Coyote Ridge (they go quickly when nobody has seen or heard anything prompting even a soupçon of suspicion) when his radio crackles, telling him to call Angie at CBI. Scott concludes his questioning and returns to his patrol car, where he dials the number of the crime lab, then punches in Angie's extension. She picks up on the first ring. "Ms. Creighton? Scott McCarthy from Larimer County here."

Scott listens to Angie for less than a minute. "I see," he responds grimly. Then he concludes the conversation. "Yes, please do send it on. Thanks, Angie." Scott's next move is to call his partner, Detective Selby, who is interviewing on the other side of the block.

"Selby here," Tom responds to the call.

"Tom, can you meet me at the car?" asks McCarthy.

"Sure. Be right there."

During the few minutes that pass while he waits for his partner to show up, McCarthy scribbles the gist of his conversation with Angie in his notebook. He is still writing when Selby knocks on the window so as not to surprise him, then slides into the front seat beside him.

"What have you got?" asks Selby.

McCarthy finishes writing, snaps his notebook closed. "You know that hair?"

Selby nods, waits.

"It isn't human."

checks and balances

Angie Creighton's news disgusts Detectives Selby and McCarthy. "Shit, that means we have even less than we thought we had," remarks McCarthy.

Selby nods. "Did you think to ask the Blackburns whether they have a dog or cat when you interviewed them?"

"Uh-uh. It didn't come up, though I never saw one when we were there. You?"

"Nope. And the damn thing could have come from Grandma's cat, or the babysitter's guinea pig, or a million other places besides. I'll ask Bonnie about possible sources of animal hair—"

"Are you going to tell her why?" interrupts McCarthy.

Selby sighs. "Yeah, I'll tell her about the hair. I just won't tell her how disappointed we are that it's not from the kidnapper." He pauses, thinking. "Anyway, so what happens to it now?" he asks McCarthy.

McCarthy shrugs. "Angie told me we have two choices. CBI can say with certainty the hair is nonhuman, but that's all they can say, because they don't do nonhuman IDs. If we don't care to take it further, the hair'll be filed, and that'll be that. But if we want to know what animal it comes from, it has to be sent to the Wyoming Game and Fish Lab in Laramie."

"Jesus. Why does it have to go all the way to Laramie? You mean to tell me CBI doesn't have the right kind of scope to look at animal hairs or something?" Neither officer has ever run into this problem before.

McCarthy shakes his head. "No, I found out it's a matter of expertise, not equipment. I guess a lot of animal hairs look alike, so identification depends on comparative analysis of a bunch of characteristics like length, width, scales, color pattern, undulation and so on. Some guy up there wrote a whole book on it—*The Identification of Dorsal Guard Hairs*—they still use."

Selby looks over at his partner. "I'm impressed," he admits.

Scott grins. "About time."

"So, now what are we looking at, time-wise?"

"If you still want results ASAP, Angie can overnight express it and Game and Fish will have it by tomorrow noon. The ID will only take a couple of hours," replies McCarthy.

"That's a hell of a lot faster than that PCR business. You know, for the time being, let's keep the pressure on," decides Selby.

Scott grins again. "As a matter of fact, I already told Ange to send it on to Laramie."

"Hell, I may as well be on vacation." Letting himself out of the car, Selby continues, "I'll go see what I can find out from Bonnie." He heads once again for the Blackburns' front door, while Scott trudges off to more friendly interviews.

Seated in the Blackburn living room again, Selby gets right to the point. "Mrs. Blackburn, do you have a pet of any kind?"

Bonnie, who has circles under her eyes from lack of sleep (the calm imparted by her voice dream has long since vanished) shakes her head. "No. Why?" The loss of her baby has left her so depleted in so many ways, even minimal responses take a great deal of effort.

"Well, we collected a hair from Zoë's infant seat that the lab says comes from an animal rather than a human. Had you left Zoë in the care of anyone who has a pet recently?"

Bonnie stares at Selby. "What?"

"We're trying to determine the origin of an animal hair that was found on your daughter's infant seat," Selby tries again, speaking slowly. "Do you recall spending time, or leaving her, with anyone who has a pet?"

Bonnie struggles to think back through the dark vortex that has become her reality since Zoë's disappearance. Finally, she offers, "Pat's. We stopped at Pat's for a minute the day before—"

"That would be Pat from next door?" Selby understands her inability to complete her sentence.

Bonnie nods.

"Thanks, Mrs. Blackburn." Anxious to disturb Bonnie as little as possible, Selby closes his notebook and leaves the house quietly.

When his ring of Pat's front doorbell prompts no answer, Selby walks curiously around to the gate in the privacy fence enclosing the older woman's backyard. Peering over the fence, he is rewarded with a view of Pat—her back to him—on her knees, apparently working on her flower garden. A yellow lab lies close by in the shade.

Selby admits himself quietly to the backyard but, as he turns to re-latch the gate, the dog appears at his side, wagging his tail. "Ah, just what I need." The hand Selby runs firmly across the animal's flank comes away with several dog hairs on it. After placing the hairs in an evidence bag, the detective exits the yard without Pat ever having been aware of his presence.

Had he approached Pat, Selby would have observed a strange sight. Her hands—the hands he assumes are doing whatever gardeners do in their gardens—instead rest upon the older woman's knees, strangely motionless. Her ringless fingers pluck neither dead blooms nor bugs nor yellowed foliage from the gay array of flowering plants before her, but interlace loosely with one another, forming a small cave into which Pat peers wordlessly. This most likely would have puzzled Selby enough to ask whether everything is okay, at which point Pat would have brushed him off with an embarrassed laugh.

She would never have revealed the real reason for her posture, which has nothing to do with her garden and everything to do with the fact that she is praying. Having been a Sunday churchgoer for years, Pat keeps to herself the knowledge that she prays Mondays through Saturdays as well. She prays anywhere and everywhere the notion strikes her, including her own backyard. She does not make a big to-do about her spirituality because she deems it wanting.

Had Selby asked, Pat would have had to tell him that, even after years of practice, she finds it easier to pray for the dead than the living. She would have had to explain that, because the dead don't argue back or throw up or intrude upon your affairs with any of the thousands of strength-sapping, time-taking, trouble-causing behaviors of the living, they are a snap to pray for. How could one *not* wish only well for those who, having crossed from the physical to the spiritual realm, no longer bother you with anything, wonders Pat. She considers her relationships with the dead to be cloaked in the perfect benevolence of distance. Whatever separates where she is from where they are—not miles or leagues but something unnamed, maybe even unknowable—also serves as a buffer that allows her to forgive all and accord each dearly departed the status of saint in one fashion or another. What could be easier?

But the living—ahh, they are another matter entirely. Pat would have died rather than admit to Selby that she thinks it easier to pray for perfect strangers than those she knows and loves. But the logic is clear, she argues in her own defense. Strangers' sins—no matter how wicked—don't affect one personally, so praying for the perpetrators is simple. One's breast need only heave with generic good will toward men to salve the souls of unknown evildoers. That doesn't take much effort.

Thoughts drifting gently, Pat recalls a beauty pageant Rita had entered in her teens. One by one, each trembling young contestant had been thrust before the microphone and asked by the middle-aged, self-important judge to describe her dearest wish. One by one, each beautiful young woman except Rita had broken into a smile of radiant joy (or was it relief at the fact that they never changed the question, wonders Pat now) and replied, "World peace." Her Rita had unhesitatingly spit out, "Winning the lottery."

Some time after that debacle, Pat had seen a documentary about a camp for kids from two nations that had been at war for decades. The theory was that the friendship fostered between the children at the camp would promote new understanding between the feuding countries. After six weeks of intensive mingling, the question posed by the young campers was: "If we have grown to know and appreciate each other after so brief a stay here, how can we go home and allow the hatred between our nations to continue?" The camp concluded with the youths exchanging tearful smiles and bear hugs. Would these embryonic gestures of humanity between children develop into full-fledged peace between their warring homelands? Only Scrooge could say no.

Time passed, and the days following the documentary strung themselves into weeks, months, years. Then came an evening when a newly widowed Pat again sat before her television and by chance, tuned to a documentary that was a follow-up to the original. Journalists and cameramen had traveled to the homes of the former campers to see what they had to say. Pat will never forget the shock of hearing how things had changed. The youths who had left the camp so hopeful for peace had become young adults who had seen fathers, cousins, brothers fall to enemy bullets. Having felt the hammer blow of loss strike heavily upon their breasts, they were (to give them credit) wise enough to know that the resultant bruise precluded any possibility of peace.

Pat sighs. She feels much the same about sin. Easy enough to pray for the unknown prostitute, but praying for Rita's hurtful behavior to end takes devotion Pat is no longer sure she can muster. It's not so much that she feels tired as *worn*. Yes, that's the word, reflects Pat. Rita's continual selfishness has worn such grooves in Pat's psyche, any prayers she might make on her daughter's behalf will resound not with the fervor of the freshly injured, but the annoying whine of an old beggar. If she were God, she wouldn't listen, either...

Luckily, however, Pat is spared having to make any humiliating confessions by a busy detective's disinterest. But as Selby makes his way back down the block to his car, a mini-van he hasn't seen on the street before does capture his attention. Selby turns to watch the van and is surprised to see it turn into Pat's driveway. A big-boned woman wearing a hot-pink jog bra and short shorts with—of all things—a tattoo on her left shoulder exits the van, marches up to Pat's screen door and lets herself in. Selby wonders who Pat would know that would look like that. The cleaning lady? Shaking his head, the detective continues on his way.

"Ma!" Rita calls as she enters her mother's home. Receiving no response, she tramps through the house to the kitchen, where she catches sight of Pat still working in the backyard. Intending to summon her mother from the deck, Rita is headed in that direction when she notices Pat's checkbook, statement, and cancelled checks strewn across the kitchen table, along with a calculator and legal pad covered with figures. This is too much to resist. Rita sits down at the table, checks the balance in the account, and leafs curiously through her mother's cancelled checks.

After a moment, disappointed to find that the small documents contain nothing extraordinary—indeed, Pat's spending habits seem singularly boring for a wealthy widow—Rita transfers her attention to the yellow legal pad. Here she finds immediate reward, for the crooked columns of numbers running up and down the page clearly indicate Pat's repeatedly unsuccessful attempts to balance her checkbook. Though erasures and cross-outs dot the page like punctuation marks, Pat's labored arithmetic has not once yielded the magic (five-digit!) sum encircled over and over again at the top of her statement. Rather than provoke in Rita an attempt to help her mother by re-doing the math, however, the pathetic columns of numbers merely cause her to tuck her chin in her manicured hands and think.

A moment later, satisfied with her mental exercise, Rita rises from the table and walks out onto the deck. There, she exchanges the peremptory "Ma!" she was going to holler at Pat with an almost (but not quite) lilting, "Oh, Mother!"

Startled (she wasn't expecting visitors), Pat raises her sweaty, dirt-streaked face from her work. The sight of her daughter causes her to drop her trowel and, one hand on her back, rise stiffly from her grungy old kneeling pad. "Rita! What brings you here?" Pat asks with a smile.

Rita is not about to confess that she had come armed to the teeth for a serious talk about Pat's interfering ways with her children— especially that stupid story about the ocean that has Laura telling everybody it's made of tears ("*Really*, Mother! I go out of my way to stimulate my daughter's interest in real science, and what do I get from you but this, this *drizzle* you make up as you go along.") Instead, Rita waves her lacquered nails breezily in the air and almost (but not quite) gushes, "Oh, I just thought I'd check in, see how you're doing."

Pleased, Pat replies, "Wonderful! I'll be right up." She and Jethro head for the back garage door. A moment later, the pair clomp their way into the kitchen, where Rita waits innocently.

"How about some Raspberry Renew, honey?" asks Pat, opening her cabinet for glasses.

"Sure." Rita never could resist her mother's fabulous concoction. Besides, she thinks, the color perfectly matches the Flashy Fuchsia she's wearing on her lips and nails.

"So, what have you been up to?" asks Pat.

"Oh, the usual. I can't believe it's almost time to start buying school clothes for the kids again, you know?"

Pat nods. "Summers still go by quickly for me, but never as quickly as when I was in school!" she confesses.

"So, Ma, you having a little trouble here, or what?" Sipping her drink, Rita gestures to the mess on the table and pretends her comment is an innocent attempt at small talk.

The question flusters Pat. "Oh, I'm having a horrific time getting the darn thing to balance. I worked on it 'til I got so mad I had to get outside and let off some steam."

Rita looks at her mother over her glass. "Mmmm." The expression is not so much sympathetic as considering. "You know, Ma, maybe you should put me on your accounts with you and give me power of attorney. That way I could keep the books, make things easier for you," Rita offers.

"I didn't know you had a head for figures, honey," responds Pat. "Tell you what, you figure out what my problem is here and I might just do that." She pushes the calculator and pencil over to her daughter with one hand, the statement with the other.

Surprised by her mother's offer (challenge?), Rita takes pencil in hand and sets to work.

Ninety minutes later Pat, who has busied herself concocting a casserole that smells delicious, interrupts her daughter's intense labor. "Would you like to stay for lunch, honey?" she asks cheerfully.

Tossing the pencil down in disgust, Rita scrapes her chair away from the table and checking the time, rises in alarm. "Oh my God, I'm supposed to be at my hairdresser's in fifteen minutes! But look, Ma, I'll come back and work on this some more, maybe tomorrow or something, all right?" she adds anxiously. "I'm sure I've almost got it. This has to be just some little thing we're overlooking."

Pat nods. "I'm sure it is, darling. I've grown quite good at overlooking things these days."

Rita, whose mind has flown to the Sun-Kissed Kopper highlights she will soon be sporting in her hair, is no longer listening. "Bye, Ma," she offers over her shoulder as she exits the kitchen.

Pat raises a gaily colored potholder in silent adieu, then wanders over to the kitchen table, where she stands looking down at her daughter's messy columns of figures for a long time.

When Rita returns home after her appointment at the beauty salon, she is disgusted to find her house in uproar. Kayla, the young college student she hires to baby-sit when the pressure of having the kids home all day gets to be too much, apologizes. "I'm so sorry, Mrs. Wonsawski. It's just that Cat O. Lick's gone. We've looked everywhere, haven't we, kids, and we just can't find him."

"But Protest Auntie's here?" The Wonsawskis inherited their two cats from a pun-loving uncle on Ed's side.

"Yep, she's sleeping under my bed." Greg loves that the cat chooses *his* room to hang out. He takes this as a sign that he is better than his sister.

"Well, then, I'm sure he'll turn up sooner or later," Rita glibly dismisses the problem and reassures her children as she pays Kayla, who leaves immediately. (Mrs. Wonsawski is generous with neither her hourly rates nor tips.)

Greg is willing to take his mother's word on this. He is tired of looking for a stupid cat, wants to do something exciting like help the search and rescuers look for that missing baby who lives next to Grandma. As he and Laura wander off, Greg speaks to his sister in confidentially low tones: "Do you know how you make a dead baby float?"

Pleased at this rare attention from her brother, Laura takes the question as seriously as it was posed. "Uh-uh. How?"

"Two scoops of ice cream and one scoop of dead baby!" hollers Greg gleefully, jabbing his sister in the ribs before running outside.

Rita ignores the shriek from the other room, is *that* close to shrieking herself. Nobody (not even Kayla!) has said one word about her hair.

a hair's breadth

Five o'clock the following afternoon finds Detective Tom Selby on his way down the steep stairs connecting Coyote Ridge to the Cathy Fromme Prairie. A fit man, Selby nonetheless takes the rough stairs, formed of railroad ties and filled with dirt and gravel, slowly. Though he appears to be looking down at his feet, he doesn't notice that each step powdercoats the shiny tips of his brogans with buff-colored dust. At the midway point, he looks up, shifting his gaze from his dull shoes to the distant searchers. They have covered so much ground since the day before yesterday, they now look like ants. Their ant-like line rises and falls with the topography of the prairie, but it never breaks form. Selby isn't surprised that today the line is much shorter than yesterday.

The prairie's heat, rough terrain, spiny plants and venomous snakes have made short shrift of most people's urge to Do Good. When push came to shove, thinks Selby, not even free coffee and donuts were enough to counter the demon Discomfort. Besides Richard and a few other hardy souls, Chris Reid's large volunteer army has shrunk to the tough Larimer County Search and Rescue Team, doing the dirty work without complaint as usual. Just as well, thinks Selby, whose dark blue shirt further darkens with sweat as he crosses the prairie.

Glad to interrupt their horrible preoccupation with the ground, the searchers pause to watch the detective approach. While some lean casually on gnarled walking sticks, others remove wide-brimmed hats to wipe their glistening brows, swig warm water from plastic bottles that have been too long in the sun. Richard's strong, steady heartbeat accelerates. Is there finally news of his daughter, maybe a ransom demand? Other than Zoë's blanket yesterday, they have found absolutely nothing to indicate that anything out of the ordinary has happened here. At times Richard has even found himself stupidly wondering: Did Zoë's kidnapping and the discovery of the blanket really happen?

Like Bonnie, he feels caught in a strange state of the dreamlike, the surreal. The long hours he has spent out here under the hot sun exacerbate this feeling. When Selby gestures to Chris Reid and him, Richard feels badly that, deep down, he will be glad of any news whatsoever. He also feels ashamed that, except for the horrible moment when they found the blanket yesterday, this entire search effort has been one of tortuous boredom. The single impression of the prairie that has burned itself into Richard's brain is that it is distinctly undramatic. To him, the place seems nothing more than a stage so somnolent, only insects act upon it.

The three men move a little ways off from the rest of the line. "What's up?" Chris asks so Richard doesn't have to.

"Uh, I don't know how to tell you this," the detective stalls. "In fact, I wish I didn't have to tell you this at all," he says, looking uncomfortably at Richard.

"What?" Richard has already been through so much hell, he isn't in the mood to cut Selby even an inch of slack. *Just spit it out, man.*

Selby inhales; momentarily, his gaze travels out across the distant prairie. When his eyes return to meet Richard's unfriendly stare, he speaks in a low, quiet tone. "Well, we have some new evidence that indicates your daughter wasn't kidnapped after all, Mr. Blackburn."

"What?" repeats Richard in an irritated tone. "But what happened to her then? *Somebody* left that bloody piece of blanket," he insists stubbornly.

"Well, that's just it," corrects Selby gently, "apparently, somebody didn't. You see, we've just been informed that the hair we collected from your daughter's infant seat comes from—" he pauses briefly, looks out over the prairie again while Richard and Reid try, but fail, to second-guess the detective—"from a coyote." Selby flicks his gaze sorrowfully to Richard's face before turning it apologetically downward. Suddenly, the thought that he needs to polish his dusty shoes becomes paramount.

Selby's statement is met by shocked silence from both Reid and Richard. Reid grasps the implication immediately, but waits until he sees comprehension register on Richard's face before he says the only thing possible under the circumstances: "I'm so sorry, Richard."

Richard looks as if he has seen the face of Lucifer. His eyes close. Briefly considering whether such a place even exists anymore, he raises his face heavenward. "How am I going to tell Bonnie?" he asks nobody, everybody.

Selby nods, accepting this new burden. "I think that's my job. But I'll need you there to help her through it." When Richard turns toward the ridge, however, Selby waylays him with a touch on the arm. "One more thing, Richard. Now that we know no crime has been committed, I need to know what your feelings are about this grid search. Do you want to continue looking for your daughter's remains or…?"

Now it is Richard's turn to gaze out at the prairie, the place he had thought so sleepy nothing ever happened. He is silent for a moment, realizing how badly he has been fooled. Then, "Call it off," he responds. Neither Reid nor Selby ask him to explain this decision.

As Richard and Selby begin the journey back across the prairie and up the ridge, they hear a short blast from the whistle Chris Reid wears around his neck. "All right, people, listen up…" Reid hollers.

Whether because of the men's long, hurried strides or Reid's adjustment in volume once he has his team gathered about him, the rest of what he says is incomprehensible.

Richard and Selby enter the Blackburn house from the backyard. They find Bonnie and her parents seated at the kitchen table. All three look expectantly toward the newcomers. Richard speaks first. "George, Trish, would you excuse us for a minute?"

"Of course."

"No problem." The elderly people are well above the pettiness that could construe Richard's request for privacy as a slight. They vanish quickly, quietly.

Richard sits down next to Bonnie and puts his arm around her; Selby sits across from the couple and looks so sad Bonnie's hand flies to her mouth. "Did you—"

Selby shakes his head. "No, we haven't found her, Bonnie." His use of her first name indicates his empathy for the young woman across from him. "But we have learned something that sheds new light on the case." Selby pauses, trying to figure out the least hurtful way to say what he has to say before concluding there isn't one.

Bonnie feels Richard tighten his grip on her shoulder as the detective puts both hands on the table and leans forward. In an unconscious attempt to impose control over the situation, he reverts to formal address: "Mrs. Blackburn, I'm afraid your daughter was taken by a coyote."

Bonnie gasps. Then her eyes close and she leans her head on Richard's shoulder. Richard's other arm encircles his wife. When she exhales, a small mewling noise of pain accompanies the air expelled from her lungs. The sound is so soft neither Trish nor George, waiting patiently in the living room, hears it, but on his way out Selby catches sight of the grandparents, makes a determined detour. May as well get this all over with at once.

Outside, Scott McCarthy has the unpleasant task of notifying the reporters camped outside the Blackburn home of the real nature of the Baby Zoë Kidnapping. He marshals the group together, raises his hand for silence, then states, "Ladies and gentlemen, at this time I'd like to inform you we have evidence showing that Zoë Blackburn was not kidnapped." Wishing he could leave it at that, McCarthy faces the barrage of questions hollered at him, the microphones stuck in his face, with another upraised hand. Only when the crowd quiets does he tell of the hair sample indicating Zoë's kidnapper is a coyote. For a brief moment, McCarthy's simple statement shocks even the press. An eerie second of silence ensues before the newsmongers revert to the rapaciousness that is their trademark. At no time in the resultant frenzy does any reporter draw an analogy between his own behavior and that of a hungry predator.

coming to consensus

Zoë Blackburn's gruesome death has become such a hot political potato, nobody in the county wants to touch it. Half the public is so outraged by the manner of the baby's death, they want it avenged immediately at any cost. The other half, convinced the coyote simply acted as nature intended, believe the animal should suffer no consequences whatsoever. What's a county to do, except host a meeting for the rank and file to tell each other—no, make that the county—oh, hell, why think small, they really mean the world—what they think.

The stage for this event, a room down at the courthouse, has a raised platform at one end. Across this platform runs a long built-in desk, behind which five padded chairs hold the beleaguered hind ends of the county commissioners, all. The dais not only separates the commissioners from their agitated constituency this Tuesday evening, it also puts them in easy view of the standing-room-only crowd. A podium with microphone attached stands on the main floor about fifteen feet in front of the commissioners.

Shifting to his right buttock, Commissioner John Carlton pounds his gavel, calls the meeting to order, then quickly establishes the rules. "Good evening, ladies and gentlemen. Because we have a capacity crowd tonight, we'll have to restrict you to a maximum speaking time of four minutes. Speakers will be called in the order they signed in, so the later you arrived, the longer you'll have to wait. Please restrict your comments to the issue at hand, and folks, let's all work real hard to keep it civil tonight. There's a lot of emotion surrounding the death of Zoë Blackburn, and things could get out of hand quickly if we're not careful. I'm asking you to prevent that from happening by, first, stating your views in a reasonable manner, and second, holding your silence while someone else is speaking.

"Now, we already know everybody's not going to agree with everybody else here tonight but, in the memory of that little girl, let's all keep our composure and treat this matter and one another with respect. If you can't comply with that request, the sheriffs, there, will be happy to escort you out." Carlton gestures to two uniformed deputies standing conspicuously near the door, shifts to his left buttock, then continues addressing the crowd.

"Now, when the secretary calls you to the podium, please state your full name and address for the record, then make your statement. You'll get a thirty-second warning before your time expires so you can wrap things up." Carlton pauses. "Well, I think that's about it, except to inform you that Mr. and Mrs. Blackburn have opted not to attend tonight's meeting. I think that'll make it easier for you to speak your mind on this coyote issue. Other than that, I think everything's pretty self-explanatory, so let's just get this process underway. Mr. Secretary, will you call the first speaker, please?"

"Angela Verneen."

A thirty-something woman about whom everything—arms, hair, dress, earrings—hangs in elongated manner takes the podium. "Uh, hi, I'm Angela Verneen, 5347 Sandstone Court, and I just wanted to say that it's ridiculous to blame the animals when it's we who have encroached on their territory. I mean, we move into their backyards and destroy their habitat and reduce their food supply and then we cry 'wolf' when something like this happens, and who can blame them, the animals, I mean—"

In spite of Carlton's plea, Verneen's words create an angry stir behind her. "Aw geez, lady, it was a coyote, not a wolf. If you're gonna defend 'em, at least get their names right!" The deputy standing nearest the door shifts his weight restlessly, but he does not attempt to oust the critic.

In spite of the gavel pounding at the front of the room and a call for order, Verneen turns to face her anonymous accuser. "I *know* it was a coyote, I was speaking figuratively, not literally. What I meant was—"

"Yeah, yeah. We should all leave our babies out so the poor coyotes don't starve, right?" This comment, from another place in the room, causes more consternation. Hand on his holstered weapon, the deputy proceeds three steps up the aisle before the room settles down and he retreats to his original position.

"No! All I meant was, we shouldn't slaughter an animal just because an unfortunate series of circumstances caused this tragedy. The animal is not at fault and shouldn't be punished any more than a child should be punished for taking candy its mother leaves out on a plate. Who would punish a child under those circumstances? Well, this is the same thing. How can we punish the animal for behaving in a perfectly normal way, which is to take prey where it finds it? The fact that that prey just happened to be in someone's backyard—"

At this point another male voice in the audience interrupts with "It was a *baby*, for God's sake, woman!"

"—well, that's not its fault," continues Angela, becoming flustered. "It's—"

Buzz. "Thirty seconds, Ms. Verneen."

"Oh. Okay." Clutching the mike with both hands, Angela Verneen leans determinedly forward, says in one last rush, "I mean I never had children of my own—"

"Thank God for that!" interjects another heckler.

"—but the animals, the animals are my children and I think you should respect *that!*" Angela concludes her statement defiantly, not tearfully, then turns and makes her lonesome way back to her seat.

Her confession is followed by an uncomfortable silence in the room, but the somber voice of the secretary intervenes: "Charlie McGuire to the podium, please."

A big man in pointed cowboy boots with a gray ponytail hanging down his back steps up to the mike. "Charlie McGuire, 1394 North County Road Sixty-Eight E." The formalities of name and address over, Mr. McGuire turns away from the commissioners and toward the ill-fated Angela Verneen. "Weell, ma'am, I'm sorry you ain't never had kids," he continues in a drawl now inaudible to many in the room. "I'm sure you'da made somebody a fine mother, too."

"Mr. McGuire, please speak into the mike," interrupts one of the commissioners. McGuire pivots toward the front of the room again.

"But the fact of the matter is, once a animal discovers a easy prey, it's just like you said," (though he's looking at the commissioners, McGuire is still talking to Angela) "that animal's gonna do what it 'uz born to do, which is remember how and where it got that prey and then go back for more. That's why this here coyote's got to be killed." McGuire pauses, then resumes his friendly teacher/philosopher manner of speaking:

"Coyotes is smart, real smart. Hell, down to Texas when I 'uz a kid and the ranchers'd try to get 'em with baited poles that had cyanide-tipped darts attached, well, them animals not only learned not to mess with them poles, purty soon they 'uz actually poopin' around 'em, which is their way of warnin' their friends to stay away. It 'uz almost like they could talk, or somethin'. That's why we just can't afford to let one that's learned how to kill babies hang around, else somebody else's baby'll get et, too, eventually. And I know you especially wouldn' wannna see that happen, Ms. Verneen. That's all I got to say." McGuire returns to his seat while several members of the crowd nod their approval of his statement.

The secretary calls Ed Wonsawski, and Big Ed takes the podium.

"Ed Wonsawski, 5701 Coyote Cañon Way. Now, maybe most of you already know by my address that I live right below the ridge where Zoë was taken. And the way I feel about this whole thing is, the speakers that have come before me are both right. Most of us who live out there on the prairie like the animals that live around us. We wouldn't do anything to hurt 'em, in spite of the fact that a lot of us have suffered some at their hands, or should I say paws," Ed corrects himself with a light laugh. He doesn't realize that, for many in the room, this last phrase calls to mind lurid images of pink blankets, babies, and beasts. Unaware of this blunder, he continues.

"For instance, I know my family and several of my neighbors have lost cats to coyotes, but you don't see us forming a hunting party to go out and kill every coyote that comes down the pike. We accept the loss of our pets as part of the price of living where we live. We know the animals have to eat, too, and we're very aware that our backyards run right into theirs.

"But a baby, well, that's different. Obviously, losing a baby is on a whole different level than losing the family cat. I say this is a situation that calls for redress not only for the Blackburn family, but all of us who live around there as well. We as a community just can't take the risk of this ever happening again. That coyote definitely needs to be put down, so those of us with small children don't feel there's danger lurking in our own yards.

"And I might add, it's not like coyotes are endangered, or anything. Hell—"

Buzz.

"—well they're a dime a dozen out there. Summer nights they make so much racket, sometimes I swear there are more of them than us." For the first time all evening, people in the room enjoy a brief laugh as Ed returns to his seat.

"Carol Alvarez, please."

A young woman whose thick black hair is so glossy it looks blue states her name and address, then shoots rapid-fire speech at the five beings before her. "Commissioners. I'm here to once again bring to your attention the matter of the poor drainage in my development, which the county has promised to amend at least three times within the last six months but—"

Bang. The sound of the gavel is not half-hearted. "Ms. Alvarez, we've been over this matter before, and this is not the occasion to—"

"Yes, but what I want to know is, when *is* the occasion because it seems to me like even though I've brought this matter up at least a half-dozen times, you never listen I mean you still haven't done anything and every time it rains there's more water in my basement—"

Bang. "Ms. Alvarez! If you care to comment on whether the county should attempt to exterminate the coyote that ate Zoë Blackburn, fine. If not, Officer Sanderson will escort you to your seat."

Art Sanderson takes the arm of Ms. Alvarez and tries to pivot her away from the microphone, but Ms. Alvarez does not go gently. "Well, I'm telling you you're going to have to listen, because I'm circulating a petition in my neighborhood right this minute and when you get slapped with a class-action lawsuit you won't have any more excuses." Shaking her finger at the commissioners much the same as if they were naughty children, Carol Alvarez simultaneously shakes Sanderson off her arm, turns and marches from the room.

"Folks, once again, if you would please restrict your comments to the subject at hand," an exasperated commissioner reminds the crowd.

"Lisa Warner to the podium, please."

A heavy-set woman in a swirl of brightly colored caftan marches up and takes the mike with authority. "Lisa Warner, 333 East Magnolia. Hi. Like I said, my name's Lisa and I just want to point out something that hasn't been mentioned so far, which is that none of this would have happened if some asshole wouldn't have poisoned the entire prairie dog colony out there on the Cathy Fromme Prairie.

"The Bible says, '*But if ye had known what this meaneth...ye would not have condemned the guiltless.*' Well, let's not make the same mistake here. I mean, it's perfectly obvious that the coyote wasn't at fault here so much as whoever poisoned its natural food supply, which was that prairie dog colony. So if you're going to kill the coyote that ate the baby, maybe you ought to hang the fellow that poisoned that prairie dog colony, too.

"Because the Bible also says '*Thou shalt not kill, and whosoever shall kill shall be in danger of the judgment.*' Well, if we inflict the punishment of death on that poor coyote and stop at that, I'm saying that'll make us a bunch of hypocrites because Zoë Blackburn's real killer wasn't the coyote at all. It was whoever killed the prairie dogs." Lisa strides triumphantly back to her seat while Ed sits stonefaced.

Damn. He never thought of *that.* Shrinking into himself, he considers what he has just heard. If this woman is right, then that makes him responsible for Baby Zoë's death. Suddenly, cold snakes of doubt slither into Ed's easy self-confidence. To give him credit, he experiences a brief moment of honest remorse—he only meant to kill some rats, for god's sake—before self-defense kicks in and he excuses himself from guilt by pleading ignorance. He's no biologist. How was he to know getting rid of a few rats would cause such a ruckus?

But what if they find out he did it? Now Ed feels the doubt in his gut replaced by the uncomfortable sensation of fear. He can just imagine how this PC community would respond to knowing he was the one who wiped out the prairie dogs. Hell, he'd be lucky to escape jail, much less keep any customers. He reminds himself to get rid of that strychnine stuff, ASAP.

"Dave Gray." The secretary calls the next speaker to the podium.

A bespectacled, bearded young man holding a sheaf of paper takes the microphone. "David Gray, 619 Remington. Uh, I just wanted to say, I'm a grad student at CSU and a lot of my work happens to be out on the Cathy Fromme Prairie. There are two things I think you should know. First of all, although the poisoning of the prairie dog colony was indeed unfortunate and certainly had a negative overall effect on the food web, it's not as if that colony served as a free lunch for any of the animals that preyed on it.

"I mean, there's one study—let's see, I think I have it here," Mr. Gray stops speaking and riffles through some papers he has brought to the podium with him. "Oh, yeah, here it is." He raises his face back up to the commissioners. "Anyway, in this study, seventy-three thousand hours of observation of a single prairie dog colony yielded only twenty-two events of predation." Mr. Gray shakes his head while most of the commissioners and other people in the room look back at him, waiting for the punch line. It is not long in coming.

"Let me put it another way: the prairie dog system of posting sentries to watch for danger and sound the alarm is so effective that, in one colony that was observed for the equivalent of forty hours a week for fifty weeks a year for over thirty-six years, only twenty-two animals fell victim to predators."

A look of relief crosses Ed Wonsawski's face while Dave Gray continues. "I mean, to put it bluntly, the eradication of the prairie dog colony may have deprived the coyote in question of a meal. However, it certainly wouldn't have reduced him to a state of starvation or come remotely close to 'causing' its attack on Zoë Blackburn. Prairie dogs are just too difficult to catch to constitute the backbone of any predator's diet with the exception of the black-footed ferret. That nearly extinct little guy is what we term an 'obligate' species, because his diet consists almost exclusively of prairie dogs." When Gray adds, "The exact figure, for those of you who are anal, is ninety-one percent," laughter follows, but it doesn't derail Gray from his train of thought.

"In direct contrast to an animal like the black-footed ferret that must feed primarily on one thing to survive, coyotes are what's known as opportunistic feeders. That means just what it sounds like. A coyote will take advantage of any opportunity, any place, any time, to fill its belly with anything remotely edible. The last thing in the world a coyote is, is picky about what he eats. He'll swallow anything from insects to reptiles to rodents to road-kill before he'll give way to hunger. If push comes to shove, he'll even eat grass. The only eating pattern he can be said to have is the pattern of consuming whatever food is available in his territory at any given time.

"The Zoë Blackburn incident was simply one of those 'in the wrong place at the wrong time' mishaps we've all experienced to a lesser degree at one time or another."

David Gray's four minutes' of fame have expired, but the commissioner manning the timer has been so engrossed in his speech, he has forgotten to press the buzzer. A nudge from his neighbor reminds him.

Buzz.

Totally in control of his thoughts, David Gray looks around the room. "To assume that this single unfortunate incident will result in a rash of similar incidents would be a mistake. In reality, the chances of a similar incident ever occurring again are so small as to be almost nonexistent. And to impose our human judgment system on an animal—note I didn't say 'dumb' animal—seems inherently ridiculous, except to appease us humans. That's all."

Whoa. If knowledge is power, Dave Gray has just been promoted to commander-in-chief. His statement provokes nothing but respectful silence from those listening. But, as usual, there are more who want to share their views. The secretary continues down his list. "Mitch Johnson, please."

Undaunted by what he has just heard, the next speaker eagerly approaches the podium. He has a different point of view, and by God, he'll do what it takes to make the rest of these loonies see reason.

The following day, Ed Wonsawski is making his rounds as usual when he makes a slight detour. Pulling around to the back of a machine shop he has called on for years, he stops in front of the dumpster located by the shop's closed back door. Seeing nobody around, Ed gets out of his car and quickly tosses an old cannister into the dumpster, then gets back in his car and drives away. He feels very good about disposing of the evidence so handily. The can'll just end up in the city dump, where it won't cause any harm because there's not enough poison grain left in it to amount to anything, anyway.

pep talks

Two weeks after Zoë's disappearance and one week after a memorial service attended by half the town, Pat knocks quietly at the Blackburn's screen door, but nobody answers. Because she has another armload of food for Bonnie and Richard, she lets herself in, calls "Bonnie?" in low tones, then makes her way back to the kitchen. She deposits her gifts (glazed ham, herbed potato salad) in their refrigerator, then looks about in dismay. The Blackburn kitchen is a disaster. Countertops are piled with dirty dishes, glassware, old newspapers, and half-empty coffee cups. An overturned bottle of wine has left a puddle of dark burgundy on the floor; the puddle's sour scent masks the smell of everything else. Brushes caked with dried paint, a dirty palette and open tubes of acrylics litter the large oak table. Upon a nearby easel stands a grotesque painting of an animal. Its yellow eyes gleam primevally as its open mouth reveals fangs dripping rich, red blood onto a tiny carcass below.

Pat shudders, then turns away and sets to work. Methodically, she rinses the dried food off the dishes and stacks them neatly in the dishwasher. She turns the machine on, then gathers the old newspapers and bottles lying about and takes them out to the recycle bin in the garage, where she finds another pile of empty wine bottles. Returning to the kitchen, Pat wipes the counters, scrubs the sink, and sweeps the floor, then uses paper towels and some aerosol cleaner she finds under the sink to wipe multi-colored fingerprints off the appliances. After rinsing the brushes and capping the open paint without looking at that horrid picture again, she washes her own hands, then tiptoes toward the master bedroom.

"Bonnie?" Though it's almost noon, a peep through the door shows that her neighbor is still asleep.

Bonnie stirs, moans softly. "Huh?" She doesn't open her eyes.

"Bonnie, it's Pat. I just thought maybe you'd like to get out for a little bit, go for a ride with me or something."

"Nuh-uh."

"Bonnie, please," Pat says. She tiptoes over to the window and opens the drapes, then crosses to the bed, sits down, and puts her hand on Bonnie's shoulder, which feels bony. She gently brushes a strand of greasy hair back from the younger woman's face. "Come on, get up and at least come outside on the deck awhile," she urges. "You look like you could use a cookie, if not a square meal," she jokes.

Bonnie struggles awake. "Ooh, I can't, Pat."

"Why not? It's so nice out, you don't even have to get dressed, just throw on a robe."

"I just can't, that's all."

Pat looks around. In the corner stand an ironing board and laundry basket overflowing with Richard's wrinkled shirts. Against the wall, more garments layer an upholstered bench below which someone has deposited their shoes in an unstable mound. "Hmmm." Pat exhales, decides to try a more aggressive tack. "Bonnie, you can't just sleep the pain away."

At this, Bonnie takes offense. She struggles to sit up halfway, revealing that she is clad in an old maternity shirt. The shirt is crushed and stained. "Maybe that's exactly what I need to do, Pat." In spite of the hour, the circles under her eyes add credibility to her statement.

Pat backs off. "Oh, honey, I don't mean to hurt you. I just want to help."

At this expression of good intent, Bonnie's eyes fill. "I don't think that's possible," she whispers.

"Oh, Bonnie, don't say that. I know you're hurting worse than you ever thought possible, but you can't just give in and let it destroy you." Pat is kind enough not to add "and Richard," but she thinks it.

"What would you suggest?" Bonnie's voice is cold, but Pat is so eager to help, she ignores the warning.

"I know that losing Zoë feels like a lonesome journey you're on all by yourself, dear. But you have to realize that the exact opposite is true. You aren't by yourself at all. Richard, your parents and friends, myself, heck, half the town is going through this with you. Now, don't misunderstand me. We don't claim to be suffering the way you are. Just know that we're here with you and want to help any way we can. If you can just open yourself up to all that love, it'll carry you a long way toward healing."

"Is that all?" Bonnie is not impressed.

"No. And here's the tough part," Pat plunges on. "Besides letting us help you, you have to make up your mind to help yourself. To not let what's happened diminish you, but well, I know it sounds strange, but you must work to make it *enrich* you."

Bonnie says nothing, but raises her eyebrows in mock curiosity at the presumptuous woman across from her.

"I mean, I know you wouldn't choose to lose Zoë if your life depended on it, Bonnie, but, now that she's gone, you *can* choose how you respond."

"Really."

"Oh, yes!" Pat is filled with certainty. "You can choose to let yourself unravel thread by thread, or pick yourself up, paste yourself back together, and get on with it. What I'm trying to say, Bonnie, is that history defines heroics only in events that shaped the world. But the everyday definition is so much simpler, dear. Heroics wait in that basket of ironing." Pat inclines her head in the direction of telltale evidence, but smiles gently to soften her words.

Bonnie tires of the game she has been playing. "How would you know anything about what this feels like, Pat? As I recall, *your* daughter is fully grown and lives safe and sound just down the hill."

Pat pales. Bonnie and Richard have been her neighbors less than two years. They know nothing about the minutes, hours, weeks, months it took her Steven to die. For Pat, the phrase "inch by inch" has nothing to do with gardens. She opens her mouth to speak, but Bonnie cuts her off.

"Well, that doesn't exactly put you in a position to offer me advice, does it?" Bonnie's harsh words twist her face into a grotesque resemblance of the animal in her painting.

Shocked by the brutality in the younger woman's voice, Pat, shoulders slumped, hurries to leave.

When Richard returns from work that evening, he and Bonnie barely speak. Richard changes to his running shoes. Though his ankle can't withstand running yet, short spurts of walking are therapeutic, and he uses that as an excuse to escape the house. Richard can't stand being with Bonnie for long—she is forever sleeping, weeping, or drinking, and still seeking forgiveness for crimes she didn't commit. He has urged her to see a doctor or therapist, and she won't do that, either. He tries to be patient, but part of him just wants to shake some sense, some drive, some *life,* back into the pathetic stranger that is his wife. Before sneaking quietly out of the house, he looks up a number in Bonnie's address book and makes a hurried phone call.

Another full week passes with no change at the Blackburn home. Around noon the following Tuesday, however, the doorbell rings again. Another woman stands outside the open screen door, waiting for a response. When none appears she, like Pat, opens the door and walks brazenly into the house. This woman—tiny—is clad in tight jeans and a black spandex top. She carries nothing but a large leather shoulder bag slung over her shoulder. Proceeding down the hall as if she already knows the layout of the house, she strides into the master bedroom in high-heeled sandals that leave indentations in the carpet. Rather than wait for her eyes to adjust to the dim light, she, too, crosses over to the window and opens the drapes with a single yank on the cord. Coughing roughly, she makes no attempt to soften the noise, which rouses Bonnie from the half-sleep, half-waking state she inhabits most of the time now.

"'Lo."

Bonnie shields her eyes from the light pouring in the window, looks up at the intruder, squeals in surprise. "FAY!"

"Mind if I smoke?" Fay is already rooting around in her bag, pulling out cigarettes and lighter.

"Well, there's no ashtray," says Bonnie uncertainly. She is wearing the same shirt as before.

"This'll do." Fay grabs a half-empty glass of wine from Bonnie's nightstand and takes it over to the upholstered bench, which she sweeps clear of clothing before seating her slim frame on it. She lights her cigarette, closes her eyes, and takes a long drag before resuming the conversation. "So, how're you doing?"

Bonnie's eyes fill with tears. "Oh, Fay, not good."

Fay nods. "Doesn't look like it," she says noncommittally, glancing around the messy room.

"I just can't get over losing her," whispers Bonnie, clutching a pillow to her chest.

Fay nods again, taps the end of her cigarette on the rim of the glass. Ash falls into the wine with a tiny sizzle. Still, she says nothing.

"It's so hard," continues Bonnie. "I mean, we didn't even have her long enough to know her, really, yet I feel like there's this huge hole in my heart and my life, you know? I just want her back, Fay." Tears dripping continuously down her face, Bonnie looks miserably at Zoë's birth angel.

Fay exhales a long stream of smoke into the air above her head. "I didn't bring any miracles, Bonnie. Hell, I can barely manage everyday life," she admits candidly. "But I'll tell you one thing."

"What?" Bonnie's request is a whispered plea.

"You don't have a clue about hard." Leaving her purse on the bench, Fay rises gracefully with cigarette in one hand, tumbler in the other. Her remark shocks Bonnie into silence.

"You want to know about hard, Bonnie? I'll tell you hard." Fay stands over by the window, taking in the expansive view. "Hard is having four kids by a guy who turns alcoholic and beats you for years before walking out with every dime you have." She takes another pull on her cigarette, continues, "Hard is being three months behind in your rent and rooting through restaurant garbage cans for food to keep your kids from starving, while you try to make something— anything—of yourself that'll pay enough to keep Social Services away.

"Hard is failing to meet their specifications on that, then having to watch when they yank your kids out from under you and give 'em to somebody 'more fit' to be their mother."

She turns, looks at Bonnie with something akin to compassion. "You know, I don't mean to make light of what you're going through, Bonnie, but do me a favor. Don't make it bigger than it is, and for God's sake don't think you've cornered the market on pain, okay?"

Fay drops her butt in the wine and returns the glass to the nightstand. On her way out of the bedroom she asks, "You really want to make the pain go away, Bonnie?" All Bonnie can manage is a slight nod.

"Then get the hell out of bed."

After Fay leaves Bonnie just lies in bed, staring at the ceiling. Tears spill from the outside corners of her eyes and follow their gravitational path into her hair, but she doesn't bother to wipe them away. This has happened so often in recent weeks that the constant trickle of salty water has left red, roughened patches on the skin around her eyes, but Bonnie is not conscious of her looks these days. Neither is she *un*conscious of how badly she is behaving, but the small waves of guilt she experiences are not enough to make her change her behavior. The painful memories of Zoë that keep storming her brain like the Blitzkrieg have flattened Bonnie to the point where she has no depth—nothing to fight back *with*—left.

Miserably, she turns and reaches blindly toward the nightstand. Her hand connects with the glass, which she grasps and carries shakily to her lips. She drains the dark liquid it contains without noticing Fay's extinguished butt and the shreds of tobacco that have escaped it floating lazily atop the purple surface of the wine. After drinking, Bonnie clumsily replaces the glass on the nightstand, then rolls over and closes her eyes. Though the stained butt on the bottom of the glass emits a rank odor, its source is so small the smell does not fill the room. Afternoon sunshine trespasses through the uncurtained window and bathes the small mass of Bonnie's sheet-shrouded body in bright white light.

door busters

Side by side, Davin and Madison meander eastward on the bike trail in Rolland Moore Park. The trail is wide enough so they don't have to separate for the occasional cyclist flying toward them, but the flailing arms and legs of a beginning blader force them into single file. The new arrangement does not cause Madison to stop talking, however. Full of excitement about college—she has been accepted by American University in Washington, D.C.—she continues over her shoulder, "And they've got this great study-abroad program, Davin. My parents already said I could go to Europe sophomore year if I want to!"

"Hmmm." Davin is tired of listening to Madison talk about her dreams, which, contrary to his, seem to be based on substance rather than smoke and mirrors. He has been wait-listed by Tisch, and is beginning to wonder if he should have made alternate plans. What if he doesn't get in? Thoughts of having no destination in the fall scare him but, if it comes down to it, he's got enough money saved so he can take off for New York even without a school to go to. Anything'd be better than having to hang around here and nurse his father through his legal difficulties, which seem to have grown to monstrous proportions. Davin can't wait to be in a place where the name "Hassletree" is not synonymous with his father's crimes.

When they reach the small lake on the eastern edge of the park, the two young people wander over to its shallow banks and sit down. A little kid throws bread to ducks bobbing on the water while his mother looks on with a loving expression. Davin notes the look, wonders whether his mother ever looked at him like that. If so, he doesn't remember. Would he have turned out differently if she had?

The question hangs in Davin's mind like an old wall phone some prankster has taken off its receiver and left dangling while a voice on the other end repeats "Hello? Hello? Can you hear me?" over and over to an empty room. Visualizing this scene, Davin wishes only to replace the receiver in its cradle so he never has to hear the voice again, but somehow that action is denied him. His helplessness transmutes itself to a heavy feeling of despair he attempts to dispel through an audible exhalation. Though his sigh is small, as sighs go, it captures Madison's immediate attention.

"Davin!" she complains.

"Huh?"

"You aren't listening at all, are you?"

Davin looks across the sparkling water. "I've heard every word, Madison."

"Well, you don't act like it."

Her use of the word "act" irritates Davin "And how would you have me 'act'?" he asks sarcastically.

"How about like you care a little?"

"Ahh." Pretending relief, Davin reclines on the grassy bank while he observes the young woman next to him. "I guess I could," he admits. "In fact, I know I could." There is a deadly two-beat pause. "But you know what, Madison?" Frowning, she shakes her head. "I do so much acting already, I feel I need a relationship where I don't have to."

The harsh words assault Madison's emotions like a troop of winged monkeys. Looks of hurt, anger and resentment mingle on her intelligent face, but she does not give in to the urge to express those emotions. Wordlessly, she rises and takes her leave of the still recumbent Davin. Overhead, immense white clouds that consist wholly of water vapor sail across their vast ocean of sky like frigates bound for combat. The contradiction between the insubstantial nature of the clouds' composition vs. the imposing impression they make fascinates Davin. He lies there for some minutes staring up, enthralled.

Then a singular event occurs. All at once, for reasons speculative (the sight of a small boy feeding ducks?), an unknown number of neurons in Davin's brain fire tiny hoards of chemicals across microscopic moats. All at once, receptors on the other side of the moats welcome the discharged molecules like mothers taking their babes unto their breasts, and all at once a memory is born.

Davin is five. He is at the park with his mother, who is pushing him gently on a swing. "Higher!" he commands gleefully. He cannot see his mother's face because she is behind him, but her laughter plays a melody in his ears every time he reaches the backwardsmost part of his arc.

Then a stranger approaches. The stranger—a tall man in boots and a big hat—stands in front of Davin, smiling. He says something Davin doesn't hear to his mother, and suddenly the man and his mother trade places. Now Davin can see his mother. She smiles, but not at him. Next he feels the hands of the stranger push him hard— too hard. Suddenly, Davin feels himself flying through the air so fast he is frightened. What if he can't hold on? What if he falls off? Too terrified to cry out, he clings to the swing chains in mute panic. When the ride finally ends, Davin's palms are etched with the pattern of the chain links. As the three of them leave the park, the little boy's fingers probe the ditches the metal has dug into his soft skin. He wonders if they will last forever.

survival

Parked in the small lot next to the Cathy Fromme Prairie, Vic and Owen Parker sit in the cab of their pickup eating homemade pumpkin bran muffins and drinking orange juice from a carton they pass back and forth. It is so early the two have the lot all to themselves. Covered by heavy shirt fabric, Vic's elbow forms a triangular mass that makes a 3D statement outside his truck window: "I don't need assertiveness training." Inside, the less muscular arm of his eighteen-year-old son, Owen, reaches for another muffin from the brown paper bag sitting on the floor behind the gearshift. As the men eat, crumbs fall into the dark Vs of upholstery between their crotches. Two .308 rifles racked on the back window of the cab seem incongruous with the delicate dawn teasing this Thursday morning, the third week after the Baby Zoë Kidnapping, to life.

Having finished his breakfast, Vic reaches into the front pocket of his khaki shirt for a tin of Skoal. He takes a dip and places it between front lower lip and gums, then turns and removes the top rifle, which he hands to Owen, before taking his own from the rack. Leaving their vehicle, both father and son cradle their firearms with practiced ease. They ignore the smooth asphalt trail meandering westward across the prairie and instead strike out overland. "Damn shame we can't use the truck," jokes Vic. "Remember Grampa's stories about the times he and his buddies used some jalopy to chase coyotes out in the middle of hell-and-gone?"

Owen grins. "Were those the good old days? Man, even if we got the coyote, I bet they'd hang us if we drove over this prairie in a truck."

"Actually, they'd have reason to," suggests Vic. "Did you know this little prairie's one of only a handful that've never been plowed? There's not much shortgrass prairie left in North America to begin with, but places like this where the soil's never been disturbed are really rare. I'd hate to mess that up when I didn't have to, you know?"

Owen nods. "We can get him without the truck, can't we, Dad?"

Vic looks over at his son. "All it ever takes is time, Owen, you know that. And as long as they're paying, I can hunt that goddamn baby-eater 'til the cows come home." He refers to the fact that, following protracted arguing between animal rights' activists on the one hand and people rights' advocates on the other, the county has bowed to majority opinion and is seeking redress for the tragedy experienced by the Blackburn family. In effect, the government has hired Vic to hunt and kill the coyote that ate Zoë Blackburn.

Vic Parker has not been chosen for this task because he is a professional coyote hunter (they are not *that* long gone, but the days a man could collect a bounty for a coyote pelt are over in Colorado). He is, however, a self-proclaimed survivalist who practices a way of life neither popular nor easy. In short, if his wife Lara doesn't grow it or bake it or he doesn't kill it, Vic and his home-schooled kids don't eat it. Early on, these self-imposed rules of existence earned Vic a reputation as a right-wing extremist, but over the years the family's stubborn adherence to its principles has caused a slow shift to take place.

Interestingly, this shift in the community's viewpoint of the Parkers occurred primarily during the nineties, which saw an average local wage increase of 42% pitted against an average 101% increase in the price of a single-family home. This disproportionate increase in housing costs in Fort Collins found more and more families scrambling to make ends meet. And as greater percentages struggled to invent new ways to stretch the value of their income, disdain for the Parkers' do-it-yourself lifestyle gave way, first, to respect and ultimately, to unqualified admiration. Now the general consensus is something like, *if only the rest of us could fill our freezers on the few shotgun shells it takes Vic Parker to do it....* Similarly, Vic's expertise keeps his name at the top of the list of hunters the county keeps for the rare emergency like the occasional bear who, having become an expert forager (which is, after all, the goal of bears everywhere), turns up once too often at some slob's overflowing garbage can.

But walking apace now over the dry terrain, father and son gaze from beneath the curving bills of their caps as if the prairie holds answers to the universal riddles (wherefrom?, whereto?, and the lesser—but no less troubling—now what?) every human feels he must solve within the framework of his own experience. The prairie feels Two-Legs' gaze upon her, but if she does indeed hold the answers to such questions, she is too wise to divulge them immediately to passing strangers. *Perhaps*, she promises, *if you stay with me awhile, I'll give you a hint. Watch a hundred summer suns temper the frantic growth of just a hundred springs, and you may begin to understand that your burning questions are not larger than life. A century of seasons will teach you that you will not work your way closer to enlightenment in the simple linear progression you imagine.*

But Vic and Owen wouldn't squander a hundred summers on the prairie if they had them. Their searching eyes seek not answers to the puzzle of existence but simple motion: like most wildlife, coyotes pop crazily out of nowhere when you aren't looking for them and vanish without a trace when you are. This is okay with the Parkers.

Neither expects his quarry to sit atop a hill waving a flag that says, "Here I am, come get me."

In truth, neither Vic nor Owen expects to get lucky enough to even use his rifle this morning. This morning, they will simply walk the prairie looking for sign—tracks and/or dung—and promising spots for dens like culverts or sandy soil beneath sheltering overhangs. Neither will they rush this part of the job, for patient scouting now means more chance for success later. So the two walk steadily, first south to put some distance between themselves and the asphalt trail, then westward, toward the foothills. There isn't much to look at or even investigate in terms of likely den locations on the prairie proper. "I bet he's in one of those draws that feed down to here," says Owen, breaking one of the rules of firearm etiquette by pointing ahead with the tip of his rifle.

"Don't point with your gun, Owen," Vic reminds his son, then takes the sting out of his remark by agreeing with him. "But you're right, those draws do look good. Care to place a bet on which one he calls home?"

Owen can't resist a wager. "Ten bucks says that one." He points ahead, this time by gesturing with his head to indicate the rockiest wrinkle in the landscape before them. On this still morning the last week in July, the wrinkle does not look foreboding. It hasn't the preponderance of a jagged peak swathed in clammy cloud or any presence at all, really. It's just a small unevenness in terrain that marks the unremarkable place the prairie gives way to the foothills of the Front Range of the Rocky Mountains.

Vic nods, satisfied. "You got it. You want to split up when we get there?"

"Yeah. I don't like the idea of two guns jammed into one of those little draws, do you?"

"Good thinking. I'll check out that one to the north."

Content with their plan, the men drift apart. It takes a good half-hour of walking for Owen to reach the mouth of his draw, where he pauses briefly. He takes mental note of the angle of the draw relative to his dad's now unseen location, then continues on. At once, the land begins to rise gently while the terrain roughens. Though the entrance to the draw is not narrow, it is still a place where higher land cuts off the views to either side. Owen thinks this a refreshing change from the bland openness of the prairie. He knows that, while the coyote that took Zoë Blackburn probably hunts the prairie regularly, the animal will pick a place with better hiding places for his den. This draw offers the double advantage of concealment from but easy access to the hunting grounds behind him.

Owen proceeds cautiously, not from nervousness or fear (he has been hunting since he was ten), but the fact that he is searching the ground around his feet carefully. In minutes he hits pay dirt: the four-toed, dog-like print of the hind foot of a coyote. *Yeess!* Squatting to get a better look at the print, Owen is pleased. Though his dad will give him a share of whatever he earns on this job regardless, it still feels good to have made the right call right off. With luck, knowing the animal's home base will shorten the time they have to spend hunting him considerably.

Owen straightens and heads up the ever-steepening draw with new purpose. Moving quickly but quietly, his long legs take him easily up the pathless, rocky ground. While his eyes no longer search the ground for prints but scan the surrounding area for the telltale hole marking the entrance to a den, in his gut Owen feels that structure will be further up the draw. He knows that, though coyotes are amazingly adaptable animals that take the increasing presence of humans on or near their territories in stride, they are nonetheless still shy and secretive. To Owen, these facts are not contradictory but complementary. *If I was a coyote, I'd give us humans a wide berth, too.*

As the young man nears the top of the draw, its sides close in significantly. It is so early that the sun has not yet risen high enough to fully illuminate the area. Even in his heavy shirt, Owen shivers, but the shiver has nothing to do with temperature. The small spasm that ripples soundlessly through the boy's body is purely anticipatory in nature, the sign of a good hunter knowing that he is closing in on his prey. Owen does not ignore this sign but accords it utmost respect by at once becoming motionless. Standing silently in place, he caresses everything in his visual field with eyes that move back and forth, up and down, searching for whatever it was that triggered his awareness on some primal level he cannot name.

Seconds later, he spots an unobtrusive crevice—nothing more than a narrow slit, really—in an unimposing rock face to his left. Even from where he is standing, he can see that the ground in front of the slit is chock full of paw prints. Rather than move closer to inspect the prints, however, Owen turns on his heel and backtracks quickly down the draw. Having gotten what he came for, he is neither so proud nor so foolish as to think he can stay and carry out a one-man kill successfully. Coyotes are so smart Owen knows that, all promises aside, he and his dad will be damn lucky to score even if they stake out this place together.

When he leaves the draw, Owen turns north toward the area his father is investigating. He doesn't call out or whistle, but waits silently until he sees his dad's tall figure come into sight. Waiting a moment more until he's sure his dad sees *him* (any sudden movement can be disastrous at this point), Owen removes his cap and waves it once in the air, signaling his father that he has found something. His dad approaches rapidly.

"Whatcha got?"

"There's a den about ten minutes up the draw."

Vic nods, pleased, then checks his watch. "You want to stake it out from up top for awhile on the off chance he might show?"

"I'm good to go, Dad."

"Okay, you take the south side." Once again, the men separate, but instead of heading up different draws, each begins to make his way topside along opposite edges of Owen's draw. This time each has the other in view across the ever-narrowing gully that marks the draw between them. When they have climbed parallel to the location of the den, Owen once again removes his cap and waves to let his dad know they are there. Vic nods, checks the immediate terrain, then drops to his belly in a secluded location between two boulders. On his side of the draw, Owen follows suit.

By now the sun is fully up, but Owen is grateful that his arms and legs are fully covered by the tough fabric of his shirt and jeans. He knows from prior experience that, no matter how smooth the ground beneath him looks, there'll always be *some*thing poking itself into some part of his body, or some tiny insect trying to stick him in what feels like ten different places at once. But Owen hasn't spent all those hours hunting with his dad for nothing. From long practice, he makes his body settle over whatever unevenness it finds as if he is just another layer of earth, and when he gets an itch, he ignores it.

He lies totally still. When he becomes bored waiting for the Coyote that, so far, Isn't, he amuses himself by trying to will certain muscles to cause his ears to twitch. Most animals can make that simple motion with ease. Owen doesn't see why he shouldn't be able to, too. But ten minutes of concentration yield not the slightest tremor in his ears, and he abandons his effort. *Damn!* Time and again, Owen is frustrated by animals' superiority to humans. *They see better, hear better, smell better, and move better,* thinks Owen. *Do our brains really make up for all that?*

This is something Owen has thought about before. He's a member of a species that can count calculus among its achievements, sure, but can only smell and see dinner when it's at short range. And Owen is firmly convinced that animals behave better than humans, too. (He holds the common misperception that all animals nurture their young kindly and gently. The underground infanticide practiced by adult female prairie dogs falls outside of his range of knowledge.)

As the sun rises higher, the temperature on the prairie climbs. Owen uses his sleeve to surreptitiously wipe the sweat that beads his face, but he knows better than to ask his dad how much longer they have to watch for the coyote. His dad seems to follow an internal clock more in keeping with the erosion of rocks than anything else. This thought brings a smile to Owen's face. There could be worse things. He thinks briefly of that Davin guy he's met a couple times and now knows is the son of the "Cardiac Quack." Jeez, better a rock.

But the rock-like man across the way must have reached even his own limit, for now he nods across the gully to his son and, depositing his rifle on the ground, resumes a standing position, from which he expands into a full body stretch. Gratefully, Owen copies his dad, unkinking every muscle on his frame.

As expected, father and son trudge back across the prairie empty-handed, but Owen knows today was just the beginning. They'll be back, shortly, to try again. Rocks don't give way to anything, including hard luck, easily.

resolutions

After work, Richard takes himself out for a bite of something decent. Chewing through blackened salmon, he thinks about how fed up he is with Bonnie's behavior. Losing Zoë was one thing, but the way Bonnie is carrying on about it—or, more accurately, refusing to carry on—is ridiculous. *Christ, we only had the kid for five lousy weeks, not even enough time to get to know her.* Why can't Bonnie put the whole sordid incident behind her and move on, like he has?

Truth be told, Richard is more offended by his wife's lack of consideration for *him* than anything else. Maybe he isn't taking Zoë's loss as hard as she is, but maybe that's because he makes himself get up and go to work every day. Even if he felt like moping around all day, he couldn't. Richard feels that he has truly tried to be patient with Bonnie, but she has used their loss to shut him out of her world as completely as if he didn't live there anymore.

Skipping dessert and coffee, he grabs his napkin and swipes it roughly across his mouth, then settles the bill and makes his way awkwardly out to his car. Toward the end of the day, his ankle still bothers him. The damned thing is taking so long to heal, Richard senses the ominous shadow of middle age hanging over his head. To thwart this unwelcome presentiment, instead of going directly home, he heads for the mall. His physical therapist has recommended exercycling and he wants to check out some equipment at Gart's. But after comparing features on various models for half an hour, Richard is more bummed than ever. He likes/is used to being outside when he exercises: the idea of sitting on one of these stupid things and pedaling away in his gloomy basement just doesn't cut it. He's a *runner*, for crying out loud, not some sissy-ass.

When he finally returns home, Richard doesn't go out of his way to find Bonnie. Why should he? She is drinking so steadily these days, he doesn't think she's even aware of his comings and goings. She's in a constant fog that precludes awareness of anything so mundane as his work schedule. Changing to shorts, shirt and Birkenstocks, Richard now considers the community's sympathy for the Blackburn name from a different angle. He wants a divorce, but the fact that the whole town knows who he is makes it unlikely he will get one soon. Divorcing Bonnie right now would tarnish Richard's public image so badly, he might *be* middle-aged before he could overcome the negative press. The freedom he'd gain from the divorce wouldn't be worth the risk. So he'll continue to pay the bills and go through the motions, but as far as he is concerned, Bonnie can kiss their marriage goodbye.

Making his way to the kitchen for some ice water, Richard notes that hiring that strange woman—Fay somebody—who helped Bonnie in the hospital was a stroke of genius. When he'd learned Fay ran her own cleaning service, he knew he could at least sign *her* on without fear she might gossip about Bonnie's predicament. Something about the woman said she knew how to keep her mouth shut. Fay's comings and goings take place while he's at work, but at least the place isn't totally trashed when he comes home. Richard doesn't intend to suffer the loss Bonnie's negligence would cause when he eventually dumps the place.

Hearing a noise through the screen door, Richard glances outside and at last locates his wife. She is out on the deck, reclining on the chaise lounge. He can see even from inside that the muscles of her entire body are limp and unresponsive. What Richard finds even more repulsive, though, is that the flaccidity now so characteristic of Bonnie's once beautiful and singularly responsive body has, like some inexorable plague, seeped tellingly into her mind as well. When he steps outside to greet his wife, Richard looks into eyes that are non-eyes. Void of expression, they stare at him bleakly.

Richard takes a deep breath. Seeing Bonnie like this causes emotion neither simple nor predictable to surge through him like floodwater cresting inadequate banks. Having been through this before, Richard is wary—at times, frightened— of these feelings. Occasionally, he has been so stricken with rage at Bonnie's failure to pull her own weight in their relationship since Zoë died that he has had to fight the urge to shake her 'til her neck snaps. Though he has never given in to this urge, knowing it exists makes Richard perceive himself differently now. And that altered perception—the not-so-subtle knowledge that Bonnie's ugly behavior might somehow be "catching," because it may provoke ugly responses in *him*—is the main reason he wants out from their marriage. Always conscious of his image, Richard doesn't care to live with someone who will be a constant reminder of his own shortcomings.

At the moment, thankfully, the only feelings Bonnie rouses in him as he stands before her (he is not so brave as to sit down next to her) are the old classics, regret and pity. *God, Bonnie, how could you let yourself—us—come to this?* Richard wonders for the thousandth time. But it's a question he's tired of asking, so he limits himself to the far less combative, "Hey, hon, I'm home."

With cold detachment now, Richard watches the struggle his simple statement brings about. Clearly, Bonnie hears his words, but whether she knows he is the speaker is another question. Richard imagines that her beleaguered brain rouses to the interruption by sending its owner a panicky refrain: time to muster, time to muster! He observes his wife stir ungracefully, then mumble a response that sounds like "coffee in the fridge." This effort must give rise to the conviction in Bonnie's mind that she's still here—still capable—when she wants to be. And she must find this thought so consoling, she takes it as permission to drift off again, for now Bonnie groans, closes her eyes and turns her face abjectly away.

Just as abjectly, Richard withdraws into the house. Momentarily, he pities himself. Slowly, he is coming to understand that eyes that are non-eyes crush hope so thoroughly, no residue remains.

The next morning, soon after Richard leaves for work, Fay arrives at the Blackburn home. Knowing better than to ring the doorbell, she lets herself in with a key and sets immediately to work. Though business has grown so steadily over the years Fay now employs a half-dozen people, she doesn't use this an excuse to quit cleaning houses herself. She takes pride in her work and gives her clients what they consider to be their money's worth. (Fay still can't quite believe what people are willing to pay to have somebody else scrub their tubs, sinks, and floors, but she does not hesitate to ask the going rate.)

Anyway, Fay's take on what's going on at the Blackburns' is such, she figures she better handle this one on her own. No stranger to alcoholism or addiction, Fay would not charge Richard extra for her discretion were it not for the fact that, on cleaning days, Bonnie has taken to following her from room to room in a pathetic effort to rekindle whatever they shared at Zoë's birth. This slows Fay down considerably, but she gets the job done regardless.

"So can ya go ta lunch with me today, Fay?" Bonnie asks this question every time Fay comes, but doesn't seem to remember the string of rejections she has received.

"Oh, I'm really booked today, Bonnie. Maybe next week." While Fay vigorously polishes the bathroom mirror and sinks, Bonnie is seated on the closed toilet.

"But I need help, and you're my angel, aren't you?" whines Bonnie.

"Yes to the first, no to the second, darlin'," responds Fay, knowing the form of her answer is such, Bonnie will lose it in the murk of her mind.

Bonnie frowns. "I think I have a problem," she reiterates.

This Fay has no problem confirming. "Well, that's for damn sure."

The bluntness of this response provokes another frown. "But I don't know what to do about it," protests Bonnie. "Can't you help me, like, stay with me awhile or something?"

"Oh, kiddo, you're in way over your head," replies Fay. "And you couldn't pay me enough to take you on. My staying with you wouldn't make a hill of beans worth of difference, cuz every time you want another drink, you know what you'll do?" She looks over at Bonnie to see if she's following.

"Uh-uh." It's an honest denial.

"Oh, you'll take it," replies Fay bitterly. "You'll chug that sucker like soda and then, for a little while directly after, you'll be *really* sorry 'til the stuff kicks in and takes the edge off. And when you're finally sober again, all's you want will be more."

There is a moment's pause, then Bonnie whispers, "I can't stop, Fay."

Fay's laugh is harsh, unmusical. "Of course you can't. You're an *alchie,* Bonnie. You don't care about anything except your next drink, and to hell with everything and everybody else, including your husband."

"Richard?"

"You seen much of him lately?"

"But he doesn't understand anything at all. He doesn't even know what it feels like to—"

"—to what, Bonnie, get high, or low, or whatever the hell you do? Nah, he's too busy supporting your habit to have time, is my guess. And after seeing you, who'd want to be like you? You're not exactly honoring your daughter's memory by acting this way, Bonnie."

This charge sends Bonnie's hands flying to her mouth. "Have you taken a look at yourself in the mirror lately, Mrs. Blackburn?" Fay continues. "Here, be my guest." Fay reaches down a hand, helps Bonnie to a standing position in front of the mirror that extends from countertop to ceiling above the sink. Bonnie stands staring at her reflection. If she recognizes the stranger in front of her, she gives no sign. Now Fay takes hold of one of Bonnie's arms, lifts it straight into the air, and pushes Bonnie's head down toward her armpit. "Take a whiff of that, dear. Now, excuse me, but I have to clean your house." Fay picks up her cleaning bucket and leaves.

Alone, Bonnie continues to stare at herself in the mirror for a long time. Then she slowly reaches down and peels off her nightgown. She drops the nightgown where she is standing and turns sideways to her reflection, which looks gaunt even from the side. Her body is all sharp angle and bony edge. The lines of her ribcage look like a sheet of music upon which someone has forgotten to write notes.

Slowly, carefully, Bonnie reaches into the shower and turns on the water. It takes her a long time to adjust the temperature; when she finally gets it to her liking, she steps gingerly under the spray. She does not use shampoo or soap but stands motionless under the cascade, holding herself. The warm droplets mingle with, become inseparable from the tears streaming down her hollow cheeks. When Bonnie finally emerges from the shower, her skin is an angry red.

She just manages to apply deodorant and lotion before donning her robe and heading to the kitchen with new purpose in her step.

Bonnie knows that Fay is right. She *has* been disrespectful to Zoë, and she hates herself for it. She also knows that if she can just start painting again, she can make everything right for Zoë and Richard, both. It's not too late. Lots of people pick themselves up and start their lives over after something tragic happens to them. And that's exactly what she's going to do. She's a good artist. She'll just allow herself one tiny drink to calm her nerves—put the old "steady" back into her hands—and then hit her canvas like she used to.

Oh, if only she had known that those days— when all she had to worry about was whether she could squeeze some time for her art in between taking care of Zoë—were precious, thinks Bonnie. She wasted so much time fretting over how she was not going to sacrifice personal growth on the altar of her daughter's well-being, instead of just relaxing and savoring the chance to be with Zoë. Now Bonnie views the whole dilemma as a pathetic comment on her own self-centeredness.

How could she have been so selfish as to think *any*thing more deserving of her time than her own daughter? What kind of a mother would do that except the undeserving kind? This thought makes the hand holding the bottle tremble harder, while the eyes that watch it fill again with tears. Instead of the medicinal dose she means to pour, Bonnie blindly pours a tumblerful of roseate liquid. Too late, she realizes she has forgotten to ask Fay where she put her art supplies. Her painting will have to wait until tomorrow...

car trouble

Davin's fingers play the steering wheel of his big old Lincoln like a virtuoso at the keyboard of his favorite instrument. Now that he's been wait-listed by Tisch, he's been thinking a lot about New York. But the beautiful machine he's driving is a problem. He can't drive it to New York (nobody drives a car in the city of New York), he's afraid to sell it without asking Pat if she'd mind, and he's afraid to ask Pat if she'd mind. Of course she'd mind. But money from the sale of the car would sure jump-start his move. What to do?

He could just sell it and not tell her. But that action smacks of how his dad betrayed his patients, and Davin won't go there. Instead, he forces his hands to turn the car into Pat's driveway. "Just *ask* her," he orders himself as he gets out of the car and rings Pat's front doorbell.

At the sound of the bell, Jethro trots to the screen door and wags his tail, but Pat doesn't appear. Hmm. The front door is open, so she must be home, thinks Davin. "Pat?" he calls after another moment passes. Jethro gives a short bark, then disappears toward the kitchen with his tail wagging behind him. "Pat?" Davin calls, louder this time. No answer except the reappearance of the amiable Jethro.

"Well, what's going on, boy?" asks Davin, letting himself into the house, then reaching down to scratch Jethro's ears. "Where's she at, huh?" Jethro trots kitchenward again, with Davin following close behind and noting that, as usual, Pat's whole house smells good. What's cooking this time?

"Pat?" Davin tries again as he comes into the kitchen, which appears to be empty. He's about to turn around and retrace his steps when a soft sound seems to come from the floor on the other side of the island, where Jethro has disappeared again. Stepping around the island to investigate, Davin almost trips over Pat, who is prone on the floor in front of him.

"*PAT!*" Kneeling, Davin places a gentle hand on the woman's shoulder and tries to rouse her.

"Uh-h-h-h," replies Pat, which reassures Davin that she is, at least, alive.

"Pat, can you get up if I help you?" Davin tries again.

"Uh-uh," labors Pat, trying hard to retain her tenuous grasp on consciousness. "Hip."

"Your hip?" prompts Davin. "Oh, God. Do you think it's broken?"

"Ahah…"

"Oh, God, I need to get you to the hospital." Thoughts speed through Davin's mind like bees swarming from their hive. He knows broken hips are bad things for old ladies, but he's got to figure out if he should try to get her to PVH himself or call an ambulance. Because moving her himself would hurt like hell, Davin reasons, he grabs the phone and punches 911.

After giving the dispatcher the information, a frenzied Davin runs around the house until he locates a pillow, which he snatches off a bed, then gently inserts under Pat's head. "Okay, hang on, Pat, the ambulance is on the way," he counsels the woman who has become his friend. "They'll be here any minute, and we'll get you to the hospital. Do you want a drink of water or another pillow under your hip?"

Davin's constant stream of talk rouses Pat slightly. "Davin."

"Yeah, it's me, Pat!" the young man responds with delight.

"If you so much as breathe on my hip, I'll kill you."

This sounds like the old Pat, but her remark so unnerves him that Davin sucks in his breath and squats back on his heels, unsure what to do next. His silence causes Pat to open her eyes and check on her rescuer.

"Not really, dear, not really," she reassures the young man, giving his thin wrist a grandmotherly pat. Davin smiles down apologetically.

"What happened? How'd you fall?" he asks.

Pat rolls her eyes. "It was so stupid. Tripped over that darn rug in front of the sink once too often."

"When did it happen?"

"Ohhhh, I don't know, what time is it?"

"It's seven o'clock."

Pat thinks back. "Must have been five-thirty-ish, then."

"You've been lying here for an hour and a half? Aww, Pat, I'm sorry," mumbles Davin, visibly upset at the thought.

"Hey, but you're bringing the cavalry, right?" asks Pat.

Right on cue, a siren cuts off their conversation.

Next door, Bonnie hears the commotion and peers out her front window to see an ambulance turn sharply into Pat's driveway. *What on earth?* Next, she watches a couple of paramedics remove a gurney from their vehicle and hurry into the house. Bonnie considers following them. She vaguely recalls having treated Pat badly sometime in the past. Should she go over there and see if Pat's okay? She is still pondering the question when the paramedics emerge with what looks like Pat strapped to the gurney between them, and there's another person—*oh, God it's that guy they thought took Zoë*—standing around looking totally uncomfortable. This is too much for Bonnie. As the ambulance pulls away, she shuffles out of her house and over to Pat's, where Davin still stands in the driveway.

"What's going on?" Bonnie asks the young man.

"Looks like Mrs. Schreveport fell and broke her hip," Davin tells the woman from next door. He notes that, though it is after 7:00 P.M., she is still clad in her robe and seems to be acting strangely, then remembers she's the one whose baby got eaten by the coyote. *Jeez, isn't anybody on this street normal?* Should he say something about the kid? He decides the better tack would be silence. The woman continues to regard him silently as well until Davin shifts uncomfortably. "I better get going," he offers, moving toward his car.

"We all thought you took her, you know," Bonnie says in a flat voice.

"What?" Davin turns back toward the woman.

"We thought you kidnapped Zoë."

"Yeah, I figured that out after the cops came to see me and the headlines broke, but then—"

Bonnie nods her head up and down. No need to say more. Still, knowing the kid almost got blamed for taking Zoë stirs her compassion. "Well, I just wanted to say I'm sorry it happened like that for you, especially with everything else you've been going through."

"Yeah, we're both celebrities now, aren't we?" Davin replies bitterly. While Bonnie shuffles back to her house, Davin uses his cell phone to dial Rita-somebody, Pat's daughter, before he forgets.

The phone rings, then is answered by a male voice. "Hello?"

"Is Rita there?" inquires Davin.

"Just a sec."

Shortly, a woman's voice comes on the line. "Hello?"

"Rita?" Davin confirms her identity.

"Yes?"

Now for the hard part. "Uh, hi, I'm calling because your mom asked me to. I found her about a half-hour ago on the floor in her kitchen. Looks like she fell and broke her hip, but the ambulance came and took her to PVH."

"Oh, shit."

"Excuse me?"

"Oh, sorry, it's just that she was supposed to be *here* in fifteen minutes to baby-sit. We have tickets for Showstoppers tonight."

Davin knows she is referring to the series of entertainment productions put on every year at the city's performing arts hall, the Lincoln Center, but he doesn't know how to respond to her remark, so he says nothing.

Then, "Who are you?" asks the voice on the other end.

"My name's Davin," replies Davin, carefully avoiding use of his last name.

"Oh, yeah, you're that kid that acts Mom told me about, right?"

"Yeah."

Rita thinks fast. "Well, say, Davin, is there any chance *you* could sit for us tonight instead of Mom? My kids are ten and eight, a boy and a girl. I'd pay you well." Rita is not about to miss tonight's event even if it costs her top dollar.

Davin thinks it strange that Pat's daughter doesn't want to go to the hospital to see Pat, but he doesn't comment. Anyway, a few bucks is a few bucks. "Okay. Where do you live?"

"Just down the hill, really," Rita informs him. She gives Davin directions to the house. "See you in five, then."

Shortly, Davin pulls up to the Wonsawski house and rings the bell. He is met by a tall, heavily made up woman wearing spike-heeled gold sandals and a glittery dress with spaghetti straps that clings to her ample body like Saran wrap. She makes short shrift of introducing him to her husband and kids (who stand there looking like Davin used to feel all too often when he was their age), then sallies out the door like a dowager queen. The husband, Ed, lingers to give Davin a few friendly instructions and pat the kids on their heads, but is interrupted by a loud shriek from the driveway. In seconds, the queen storms back into the house.

"WHERE DID YOU GET THAT CAR?" she rages, aiming a crimson-tipped nail at Davin's chest.

Davin takes a step backward. Her weapon looks as if it could inflict real harm. "Actually, I got it from your mom," he replies, then waits to see what's coming next while Ed steps outside to investigate.

"WHEN?"

"Hmm, it was before I graduated, so must have been May something-or-other." Davin tries to humor this strange lady, who, if she is Pat's daughter, is about as different from Pat as he could imagine.

"HOW MUCH DID YOU PAY HER FOR IT?"

Too young to know better, Davin answers the question. "She sold it to me for a buck."

Re-entering the house from his own inspection of the vehicle on the driveway, Ed catches this last phrase and knows he is too late to prevent what's coming.

"A *BUCK*?" Rita sputters. "My mother sold you Daddy's car for a *buck?*"

As he did when the cops came to talk to him, Davin reaches his own limit. He draws himself up to his full height and replies, "Look, I don't know what business this is of yours. Your mom sold me the car for a dollar and I have the title to prove it. Now if you have a problem with that, take it up with her, not me. By the way, she's currently at PVH, not the Lincoln Center, probably having surgery on her hip. Looks like you really care." With that, Davin turns on his heel and walks out the door while Greg and Laura stand there, goggle-eyed.

ambush

Though no calendar marks the passage of July into August on the prairie, she is well aware of the transition. Her once green foliage turns a thousand shades of beige as it crisps under the desiccating sun of late summer. Wildflowers with names as picturesque as their blossoms (Mexican hats, gayfeathers, broom snakeweed) give way to seedheads so somber, they belie the rainbow of color they'll produce next year. From hillock to vale, lessening minutes of life-giving sunlight give daily warning of greater change to come. And the prairie's living things take note, for they know that to maintain the profligacy of summer overlong is to invite harsh consequence.

That the prairie must be so stern a mistress does not distress her, however. Her seasons are *supposed* to come and go, and she finds their cycle not deplorable but proper and good. The waxing and waning of summer, fall, winter, and spring serves as a kind of timepiece for her entire ecosystem, without which things would be chaotic indeed.

For the coyote pups Liza and Banks, the appearance of August signals not so much the coming of autumn (it is still too early for the pups to don their winter coats), but a continuation of school. While the pups continue to gain size, strength, and survival skills six weeks after Kaia first denied them her milk, they still depend primarily upon their parents for food. Thus Marcus and Kaia still double-time their daily search for nourishment, and thus the family's struggle to survive continues unabated.

This early August morning—the sun has not yet cast the shadows from the draw—finds Marcus returning to the den after a long hunt. Footsore and weary, he wants only to feed his youngsters and hole up for a long sleep, but when he arrives only Kaia and Liza emerge to greet him. The independent Banks is off on an excursion known only to him. Kaia approaches to touch noses with her mate, and in fact just feels the reassuring contact of his moist snout on hers, when twin explosions occur on either side of the draw above the coyotes' heads.

Instantly, Marcus and Kaia fall to the ground, dead. When Liza makes a belated attempt to dive for the shelter of the den, she, too, is shot. The slaughter of the three animals is so quick that, for a brief moment afterward, the onlooking prairie forgets to breathe. In shock, she who daily regards deadly combat between predator and prey with cool detachment neither in- nor exhales, but stares in stupefaction at the carnage she has just witnessed. For a heartbeat's worth of time, the prairie's pulse stops.

In their concealed positions above the draw, Vic and Owen Parker note only that, in that same heartbeat's worth of time, a surreal stillness descends over the killing site. As if even coyotes merit a moment of silence at their passing, nearby songbirds stop their singing and insects, their whirring. Then Vic rises to stretch his cramped muscles and the moment vanishes. At this point Owen doesn't ask his father why he shot the pup, too. Owen knows it was a mercy killing, to spare the immature animal death by slow starvation.

Well pleased with their effort, the Parkers collect their carcasses and leave the area. Not for long minutes afterward does the frightened Banks return to a strangely empty den. Then he hangs around for a long time in anticipation of the reappearance of his parents and sister, whose failure to materialize confuses the young animal. Eventually, however, Banks' increasing hunger causes him to wander off again. Whether he is lucky enough to find enough nourishment to sustain him through another day, only the prairie knows.

affirmative action

"Hi, Pat, how're we feeling today?" The young social worker's bright tone and countenance annoy Pat, who is feeling anything but cheerful. It's hell not being able to get around by herself, and she's worried about her plants and the work that must be piling up in her yard. On top of that, she's hungry for her own oatmeal cookies and feels like she's catching a cold.

"Well, I have good news for you," continues the young woman. "I know you must be getting tired of this place. But luckily for you, a bed has just opened up in Assisted Living over at the Ponderosa." The Ponderosa is a nearby old people's home. Even with a private room the hospital is bad enough, but Pat knows the Ponderosa will be worse.

"Oh, honey, I'm all right here."

"Well, you know, Pat, the problem is, you've used up the maximum allowable hospital stay that your insurance allows for your condition, so we really have to transfer you for you to continue to receive benefits, see?"

Pat considers this piece of information. "You mean, I have to go there whether I want to or not?"

"Unless you can arrange home care, or have someone who could take you in for awhile?"

Hah. Pat can just imagine how long Rita would last helping her go to the bathroom.

"But you'll get good care there, I promise." Pat doubts Bright Face has ever set foot in the Ponderosa, but *she* has. As a volunteer driver for SAINT (Senior Alternatives in Transportation) a few years ago, she made many a pick-up and drop-off at the facility. She remembers thinking it gloomy and depressing even then. A small moan of dread escapes her.

"Are you having pain?" quickly interjects the social worker.

"Yes," lies Pat. "Do you think I could have some aspirin?" That would help her cold, at least.

"Well, I'll ask the nurse to ask your doctor to prescribe something."

Drat, foiled again. After the social worker leaves, Pat lies there, thinking about how she used to wonder why things never turned out like they were supposed to, until she finally figured out there *was* no supposed to. The idea was to accept everything that happened to you without rancor but grace. And that was the hard part. Even now, when she should know better, part of Pat wants to throw something across the room in protest of this hip thing. *For crying out loud, what next?*

A soft knock at the door interrupts her reverie. *Now what?* Rita has already made her weekly trek, and the bridge ladies' sympathy visits are long over.

Bonnie tiptoes sheepishly into the room. "Hi, Pat."

Well, if it isn't the fog entering on little cat feet. "Hello, dear." Pat's greeting is restrained. The memory of her last encounter with Bonnie still lingers.

"I, I brought these from your yard. I knew you'd miss them." While Bonnie busies herself setting the vase of flowers on the table and rearranging them with her artist's touch, Pat eyes the blooms hungrily. She picks out mums, late roses, heather and flower-capped branches from her butterfly bush before her eyes fill. But she doesn't want this woman who just lost her child to see her crying over some stupid flowers, so she grabs a tissue and hastily wipes away the tears.

When Bonnie turns around, Pat has regained control. "That was very thoughtful of you, Bonnie. Thank you."

Bonnie nods, casting her glance downward as she seats herself in the bedside chair. When she looks up, Pat sees that her neighbor still has those dark circles under her eyes. She stretches out a hand that Bonnie takes, but neither woman speaks for a moment. Then Bonnie, looking down at their clasped hands, breaks the silence. "I'm sorry, Pat." She glances up, then quickly re-focuses her gaze on their hands. "I know I was out of line the last time you came over. Actually, I guess I've been out of line for a long time," she confesses, finally meeting Pat's gaze. The admission comes with a rueful smile and shake of the head.

"Oh, Bonnie, I know you didn't mean it." Pat is anxious to move on, but wary of the water she must tread. "How are you doing?"

Again, that rueful smile. "Aren't I supposed to be asking *you* that?"

Pat rolls her eyes. "Hey, it's not the Ritz, but I could be doing worse." She doesn't mention her impending transfer.

"Will you be coming home soon? I've tried, but your yard just isn't the same without you."

"I should hope not." Pat laughs, her heart warm with the knowledge that someone has tried to intervene on her plants' behalf. "But it'll be a long time before I'll be able to get down in the dirt like I used to," she admits, "so my son-in-law's going to arrange for a gardener to come while I'm gone. It won't be the same, though," she cautions.

"No, it won't," agrees Bonnie, and both women know she is talking about much more than Pat's yard.

A quiet moment elapses, then Pat adds, "But it'll be okay, you know?"

For the first time since Zoë's death, Bonnie looks at her neighbor with something other than dark despair in her eyes. "All I can say is that I'm trying to learn, Pat. I have a good therapist and I'm going to AA, but you know what? They teach you that day-at-a-time business for a reason. They know that to ask any more from people like me would be foolhardy."

Pat nods. "We're so fragile, and there are so many ways to fall by the wayside. Sometimes I think it's a miracle any of us make it."

"*You* think that? But, you seem so strong."

"Oh, Bonnie, you have no idea." Pat waves the young woman's suggestion away. "If the trial is by fire, I've just been in the kiln a lot longer than you, dear."

Bonnie considers this. "I know what you mean, but I don't think the trial's by fire. It's by loss, isn't it?"

The older woman doesn't claim to have all the answers. She shrugs. "I guess. Among other things. For most people." She pauses. "It really doesn't matter what form it takes, does it? I mean, what matters is developing a faith that'll see you safely through all of it.

"The thing is, even though everybody wants to help, you still have to figure that last part out yourself. I learned that after Steven died," Pat confides softly to her neighbor.

"Steven?"

"He was my son. He died from AIDS."

Bonnie's eyes widen. "Oh, Pat, I didn't know."

Pat shakes her head. "No reason for you to. It was nine years ago, a long time before you came."

Bonnie sighs softly, then decides to broach a subject she has been wondering about for some time. "Did you ever hear from him, Pat, you know, after—?"

"After he died?" Pat does not find Bonnie's question at all strange. "Oh, yes! Steven was a bird lover, and after he died there was this scrub jay that hung around all the time. I swear it was Steven, Bonnie. That bird was friendlier than any I've ever seen. I'd be having a down day and all of a sudden, there'd be that jay hopping around as if to say, 'Don't worry, it'll be all right.' I'll never forget, he even took a peanut from my fingers once!" Pat marvels at the memory, then turns her attention back to Bonnie. "Have you heard from Zoë?"

Bonnie nods. "I think so. She came in a dream right after she died. It was so powerful, it wasn't like an ordinary dream. I could feel everything that happened, as if I was right there. She told me she was okay, Pat. Do you believe that?" The younger woman searches for confirmation of what, now, she thinks she might only have imagined.

"*Bonnie!*" Pat's voice is loud with authority. "Don't second-guess such an incredible gift," she orders. "Maybe that dream took a ton of effort for little Zoë to deliver, did you ever think of that? Maybe it took every ounce of her energy to transmit that message. For you to go and ruin it by looking at it from so many angles that it falls apart would be incredibly stupid. Just take what you experienced straight to your heart and trust in it, because spirits don't lie, Bonnie, you know that." Pat's tone is that of an impatient teacher scolding an errant student.

"Well, I—" begins Bonnie, but Pat cuts her off, holding out her hand like a stop sign.

"No. No ifs, ands, or buts on this one, Bonnie. Believe that Zoë is okay, not because I'm telling you, but because *she* told you. How much plainer can it get?" Pat is adamant.

Bonnie throws back her head and laughs, and the angels who see this laughter—it forms great arcs of joyous color that fill the room with shimmer and shine—dart swiftly near. Stealing but wee bits of color to highlight their wings with gladness, they gather the remainder of the rainbow of sound and carry it at once to Zoë, who rewards them with a precious baby smile.

"Oh, Pat, I'm so glad I came!" exclaims Bonnie as she rises from her chair. "You said *exactly* what I needed to hear. Thank you so much, and God bless you!" Bonnie bends and gives the older woman a big hug. On her way out of the room, she steps aside to make way for an orderly pushing a wheelchair in.

When the orderly tries to help Pat into the chair preparatory to transferring her, however, she impatiently pushes him away. "Not like that," she orders brusquely. "Here. Put your arms here, then lift."

success versus failure

Davin, whose future is still in limbo, battles rush hour traffic on his way over to Poudre Valley Hospital. When he found Pat with her hip broken a couple weeks ago, he forgot all about asking her if he could sell the car. So now he figures he'll check in to see how she's doing and ask about the car as well. He makes his way east down Horsetooth to College and at the intersection, waits in a long line of cars for the long light to change. His thoughts turn to his dad. Davin can't get over how his father, just like many a character in many a play, climbed to the top of the heap only to crash to the bottom again, a victim of his own greed. *Jeez.*

For maybe the thousandth time, he wonders how somebody as smart as his dad could also be so stupid. He finds his father's alleged crimes so preposterous, they'd border on the unbelievable except for all the lawsuits pending. *Didn't you know you'd get caught?* he wants to holler at his father. *Did you really think you'd get away with cheating your patients and Medicare, to boot?* But then, instead of smart vs. dumb, he looks at the whole mess from another angle that he terms strength versus weakness.

How come some people just seem to stay on top of things no matter what happens to them, while others crumple before it even gets tough? What *is* it that allows some guys to stay their course even in a hurricane, while others are set adrift by the slightest breeze? Davin doesn't think how people react to events in their lives can all be due to their genes, or the positive or negative influence (or even the presence or absence) of their mothers, or whether or not they got their full quota of calcium at breakfast. In his mind, there's more to it than that. Some people just seem sort of farther along than others.

Take him and his dad, for instance. In spite of him being the kid, Davin feels like he already knows some things his dad is just about to learn the hard way. But he doesn't feel like that's because of anything he's done, at least in this life. Heck, he hasn't even been to college yet, and he likes a good time. In contrast, his dad's had a ton of life and death experience on top of reams of education. So that brings Davin back to the original question. How come he knows what he knows about how to treat people and his father doesn't seem to get it?

The light changes, and Davin drives east to Lemay, where he turns north toward the hospital, still musing. How much of life is circumstantial, he wonders, and how much—if any—under a person's own control? What if nothing but your reactions were under your own control? He pulls into the large lot for "Visitor Parking" (there's a guy whose job is to drive a golf cart up and down the rows and give people a lift to the door), then makes his way down the long aisle of cars on foot. And how come, wonders Davin, a total stranger like Pat was willing to lend him a hand when his own father wouldn't?

Depressed by this last thought, Davin approaches the volunteer at the front desk and gladly switches his attention to the task at hand. "Could you please tell me what room Pat Schreveport is in?"

"Could you spell the last name, please?" the woman replies. As Davin complies, she types it into the computer, then checks her monitor. "Why, I'm sorry, sir, Ms. Schreveport was released earlier this afternoon."

"Did she go home already?" asks Davin, surprised. He thought broken hips took a long time to heal.

"Hmmm, well, no, it looks like she was discharged to the care of the Ponderosa Nursing Home."

"Oh." *Poor Pat.* As Davin makes his way back to his car, he feels guilty because he really doesn't want to go see Pat at the nursing home. But his better instincts prevail, and he heads over there anyway.

Once inside, the receptionist tells him Pat's room number and points the way down a long, windowless hall. There are grab bars running along the walls the length of the hall, and an old woman in a wheelchair parked forlornly in the middle of it. The woman watches Davin approach but, instead of returning his greeting, stares wordlessly until the moment he must squeeze by. Then she grins toothlessly and reaches out to take hold of his shirt. She appraises the cloth with practiced fingers. "This won't wear well," she informs the amazed Davin.

"Thanks," he replies before escaping. Outside Pat's open door he knocks gently.

Pat looks up from her crewel. "Davin!" A smile lights her face as she sets aside her needlework, but Davin notices that Pat's nose is red and she doesn't look well. Has she been crying?

Davin takes the chair by the side of the bed. "So how soon are you getting out of this joint?"

Pat grimaces. "Not soon enough." She reaches for a tissue, blows her nose. "Sorry. I have a cold," she confesses. "How're things going for you, Davin?"

Davin responds with a grimace of his own. "Dad's the talk of the town."

"Oh, dear, that must be awful for you. Have you spoken about it with him?"

Davin shakes his head. "What's there to say? He's guilty, Pat."

"Mmmm," Pat commiserates, but that's all.

Davin looks surprised. "Aren't you going to tell me to stick by him?"

Pat smiles tiredly, shrugs. "I probably should. But I don't want to stick my nose where it doesn't belong."

Davin gives her that raised-eyebrow look, and Pat laughs. "Don't say it," she orders curtly. Now it's Davin's turn to laugh while Pat becomes serious again.

"The thing is, sometimes people have their reasons, you know," she says. "I mean, I'm not excusing him. It's just that sometimes trouble can sneak up on you. And maybe you think it's okay to bend the rules 'just this once,' so you do something not-quite-right to fix things. And you get away with it and figure you're in the clear when who comes knocking but more trouble. So now you figure, 'Well, once more will turn the corner.' Next thing you know you're in over your head with no way out but jail."

"Jeez, Pat, you make *him* sound like the victim!"

"Oh, I know your father committed grave crimes, Davin," admits Pat, coughing and reaching for another tissue. "I'm just trying to get you to see there are always two sides to everything. You're such a good actor, because you look into yourself to gain understanding of the characters you play. Try looking into your Dad for awhile, is all I'm saying."

Davin considers this statement. Pat can see by the expression on his face that she's touched a nerve, but she's not sure if it has to do with what she said about his acting or the situation with his father. Davin gives her a half-smile. "Well, at least *you're* back in character."

"It's not hard when you only play one," laughs Pat, but Davin can see she's getting tired. He rises to leave. He still hasn't asked her about the car, but this just doesn't feel like the right time. Next visit, for sure.

When he gets home, Davin finds a large envelope from Tisch in the mail. He brings it into the house and opens it anxiously to learn that he has been admitted to the school of his dreams at last. Alone in his room, he whoops, then leaps into the air and clicks his heels together, but he does not call his father to share the news. What would be the point?

a surprise ending

Three weeks later, Pat is vaguely aware of people hovering around her bed at the Ponderosa, and she wishes only for them to be gone. She has an important job to do, and she can't do it while everybody's interfering. She resigns herself to taking another painful breath while she sits tight, waiting for an opportunity. Then someone grabs her hand and begins rubbing it rapidly, and Rita's voice comes through. "Mother? Can you hear me, mother?"

Of course I can hear you, I'm not deaf, daughter! Though Pat responds to Rita's query in her mind, no sound escapes but a horrific wheeze. That is all she can manage in the way of breathing now that the cold she caught her last day in the hospital has, like a train bound for glory, progressed into double pneumonia.

"You have to hang in there, mother. Keep fighting," commands Rita in her usual I-will-brook-no-interference style. "I brought Greg and Laura to say hello. Here they are."

Wrong move. You always were hard to get through to, Rita, but I should think even you could see this isn't the time for "hellos."

Now Pat feels both her hands being taken, one per grandchild. "Gramma?" Little Laura's voice is soft, tremulous. Pat wants only to take her granddaughter in her arms and hug her, but she hasn't the strength. She puts everything she has into a hand-squeeze that turns out so ethereal, she doubts even a fairy could feel it, but she should have known better. She hears Laura's quick intake of breath and the child whispering, "She squeezed my hand, Mommy!"

On the other side of the bed, Pat can feel that Gregory-trying-to-be-a-man is scared stiff. She wills herself to open her eyes and smile the tiniest of smiles at him. He gazes back, unflinching. She then gives the tiniest of nods, continues looking until she knows that *he* knows it's okay. Then she closes her eyes, exhausted.

Now Big Ed steps up to the plate. "Hey, Pat. Listen, I've arranged for that gardener but you and I both know he just doesn't have your touch, so you hurry on home, okay?"

Okay, but home's not where you think it is anymore, big guy. As Pat's physical presence wanes, she feels a door leading to a higher degree of mental clarity open. She steps through that door and, immediately, becomes impatient with her family's pretence. Her decline since the onset of the pneumonia has been so steep, they should know she won't be returning to Coyote Ridge. *Come on, face it,* she urges. She wants to tell her loved ones to relax, that it's all right, but words are beyond her now. The horrendous effort it requires to get what feels like a pinhead's worth of air into her lungs, even with oxygen, is exhausting.

"I think we should let her rest," suggests Big Ed.

Ahh, thank you, kind sir.

"Why don't you take the kids down for a drink in the cafeteria and I'll stay with her awhile," Rita offers.

Hmmm. It's not like you to volunteer for duty, dear.

"All right. We'll be back in half an hour."

Pat feels the departure of the three, then the annoying intrusion of the nurse taking her vitals for what feels like the millionth time since this siege began. *Honestly, honey, can't you see I'm beyond this? There's no need, really...* But the nurse ignores Pat's unspoken advice and performs her tasks with dispatch. Then she, too, departs.

"Mom?" Rita feels a tad guilty before she even starts this one-way conversation. She hates these daily trips to this depressing place, hates seeing her mother here, wants only for this whole unpleasant business to end so she can resume life as it was before Pat required her constant attendance. God, her mother looks gross.

"Mom, I just wanted to say that, I know there've been some hard feelings between us, but overall, you've been a good mother. You took good care of us all along—you know, I know now what all those meals and clean house and clothes cost you—and I just wanted to say thanks." Rita pauses. That's about it, from her viewpoint. She's leaving a lot of things unsaid, but what does her mom expect after all those years of criticism?

Rita looks up, sees tears rolling down her mother's cheeks. The tears unsettle her. Is her mother trying to apologize at this late date, or simply overwhelmed by Rita's generosity? Rita wipes the droplets away brusquely, then hurries to leave. "Bye, Ma. I'll be back tomorrow."

Pat lies very still. *Oh, daughter. Of course I'm trying to apologize. But not for scolding when I thought you were failing to be the best you could be. (I know now I should have spoken only with gentle encouragement and nothing else, but it's too late for that, isn't it?) I just wish I could tell you that, of all the ways I wronged you, dear, ranting was a minor offense. The worst thing I did was allowing you to grow up thinking that the center of the universe was you. Forgive me for that, Rita, and we'll be even.* But Pat knows it's too late for that, too.

It isn't until the small hours of the morning, when even the endless churning cycle of activity in the nursing home halts, that Pat feels a subtle change. She opens her eyes, clearly sees both Hal and Steven over in the corner of her room, smiling. *Finally.* She smiles back. The next moment, the great downward dragging force that scientists term gravity (but is really the growing weight of sorrow and pain and worry that people accumulate in their lifetimes like ever-thickening coats of barnacles) falls away. Freed from the heavy garment she has worn for decades, Pat becomes as light as pure prayer. At once, she moves to join her loved ones.

Two days later, Rita struggles to write her mother's obituary. (The paper lets you write your own, now.) She wants it classy but not too formal. She writes:

On Wednesday, August 25, the almighty archangels sounded their trumpets for our beloved Patricia Marie Svitec Schreveport, sixty-eight years of age. The great God of Heaven and Earth took mercy on her pain and suffering and we rejoice, rejoice, Emmanuel, for now we know she is rejoined with her dear husband Hal and dear son Steven, who receded her in death. Though our hearts are broken from the loss of our dear mother, mother-in-law and grandmother, her memory will live on in each of us who malingers here a little longer.

A Mass for Patricia will be celebrated at 2:30 P.M. Saturday at St. Elizabeth Ann Seton Parish, 5450 South Lemay. Internment will be in Grandview Cemetery.

Patricia was born April 26, 1934, in Oklahoma to her parents Roger and Theresa Svitec, who owned a ranch. She married her life partner, Hal Schreveport, in Kansas City in 1957. The couple moved to Fort Collins when Hal bought his own dealership there in 1962.

Patricia was a loving wife and mother who enjoyed cooking, gardening, and bridge as well as training seeing-eye dogs for the blind. She is survived by her loving daughter Rita Wonsawski, her son-in-law Edward Wonsawski, and her grandchildren Gregory and Laura. In lieu of flowers, memorial contributions may be made to the Patricia Schreveport Memorial Fund in care of Elizabeth Ann Seton Church.

There. Rita puts her pencil down. Considering that she is still disgusted with Pat for leaving her estate in the form of a trust with strict disbursement rules (Rita only gets a pittance each month), Rita thinks she has done quite well by her mother, thank you very much. *But oh, what I could have done with that whole bundle!* As it is, she, Ed and the kids will move up to the house on the ridge to at least escape the road problem. After that—Rita's thoughts are interrupted here by the appearance of Laura and her bratty friend, what's-her-name. The girls are taking turns blindfolding each other, then parading through the house behind the harnessed Jethro. Their giggles and squeals seem not to bother the dog at all, though they are giving Rita a headache.

Oh, God, that's another problem. Because he had no teacher the entire time Pat was in the hospital and nursing home, Jethro flunked out of school. Now Laura has her heart set on keeping him "in memory of Gramma please-oh-please." Right. *All we need around here is another pet, Mom. As if I don't have enough to do!* Well, if there are no takers from the ad she has placed, Rita supposes she'll have to go along with her daughter's request. Planting her elbows on the kitchen table, she bends her head forward into her hands and massages her temples with fingertips painted (professionally, mind you) Lilting Lilac.

The approach of the dinner hour finds little Laura stretched on the floor in her room, drawing. Laura's friend has gone home but Jethro lies patiently on the floor nearby. Concentrating hard on her picture, Laura keeps her head down for some time. When she finally looks up, she sees a strange sight. Jethro is wagging his tail hard. That's not so strange—Jethro wags his tail a lot. But he is staring over at the corner of her room where her rocker sits, and Laura is amazed to see the rocker moving. She sucks in her breath. The next instant, she grabs her picture and with Jethro close behind, hurries over to the rocker. Curling her body into the padded seat, the little girl holds out her picture. The picture shows Laura nestled on Pat's lap with an open storybook. "Do you like it, Gramma?" she asks.

When the rocker continues to rock her small form for some time, Laura knows the answer is *yes*.

getting there

Funny how it all turns out. Davin is heading east through the nondescript terrain that borders Highway 14 to Sterling, where he'll hook up with 76 to Julesburg, where he'll catch the interstate that'll take him all the way across Nebraska to Iowa. He's not sure what comes after that, but he's not worried. He has maps and enough money to get him to New York, where he'll sell the car for a good price to a New York collector he found on the internet. Davin still can't believe Pat died in that stupid nursing home, and he feels badly he never went to see her again, but at least he doesn't have to worry about selling the car now.

Hey, I know you wouldn't have minded anyway. His hands play the steering wheel in time to Bob Seger's voice on a CD. The thought crosses his mind that maybe he should stop with the hand routine. *But what animal in its right mind would want to live in this godforsaken place?* Eastern Colorado is so boring, even the towns are few and far between. He travels along at high speed, taking his car for one last gallop across the high plains. *Yippee!*

With Pat's death fresh on Davin's mind, everything she said to him has gained import. Too young to question the logic of granting credibility to somebody just because they are dead, Davin guesses Pat was right in telling him he shouldn't cut his father out of his life. But that'll be a lot easier to do, he figures, once there are a couple thousand miles between them. Sort of like a buffer zone if anybody goes ballistic.

Of course, jail would serve the same purpose, but Davin doesn't think it'll come to that. Based on what he can tell from his reading (neither he nor his dad could ever initiate a heart-to-heart), his dad's defense hangs on a technicality that'll probably save him from doing time. Evidently, there's a legitimate type of bypass called a sequential in which the surgeon opts to take one section of replacement vessel, split the ends, then attach them at a couple of different places on a diseased heart. Apparently that was the technique favored by Davin's dad. Now, the argument is whether that'd be considered a single or double bypass. Davin is under the impression that it's mostly a question of semantics except for the large amounts of money at stake in the billing. *Oh, and don't forget that dead guy, Dad. He'd probably prefer you err on the side of caution, don't you think?*

"*Davin.*" Davin can practically hear Pat chiding him from the empty passenger seat for this way of thinking. To humor her, he makes a conscious effort to think about how his father might have gotten into the mess he was in. Why would someone who made so much money legally break the law by trying to get more? Was his dad that greedy?

Davin only knows that his dad's been interested in the stock market for as long as he can remember. *At least ever since Mom left,* he muses. Before that, they just felt like a normal family 'til things fell apart. Foot heavy on the gas pedal, Davin thinks about his parents' break-up. He'd been so little then. He didn't remember any big emotional scenes or anything. Just that one day his mother had been there, and the next she wasn't. How might that have made his father feel?

Without remembering details, Davin does recall knowing right off that he couldn't talk to his father about his mother. As he grew older that feeling had expanded to include just about everything, but it hadn't been that way at first. At first, only the subject of his mother was taboo. Consequently, a lonely little boy had grown lonelier.

But you're back to you again. What about your father, Davin? Pat's voice is insistent in his head.

A simple thought occurs. *He was probably hurting, just like me.* The instant the thought materializes, an unfamiliar feeling shocks Davin's hyperactive hands into stillness. For the first time in years, he experiences an entire minute in which he feels as one with his father. The moment so startles Davin, it provokes questions: Was his dad a man so wounded by his wife's behavior, all the blustery arrogance of succeeding years was just a pathetic cover? Could his dad's passionate involvement with the stock market have been nothing more than a desperate attempt to propel him to riches that would show his wife he was still the *man?*

Oh God, that was too close for comfort. If I don't watch it, pretty soon *I'll* be excusing him for what he did, thinks Davin. Shaking his head at the idea, he gets the distinct feeling that Pat wouldn't approve of his reluctance to forgive and forget. "Hey, you didn't have to live with him," charges Davin, wagging his finger to his invisible passenger.

Sated with a bellyful of fossil fuel, the big Lincoln purrs across the plains with the stamina of a king for whom the phrase "term limits" refers only to successive wives' lives. Now, just for the hell of it, Davin considers a positive scenario. *Wouldn't it be something if his dad eventually got used to the idea of him being an actor?* But the notion that he and his father could ever be friends seems so preposterous, Davin rejects it. *You've had nineteen years to do that,* he accuses his dad.

To Davin's disgust, Pat once again takes issue with his thought process. *Haven't you both had those nineteen years, Davin?*

He looks over at the empty seat and caves. "Jeez, Pat. All right, if it'll make you happy, maybe—I said *maybe*—I'll e-mail him when I get there, okay?"

To Davin's utter relief, her reply consists of nothing but sweet silence.

full circle

The prairie watches the couple walking the nature trail. It is Thursday evening, the first week in October. The days have shortened so markedly there is a slight nip to the air. The woman wears a heavy sweater over her thin frame; the man, walking to her right, limps slightly. For awhile, neither speaks, then the woman breaks the silence.

"You know what I'm learning, Richard?"

"I can guess part, but not all of it," admits the man.

Bonnie nods. "Well, I'm learning that we aren't at all what we eat, as the old saying goes, remember?"

"Yeah. What are we, then?"

"We are what we *think*," replies Bonnie with conviction. "Somehow, our thoughts translate into energy that makes each of us who we are."

"Mmmm. But do you think you can actually control your own thoughts, because if the answer is no, then that means you have no say in who you become," Richard points out.

"But that's the whole idea," counters Bonnie. "I'm saying that we have a lot more to do with how—no, *what*—we think than we realize. And I'm talking way more than just positive mental attitude, here, although that's worth a lot. I'm talking about love, which we usually conceptualize as a feeling but I'm saying can be translated into *thinking,* too. Do you understand?" she asks anxiously.

"You mean, if we think it, we become it?" Richard is skeptical.

"Well," Bonnie hedges, "not quite. I'll give you an example. Since Zoë died, there have been moments I've been thinking of her that have kind of, well—don't take this like I'm nuts or something, but I'm going to use the word 'shimmered.' At those times, something— I think it's love—practically vibrates like a violin string stretched straight from me to her. I just know she's on the other end of that string somewhere, Richard, and somehow, she gets the love I send her with my mind. There've even been a couple of times my mind has received love from her.

"When that happens, it's the most beautiful experience. It's hard to put into words, but all of a sudden I'll feel like I'm her and she's me and maybe, just maybe, we're all one. Have you ever felt anything like that?"

"Bonnie." Richard is trying to get used to this new person who is emerging as his wife, but there are times—"Look, thought *is* a powerful tool. Trainers always encourage their athletes to visualize themselves winning. But thinking I'm going to win the marathon is no substitute for hard training."

Exasperated, Bonnie lets out a breath of frustration. "I'm not saying to drop the training. I'm saying you have to make thinking you can win part of the training. And I'm not talking about winning, anyway—why is everything with you always about winning?—I'm talking about *loving*." When this remark is met by silence, Bonnie grabs Richard's hand and stops walking, forcing him to stop, too. "Oh, Richard, I know I've put you through a lot, but do you think there's enough left for us to start over?"

In the gloom, Richard peers down, uncertain how this topic came up. He doesn't say that, just days ago, he was dying to get a divorce. He says the only thing he can think of at the moment: "I honestly don't know yet, Bonnie."

Chastened, Bonnie walks on, still holding Richard's hand. If she replies, it is in a voice so low the prairie cannot hear it.

Suddenly movement in the draw where the slaughtered coyotes used to den diverts the prairie's attention. *Who goes there?* While she watches for the gleam of eye or glimpse of movement that will reveal which creature walks her way, her breast rises and falls in rhythm with her steady breathing. In. Out In. Out. At last, her patience pays off. There! Shadow-like as he trots along in the dusk, Jasper moves purposefully from the draw out onto the open prairie. The prairie knows from the way he moves that the coyote is hungry, but still robust. Wherever Jasper has been, it has been a place of plenty. *Like I used to be,* thinks the prairie wistfully. But she cannot waste her energy on regret.

Instead, she watches the fast-moving coyote top a small hill and continue eastward. He must cross the busy Taft Hill Road before he can hunt the prairie proper, and that is a chance none of her creatures should have to take. *But that's the way it is, these days.* When the coyote makes a safe crossing, the prairie exhales in relief. *It'd be nice to keep this one for awhile.*

After he has put some distance between himself and the road, Jasper stops to sniff a small object he finds lying beneath a clump of rabbitbrush. The surface of the light-colored object is not solid, but broken by several mysterious hollows. While the object's whitish surface invites reflections from the light of the rising harvest moon, its dark hollows consume the light entirely. This combination of the luminous and the opaque is so beautiful the prairie lingers for a moment, just to watch.

She well knows that a few years' exposure to her sun, her wind, her rain, her snow and her microorganisms will transform the object into something else entirely. Whether the process will take a decade or a century the prairie isn't sure, but she is sure of her forces and their final effect: ultimately, the little object will have no choice but to become unrecognizable from the soil around it. Then, there will be an exchange just like the one the female Two-Legs mentioned! (The prairie is excited. It's the first time she has ever heard a Two-Legs come even close to getting the big picture.) A thing that was one thing will become another. Now, when each of those things finally comes to understand that there is no "other," just a Oneness that is all, well—*now, calm down. You know better than to expect too much, too soon.*

But I can dream, can't I? The prairie smiles, thinking about her own version of Two-Legs' violin-string-thing. In her version, a *zillion* strings connect each living thing with everything else. No creature is unattached, and even the smallest has myriad connections to others. Take this unassuming little object, here.

Eyeing the small skull lying beneath the bush, the prairie fast-forwards a vision of the future. The vision shows the sun, the wind, the rain, the cold and her microorganisms breaking the skull down into tiny particles of soil, but instead of taking decades, the process is condensed into seconds. Now, the vision slows. Plants growing in the newly formed soil labor against dreadful odds to penetrate that soil with their roots. Because of the dry climate, the ground is sun-baked to an unyielding degree of hardness. Each root advances only by infinitesimal increments as it searches for nutrients the plant requires for growth. Should fortune smile upon one of these tiny seekers by allowing it to encounter such nutrients, the root must then change hats and become a microscopic suction pump, drawing nourishment from the soil even as a babe draws milk from its mother's breast.

The aptness of this imagery causes even the prairie's vision to darken; she remains quiet for a moment, thinking. Not normally given to preaching about the propriety of natural events, in this instance she feels differently. *Watch just a hundred summer suns and even you will see,* she wants to tell Two-Legs. *What you term death is never the end, but another beginning. Watch just a hundred summer suns and you, too, will know: what you term life derives from a Oneness that is all, and is eternal. Be not so vain as to think you are the whole. Understand that each is but a part that touches every other part. Because the parts join to make a Oneness that is all—and is eternal—so, too, are you.*

Following her urge to break her silence and speak to Two-Legs, the prairie looks around only to find that they have gone. For the second time this evening, she exhales with a sense of relief. *Perhaps it's for the best.* Talking to those who cannot hear a body breathe might well prove more trouble than it's worth.